SCION OF MIDNIGHT
SUPERNATURALS OF DAIZLEI ACADEMY
BOOK TWO

KEL CARPENTER

Scion of Midnight
Kel Carpenter

About the Author

Kel Carpenter is a master of werdz. When she's not reading or writing, she's traveling the world, lovingly pestering her co-author, and spending time with her family. She is always on the search for good tacos and the best pizza. She resides in Maryland and desperately tries to avoid the traffic.

To Courtney, for all of the memories that kept me sane and being the friend I have never had. You are one of the best damn people I know. I love you like the sister I always wanted.

"He's more myself than I am.
Whatever our souls are made of,
his and mine are the same."

-Emily Bronte

PROLOGUE

Pain had always brought me release—specifically, causing someone else's pain. In the past, it had always brought clarity, but now…I didn't know what was wrong with me. The killing in the warehouse hadn't sated my demons for long, nor had almost ending Elizabeth in a fit of rage. It didn't matter that I'd kept my distance after our altercation on Daizlei's campus. Nothing would quell the monster that had woken inside me, and I think Mariana saw that when she decided to push me away. She didn't kick me out, not really. But when she booked Lily's ticket to Bella, she didn't hide that she wanted me gone too.

It wasn't unexpected given what bad shape Elizabeth was in. Alexandra had caused third-degree burns two days before she'd left for Milan. But I only had to glare in her direction, and the girl went into an all-out panic attack. I wasn't the one she needed to fear, though. Blair's icy wrath was far worse than any pain I would inflict on her—and I had bigger problems anyway. People to hunt. Monsters to kill.

Months had passed, and nothing had changed. No one had come for me, or my sisters. I never forgot, though, the real reason we'd ended up in that warehouse. The reason the demons had even sought Elizabeth out in the first place, despite how easy it was to blame her for everything. Someone was hunting me.

But in this game of cat and mouse, I'd become the lion. I would find them, and they would pay for the pain they'd caused. For the scars they'd given me.

It was only a matter of time.

CHAPTER I

Eyes were watching me as the bus pulled up to my final
stop.

Nashville—home to the man who plagued my dreams, and his unrelenting little sister. Three months had passed, and I had bigger things to worry about, yet it was my green-eyed partner that kept me from peace. After everything that had happened, I should've been free. Not being dormant should've released me from what had been haunting me for years.

I wasn't free.

I turned to look out my window, swallowing the frustration like a bitter pill. Tori's crop of blond hair and bright green eyes greeted me from the sidewalk.

This is it.

I forced a smile as I moved to get off the bus. The summer had passed, and during that time, Lucas had managed to call me every single day, even though I never answered. Never responded to his texts. I danced around the subject when Tori asked what was wrong with him, because I didn't know. I could guess, though.

I cared about him. I could finally admit it to myself. But that didn't change my decision. He was my friend, and a stolen kiss at the wrong moment didn't make him more. No matter how attractive he was. I didn't really know what we were now, and showing up at his house after so long...well, it would be interesting, to say the least.

I stretched slowly, a stir near the front catching my attention. A man had risen, his features slightly obscured by the hat and trench coat he wore. He moved lithely, but slowly. As if he were waiting for something. For a moment, my mind flashed to the warehouse, and the demons that had hunted me. My pulse slowed, and the beating in my chest brought a sickening panic as the pressure behind my eyes built to a searing heat.

I needed to think. To act.

I glanced sideways. Another man was approaching Tori, dressed much the same.

Fuck.

This was an ambush.

My training overrode the panic as I grabbed my bag and swung it over my shoulder, slipping the knife I always kept on me out of my boot. I moved to get off the bus, but the first guy blocked my way.

Big mistake.

He reached for me faster than I'd expected, but not fast enough. I clutched the knife, blade pointed up as I yanked it through the air. He hissed, revealing fangs. Black blood splattered, and his hand fell between us. I was moving to get past him when a scream pierced my ears.

Tori.

I wanted to go to her, to help her, but my pursuer was relentless, even without his hand. All around me, panic rose as the humans started to recognize the monsters in their midst. I had to end this, and get to her.

I stepped back and slammed my foot into his chest when he attempted to lunge forward. His eyes widened at the last second, but he couldn't move fast enough to avoid me in these close quarters—not that there was anywhere to go but out. He flew through the windshield and onto his ass on the street. Face-up on the pavement, where the Tennessee sun would weaken his senses just enough that I had a chance of winning this fight.

Another scream ripped through the air, and it didn't take me long to find the source. Scraped and bruised, Tori was on her knees before the damn bloodsucker. He gripped her hair tightly, revealing a tanned patch of flesh he probably found appetizing. Her fear was palpable in the sweat that slicked her skin and trailed down that precious artery pumping blood like a battle drum. Her eyes were glassy.

"Come with us or the girl dies." His voice was quiet. No human could've heard him. I almost wished I hadn't, the way that unnatural voice slithered over me. Like a taint I couldn't cleanse.

"Who sent you?" I demanded through gritted teeth. The last thing I needed was a showdown in front of humans, but they'd crossed a line, and I would make them pay. The air tasted stale, and dirty blood filled my nostrils with a stench I couldn't ignore. It was the blood of the something long dead, even though they'd never been alive.

"You'll find out soon enough." He smirked, revealing

blood-tipped fangs, and I realized Tori was already bleeding from a bite wound on her arm.

My blood boiled, matching the tempo of the exposed artery on her neck.

He had touched her. Defiled her.

"I'd rather send a message," I spat. My ability rose like a tidal wave I couldn't contain. A fire so hot it could've scorched the sun.

He froze, but not out of fear. He was no longer in control of himself—of his own body. He was a puppet now. My puppet.

"Send another messenger after those I care for, and your masters will lose more than their minions."

I felt the Vampire behind me as he tried to move silently and get the drop on me.

"Freeze," I commanded, and he became a statue. There was fear in the eyes of the one who'd attacked Tori, and rightfully so. I raised my hand, palm open to reveal one of my many scars.

"I was attacked by seven demons three months ago. What makes you think you're any match for me?" I walked toward him, feeling Tori's eyes on me as she steadily became more aware again. My blood called for vengeance. For death.

I looked into the Vampire's black-tinted eyes. "Break."

Their screams as every bone in their bodies snapped were music to my ears. I wanted to push harder, grind their bones until there was nothing left but dust. Turn their warbled screams into the most beautiful melody and dance to the lovely music they were making just for me. But Tori wasn't looking so hot.

I released my hold on them, and they crumpled to the ground. Not dead. Never alive. Nonetheless, they would heal, and we needed to be long gone when they did.

I dropped to my knees in front of Tori. We only had one chance at escape.

"Get us out of here."

CHAPTER 2

Blackness. I couldn't escape. It followed me. Hunted me. I could say that the demons hadn't affected me and the Vampires couldn't hurt me all I wanted, but Tori could tear me apart. The ground rose under me in an instant, but I still clung to her. Wanting to silence the voices that screamed for me, at me.

People were shouting. Running. *They* had followed us. I summoned a wall around us, and squeezed my eyes shut. Trying to escape my nightmare. I needed to wake up.

"Selena," Tori whispered.

I didn't respond. Couldn't. Darkness was coming for me.

"Selena, you have to stop. We're safe," she coaxed.

Just enough for me to look up. Darkness. Purple and black energy encased us in a dome. Impenetrable. Unyielding. This wasn't her, though. This was me. I had summoned power, and it bent to my will.

"Selena!"

The voice shook me to my core.

My shield shattered.

Lucas was here.

We were safe.

The power withdrew into me as I came back to my senses, taking in the world around me. The wind blew softly, gently kissing my cheeks, calming my thundering heart. And standing before me was the very man I'd avoided for three months.

His hair was longer and his tan deeper, making his eyes seem brighter. Smoldering. Last time I saw him, we were both closed off and guarded, neither wanting to yield. This time, he was nothing but emotion. And I wanted him.

He cocked his head to the side, and his eyes flared. Reality hit me, and I slammed down my walls, closing him out once more. I could deal with my traitorous body later. Tori's blood dripped down my hand, and I turned my attention back to her, vaguely aware of the other Supernaturals surrounding us, who I could only assume were her parents. She shuddered and fell apart in my arms. I breathed in the smell of her hair and exhaled deeply. The scent of blood and fear wafted from her. She succumbed to tears as I rocked her.

"What happened?" Mrs. Hunter asked.

"We were attacked by vampires. One of them bit her before we escaped." Someone was after me, and they were getting desperate. Today's fight had been sloppy. Maybe they'd hoped I wouldn't make a scene and just go with them, but sending Vampires after me in broad daylight was unwise.

"Oh my god." She stumbled toward us, reaching for her daughter, who I had no intention of releasing. I'd heard enough about this woman from Lucas and Tori that I didn't trust her as far as I could throw her.

"She'll be okay. They didn't kill her, which means she won't transition as long as she lives." I moved to inspect her bite. There were two somewhat large incisions on the inside of her upper arm. They continued to bleed, but it was slowing.

"We need to get her inside. Tonight will be rough. Her body will begin the transition, but in a few days, she'll be back to normal." I stood, pulling her with me.

Her shuddering was getting worse, though, and she teetered into me.

"I can take her—" Her dad stepped forward, but I'd already scooped her up in my arms. She weighed almost nothing.

"I got it. Where's somewhere quiet with no windows?"

"My room," Lucas said instantly.

His parents followed as he led me into their massive log cabin. I took note of the high-beamed ceilings and skylights as we descended into the darkness of a stairwell. His parents hung back as the light of the sun faded, giving way to dim lighting that was still more than enough for any Supernatural.

Part of me wanted to see whatever secrets he hid down here—a part I kept shoving down because I wanted to hit her on the head for being a hormonal idiot. My attention needed to be elsewhere. Still, I had to focus on Tori to keep from gaping when the basement opened to a massive library—not of books, but music. Artists from every age lined the wall in front of me, all the way from Beethoven to the Beatles. I turned away to follow Lucas deeper into his room. Boxing equipment littered the floor, a more expected sight, really, given his commitment to the sport, and pride swelled in me. Misplaced pride. He wasn't mine. I didn't have a right to be proud of him. I cursed the attraction I was struggling to fight and forced myself forward.

On the opposite wall from the albums was his bed. It was massive, yet simple. Black wood made up the frame and gray sheets adorned it. I laid Tori down, and my gaze skimmed over his couches for a heavier blanket. He appeared at my side, throwing one over his sister. Her shuddering eased, and she started to drift into sleep. I hoped for her sake that she stayed that way for the next two days. The transition wasn't kind to the body, and with her being in shock, it was likely to be worse.

I turned away from her, only to come face-to-face with Lucas. His eyes burned with emotion. I was on edge, though, and this wasn't the time.

"Lucas, I don't have time for thi—"

He stopped me, and my words fell short at the anguish in his eyes. His jaw was hard, set, and he was far too close. Thinking of him over the summer had been one thing, but being near him caused a constriction in my chest so sharp that I didn't know how to respond when he grazed my cheek with his fingertips—scattering my sanity until I was only holding on by a thread. This wasn't how I was supposed to act, but when he spoke, I couldn't keep from being pulled in.

"Do you know I've waited three months to hear you say my name?"

I opened my mouth. Closed it. Now was when I ran. I

had to run. I needed to. He wasn't giving up so easily, though, and he reached out to stop me as I turned to leave.

"I know what you did today. I know you're struggling. You saved my sister from a fate worse than death. I can never repay that. Let me help you, Selena." His touch on my wrist drove me crazy. This unexplainable urge to touch, to feel, overwhelmed me.

I leaned into him, and the scent of the outdoors ensnared me. His scent.

He inhaled sharply, and I cursed myself.

"Stay away from me." I threw up my walls and turned to flee. Back to safety, back to light, back to his parents who were waiting to hear what had happened to their daughter.

"Anything but that," he whispered.

I heard it halfway up the stairs.

CHAPTER 3

"Mr. and Mrs. Hunter, I'm Selena. I wish I was meeting you on better terms." I extended my hand to them.

I stood in the doorway to the main house, and the stairs creaked as Lucas followed me up. Mrs. Hunter stared at the scars I never bothered to cover. Scars from a demon blade wound down my arms, and a six-pointed star was etched into my skin just below the hollow of my throat—clearly more than she was comfortable with. I didn't want to see how she would react to the one that covered my back.

"Would you rather I put long sleeves on?"

She looked taken aback that I was straightforward enough to address her very obvious aversion to my scars, but I wasn't challenging her. As stiff as it was, this was my attempt at being cordial.

Mr. Hunter stepped forward and quickly took my hand, since it was clear she had no intention of doing so. "I apologize for my wife. We've never dealt with something like this... Your scars—you aren't what we expected." He paused, drawing in a deep breath. "I'm sorry, but we need to know what happened." His voice was compassionate, but I didn't miss the suspicion rearing its head.

"The Vampires ambushed them. Selena did everything in her power to protect Victoria. This isn't her fault," Lucas growled from behind me.

His mother's dark eyes narrowed as they flicked between us. Clearly, he'd read both her mind and mine, and she wasn't pleased.

That makes two of us.

"Why don't we take a seat," Mr. Hunter quickly interjected before anyone else's toes were stepped on. He steered Mrs. Hunter into the living room by the small of her back, while Lucas and I followed. This family dynamic seemed odd, and very unlike the one I'd known until it was ripped away from me. Lucas tensed, and I carefully masked my face as I shoved him from my mind. This day had already taken a strange turn, and I didn't need to add to it.

His parents took their places on the loveseat, and I made a beeline for one of the chairs, but that didn't stop him from taking the one next to it, only separated from me by a small end table. I gritted my teeth and turned to his parents, ready for the suspicion in his mother's eyes that wasn't completely unfounded. Not like I was going to tell them that though.

"My bus was pulling up to the stop when I saw Tori. As I made my way to the front, I noticed the first Vampire." I kept eye contact with Mrs. Hunter. She seemed to be the steelier of the two, and her eyes narrowed at the mention of Vampires. Good. Even for a controlling bitch who pitted her sons against each other, she wasn't stupid. She wasn't so apathetic as not to care.

"When I heard Tori scream, I took care of them, and she teleported us out. That's all I know, but I promise you that whoever's behind this is going to pay in blood when I find them." Tearing my eyes away from the Hunters, I stared down at my palm. The six-pointed star forever sealed into my flesh. I clenched my fists.

"And how did you 'take care of them?'" Mrs. Hunter asked harshly.

"I disabled them," I murmured. "That's all you need to know."

Her mouth pressed into a thin line, but as much as she didn't like that answer, I wasn't in a good place to go into every gory detail. I needed to replay it, and dissect it, and pull apart every scream, every glance, every word until I knew what I wanted to tell them and what was too important to give away. I needed time.

"That's my daughter downstairs. I want to know what you did—"

"With all due respect, Mrs. Hunter, that *is* your daughter downstairs. You should be thankful she's still breathing, and less concerned with how I dealt with the threat. She's not the only one who was attacked, and I need to process what happened." I was careful to keep the contempt out of my voice, masking it with shock.

It should've been an easy enough sell, but something about her thinning lips and cold eyes said she wasn't buying it.

Mr. Hunter patted her knee, and something passed between them when their eyes met.

Telepaths.

Not good, but not entirely unexpected. No two gifts were ever the same, but almost all of them were passed through genes. The abilities that weren't...they were more of a curse.

"We can leave the how for another time. I want to know why they were there in the first place. Why attack?" Mr. Hunter said.

All three pairs of eyes turned to me, and the lie was out of my mouth without hesitation.

"I have no idea. I plan on finding out, though." I shook my head in disgust at what they'd done to Tori. Biting a Supernatural was an act of war, and we were already on the brink of it.

"Attacks have been happening all over the world in the last few months. Supernaturals are being attacked in their homes. On the streets. These are dangerous times," Mr. Hunter said, seemingly lost in thought.

Mariana hadn't told us. "Do you think the Council will act?" I asked. My knowledge of my world's inner politics was spotty at best.

"I honestly don't know how this is going to play out with everything else going on..." He paused, turning to his wife. "It's time to bring Alec home, provided the Fortescues can spare him."

Lucas tensed next to me, but Mrs. Hunter only nodded.

I sighed when she threw me one last disapproving look before leaving the room.

"Do you really think that's necessary?" Lucas said quietly to his father.

"I understand your hesitation, but Victoria was bitten,

and perhaps Alec can help us get justice for your sister. At the very least, he'll likely be able to shed more light on what's going on at Court to cause these attacks." Mr. Hunter pinched the bridge of his nose and inhaled slowly.

"What exactly has been happening? If Supernaturals are being attacked, why has the Council done nothing?" I asked, leaning forward and bracing my arms on my knees.

"Every week or so for the last two months, we've been getting news of Supernaturals being attacked in their homes. Most killed, but some taken." He paused, and a shiver went down my spine. Taken was a delicate way to say they'd either been turned or tortured. "The Council has been gridlocked. Some believe we need to respond with force, others want to form a coalition with the Vampires—a truce to end the killing. With Aldric stepping down soon, and Anastasia taking his place as heir...it seems very unlikely any truce will be made."

Lucas clenched his hands, no doubt remembering the invasive and aggressive heir to the Fortescue empire. "With the family member of one of the Fortescues' own *ambassadors* being attacked, though...this could change things." A crease formed between his eyebrows.

Mrs. Hunter's footsteps clicked sharply as she entered the room, a small smile on her lips. Lucas sighed, and I knew what was coming.

"Alec will be here tomorrow afternoon. The Council is meeting tonight to come to a decision about Victoria. You'll be asked to give testimony upon his arrival. Hopefully, nothing will be *forgotten* while you process." She pinned me with her stare, waiting for a response.

"Of course. I would expect nothing less." I met her gaze, ignoring the latter comment.

A wicked smirk painted her lips for a moment, and I clutched the arms of the chair, my confidence faltering.

What did I just agree to?

CHAPTER 4

Scalding hot water ran down my back. Only hours had passed since Mrs. Hunter told us that Alec would be returning. I'd hoped I would find peace here—that the demons that had plagued me for months would disappear. Here I was, though, with the people I'd missed most, only to find those demons come to life. Tori had been attacked because of me, and with her being in the transition, I couldn't confirm what she knew. She'd gone into shock when she was bitten, and it was very likely she hadn't been able to process what I was saying when I told them to send a message.

Stupid.

How could I have let my anger get the best of me? I could've taken them down without revealing anything, and yet I'd sent a message—that I wasn't their prey, but their predator. My hands clenched.

I gasped.

Dropping the razor, I stared at the blood running through the water then examined the chunk in my ankle.

It burned like a bitch for a moment, but the pain receded as my body healed. Not even thirty seconds later, the mark was gone. Vanished. That shouldn't have been possible. Healing this quickly was beyond unheard of, even for my kind. The only time I'd ever seen anything close to this was last March, when my sister had fixed her broken arm with energy she'd stolen from April. This was...not good, but I couldn't stop myself from testing it again.

I picked up the razor and bit my lip as I brought it down on my open palm. Pain shot through me, bringing me back to the warehouse. Memories flooded me as I collapsed to the floor. The razor broke apart, the pieces disintegrating into nothing, and a pounding shook the door, reverberating through the bathroom.

"Selena, open the door!"

I turned the shower off and wrung out my hair before wrapping myself in a towel. Opening the door, I stared at Lucas.

"What just happened?" His gaze roamed over me from head to toe, but my already healed palm gave nothing away.

"Nothing, I just—"

"What is that?" He was staring at the shower.

Scarlet droplets were splattered where the water hadn't washed away the evidence. I sighed.

"Goddamnit, Selena. Have you learned nothing about lying to me?" He closed the already small distance between us. I stepped back, but he advanced.

"I know you cut your hand." My back hit the glass door, and I had nowhere to go. He was everywhere.

"Get out of my fucking head." I glared at him defiantly, but he only glared right back and made no move to leave.

"How are you already healed?" His gaze flicked to my palm.

I clenched my fist and debating decking him just to remind him who he was talking to. "Since when do you get to make demands?" I snapped, digging my nails into the palms of my hands.

He snatched up the hand I'd cut and ran his fingers over the unblemished skin. I wanted to scream at him for being so pigheaded and nosy. Instead, I pulled away, hoping he wouldn't see them tremble. He was too close.

"Answer the question, Selena."

My control was slipping, and I was going to cross a line. Damn my body. Damn this reaction. Damn it all. That wasn't what I said, though, because that would've given him too much satisfaction. Instead, I said, "Get out. I'll talk to you when I'm dressed."

He cocked his head to the side, as if he'd only now realized how little I was wearing. He lunged forward, closer than before but still not touching.

He leaned close, his lips at my ear. His breath was warm, and a shiver ran through me. "Oh, believe me, I noticed," he whispered.

My eyes narrowed. Phantom hands threw him out of the bathroom and slammed the door. I exhaled unsteadily, and cursed my body, which refused to listen to my mind. Friends. We were supposed to be friends. No more.

So why do I have this reaction everytime he's near me?

I dressed slowly, taking the time to think of what I was going to say to him. My cotton shirt brushed my skin, almost painfully. Ever since the warehouse, it was like my body had awoken into a whole new level of chaos. Faster. Stronger. More volatile than ever, and without boxing to channel it for the summer. Fortunately, I wasn't the only one who'd left that warehouse changed, and it was those changes that had brought me Blair. Three months ago, I wouldn't have thought that possible. She'd been bedridden and damaged, rattled to the core by Elizabeth's betrayal. She'd grown up, though, and become the ice that ran through her veins. And it had all begun on the plane ride back to Mariana.

"I want you to train me," she said, taking the seat next to me before one of my sisters could get to it.

"You don't know what you're asking," I said dismissively. While we might've been equals, I really didn't believe she had it in her to survive me. Not then.

"Actually, I do," she said icily. She turned and swept her hair from her face, showing me the white scars that covered her skin like snow. She raised her head defiantly, not backing down, even though I was the one who'd given them to her. My power had lashed out, throwing her through a window. She didn't cower, though, when I reached out, running my fingertips across her cheek. She didn't flinch.

"Why?" I had to know her reasons. She had to *have* reasons.

Her eyes darkened. "I will never be trapped again. I don't just want to learn to fight. I need to kill. I won't spend the rest of my life looking over my shoulder." She enunciated her words clearly.

I looked into her eyes and didn't see the girl I'd once

thought was there. I saw an apprentice. A warrior. "If you train with me, that's all you do. Your old life is over." I was asking too much, more than anyone would give, but I had to know how far she was willing to go.

"My old life died when my sister traded her life for ours."

I gave her the smallest of smiles. In that moment, my cousin had sold her soul to someone darker than the devil.

Me.

Not once in these last three months had she disappointed me. Blair was strong, as strong as I had been. Both our powers were maturing, and while her strength made her a champion among our kind, mine made me a god.

It wasn't all it was cracked up to be, though. I'd taken three doors off the hinges this summer by accident, and nearly caused an earthquake the one time Blair nearly beat me to a pulp. My sense of touch was heightened in all respects, and while clothing was mildly uncomfortable, getting pounded on by fists made of solid ice was nearly unbearable. I still hadn't learned how not to feel so much, or become desensitized to every day things—like clothes and temperature.

Masking my discomfort with ambivalence, I opened the door again. Crisp air brushed my flesh, and I spotted Lucas outside on Tori's balcony. Taking a steadying breath, I walked around the bed and onto the porch. Dusk was setting, casting shadows across the mountains and forests in every direction.

"There's only one way I figure it's possible for your hand to have healed within seconds of cutting it." His voice was low as he turned to me. His eyes were molten green, so vivid in contrast to the pink sunset. "You're stronger than you've led everyone to believe. Killing the demons last spring was only the beginning."

I could've lied if I'd wanted to, but there was no point because he already knew. He wasn't guessing. "Yes."

He nodded, taking it in stride. He walked toward me, but I went to the railing, closing the balcony door with a flick of my wrist.

"Who's after you?"

I stilled. No one knew about that. No one was supposed to. Yet Lucas did. "What are you talking about?" I said, keeping my back to him. It was beginning to sound like my go-to line every time he caught me in a lie.

"I knew the second you arrived, Selena. Tori was waiting for you. I saw the entire thing through her eyes. You knew someone was after you, and you said nothing. You didn't tell me, and I can only assume you've known since last spring." He paused, and my heartbeat kicked up a notch as I neither confirmed nor denied his suspicions. The silence must've been a confirmation of its own, though, when he followed up with, "The demons weren't a coincidence, were they?"

"No, they weren't." I didn't try to hide it. We weren't around his parents, who'd only barely bought that lie, and Lucas knew me better than anyone.

"Why have you never said anything?"

I didn't answer.

"Why didn't you tell me, Selena?" he whispered in my ear. He ran his fingertips along the small of my back, grazing my sensitive skin.

I tensed. Screw him. He knew exactly what he was doing.

"No one can know. If people find out, they're going to want to know why they're after me, and I don't have answers. If it were just my ability, this would've ended in the spring. Whoever's hunting me would've gotten the hint. Which leads me to believe that there's more going on then either of us know." I turned, brushing against his chest.

If my lies wouldn't keep him at bay, maybe the truth would. Maybe he would finally see that my life was too messed up to have room for him in it. Maybe he would let me go.

"No, I won't, because even though you keep pushing me away, I love you."

Or not.

CHAPTER 5

I STILLED, AND MY HAIR WHIPPED AROUND US. I WANTED TO ASK how the hell it was possible for him to read my mind so clearly now, but even I couldn't do that. I couldn't bring myself to completely ignore his confession.

"I don't expect a response. Why would I when I called you hundreds of times with no answer?"

I stared into his beautiful green eyes, torn by indecision. By his proximity, and the ever-quieter voice in my mind that said something wasn't right here.

He laughed, a wretched, awful sound. "I wish I could've waited, that I could've told you when you were ready. I need you to understand that I love you unconditionally, though, and that I'll do anything for you. We don't have to put a label on this." He motioned between us. "Whatever it is right now. I don't expect anything more from you than I did before."

I stood, lips parted, unable to form a response.

"I need you to be honest with me, though, because I

don't think you realize the hellfire that's coming for you when my brother arrives." He paused, searching my face for something that I didn't know how to give. "Is there anything else you aren't telling me?"

I stared at him for what felt like an eternity, unable to process his proclamation of love. Truth. He was asking for the truth, and all of it. He didn't realize that what he'd asked for was impossible to give. I doubted even I knew half the secrets I kept.

"No."

He blew out a breath, and brushed strands of hair from my face. He was vulnerable, but standing here, he seemed so strong and sure of himself that I couldn't find it in me to move away.

"Good. Now we need to figure out how we're going to get around my mother. She has every intention of interrogating you tomorrow by forcing Alec's hand. The Council's going to want a firsthand account of what happened, without any of the bias that comes with recounting it. She's going to want you to drop your shields so that she can enter your mind to see the entire thing, play-by-play."

"That's not going to happen. She can kiss my ass." My tongue seemed to have found itself again.

He smiled. "Luckily for you, her ability is very different from mine, and I suspect she won't be able to get around your shields. You're going to need to be vigilant, though, especially if she touches you. She can pick through your mind and see anything she wants—something the Council's found very useful lately." His voice soured on the word *useful*.

"My shields are still up, so how *are* you getting around them?"

He caught a strand of my hair in his fingers and played with it. "Your hair is so soft," he murmured. He ran a hand through it, knotting it so he could tilt my face up.

I should've stopped him, but we hadn't crossed any boundaries yet.

It's just hair.

Yeah, just hair. Sure. We'd go with that.

What it was was my restraint slipping. I needed to stay on point.

"How, Lucas? You can't ask for answers without giving them." I batted his hand away, crossing my arms over my chest.

"Do you really want to know?" He cocked his head, monitoring my reactions.

"Yes." I gritted my teeth. His closeness was messing with my head, and the fireflies starting to come out added to the already-too-romantic mood. I cared for him, yes, but it wasn't love. It was being seventeen and stupid. I knew that. Intellectually. Just like I knew he was enjoying this, but his next words were too simple, too easy, to be anything but a lie.

"You let me in."

"Liar." I pushed him back, and as unyielding as he'd always been, he moved. His eyes widened, and I could only guess why. Maybe my sudden strength was too much, or maybe he'd been under the impression that I would believe such blasphemous statements.

"I'm not lying to you. Why do you think I started to hear more and more as the year went on? And now I can hear every *fascinating* thought that runs through that mind of yours, when you aren't actively blocking me."

Fascinating thought? Nope. Not going there right now. We had bigger things to deal with.

He sighed.

"Getting back on subject, what's your mom's problem anyway? She seems to have a serious case of being a bitch," I deadpanned.

His lips quirked up in a grin that fell short. Ghosts haunted his eyes. "She wasn't always this way...but living in this world changes people. My mother envies those more powerful. I'm surprised Tori didn't warn you..." He trailed off, but I got the distinct impression that there was a lot more to this story than he was letting on.

"She mentioned it, but I've been a bit absentminded lately."

"I knew you would be," he said. Lucas probably thought I was thinking of him, but my thoughts turned to the summer, and the shitstorm I'd been dealing with because of that warehouse.

I'd stayed away in the beginning of the summer for many reasons. Lily was, and still remained, unstable at best. She was a mess, unable to cope with the guilt of nearly getting us killed—no matter how many times I told her it would take more than a warehouse of demons. That response seemed to work less and less as the days went on, though, and her moodswings got worse. Her anger was rapid and unrestrained. She would lash out, breaking doors, throwing lamps, occasionally sending a fist through a wall. It worried me how little it took to get her there, because I recognized the demon in her eyes. I saw it in my own.

While her anger troubled me, though, it was her depression that terrified me. Just as rapidly as she could throw a fist, she could turn into a sobbing mess—or even worse, become so apathetic that she was unresponsive. It was crushing to see her in distress, because I didn't know what to do. She didn't want to be coddled, but she couldn't seem to pull herself out of it. Hell, she'd almost killed Elizabeth again last week, and I'd finally had to make the call to send her away, against her wishes. She would remain with her best friend Bella until Daizlei started up again next month. Maybe being away from everything would heal her in a way I couldn't. Maybe then I could finally help her.

I'd come here to help myself work through things, without the craziness of living under one roof with Elizabeth. To give myself time to think. To plan. I hadn't even set foot off the bus, though, before trouble found me again.

"Tori knows," I said. The subject change was abrupt, and nearly as uncomfortable as the conversation.

"What?"

"Even if your mother can't get around me, it won't matter. She can just go through Tori's mind and get a first-hand account of what happened." I leaned back against the rails, wishing I could just bask in the dying sun for a quiet moment. My brain didn't know how to shut down anymore, though, and being here with him was only making it worse.

"I'll take care of my sister." He rested his elbows on the rail next to me as he stared out.

"And what exactly does that mean?" I pushed, turning to him.

He raised an eyebrow at me, and I glared. "Not even you

know all my tricks." He grinned, clearly amused by my lack of knowledge. "I'll make you a deal, tit for tat. If you're honest with me, I'll be honest with you."

"I have been honest, you prick. What are you getting at?" I fumed, making the door fly open. I winced, refusing to look.

He only gave me that knowing look. "You need me right now, and you know it. For multiple things." There was that word again, *need*. What I needed was a straight answer. "When you're ready to be honest about that, I'm ready. Until then, I'll be waiting." He gave me a smug half smile, and the glass door shattered.

Goddamnit. Clamp it down, Selena. Hold the leash. Force the power back. I breathed slowly.

"Feeling a little on edge?" he prodded, running his fingertips along my cheek, and tucking my hair behind my ear. His scent hit me as he brushed his lips ever so lightly across mine then kissed the corner of my mouth.

I swayed a little, and started to lean in—only to have him pull back.

"I can fix that. Whenever you're ready." I didn't miss the restraint it took for him to step away, but I was livid with myself nonetheless.

"You can share my bed with Tori tonight, and I'll take her room. Hopefully, it won't be too...overwhelming." He winked at me and left the balcony, stepping around the glass.

As pissed off as I was at him for playing me like a fucking fiddle, I knew he meant exactly what he'd said. He wouldn't force a label on me, or change the way we were, even if that was what he wanted. He would become what I needed, simply to be with me. And...I knew damn well how easy it would be to play this game. When the mind games were over, though, I didn't think he would like what would be left of us. What would be left of him, when the fire burned out, and his heart was nothing but ash.

CHAPTER 6

I LAY IN BED WELL INTO THE MORNING, WITH TORI SNUGGLED INTO my side. Last night had been terrible, for more reasons than one. She was up all night moaning, and a cold sweat still covered her. I shifted her head to my chest, feeling her forehead. Cold. She was ice cold, and yet she'd sweated through her clothes. I'd taken them off, worrying that the damp clothes would only make her colder. I brushed her hair back from her face, and bright green eyes stared up intently.

"How are you feeling?" I murmured.

"Thirsty," she rasped, trying to sit up.

I eased her off me and into a sitting position against the headboard. She cringed when I opened the mini-fridge next to the bed and light flooded the basement. I quickly shut the fridge door and handed her a bottle of water. Tori fumbled with the cap until I mentally loosened it for her then watched as she drained the bottle.

"More," she urged. Her voice was slightly stronger.

I gave her another, and then another, before I held up a

hand. "That's not what you're thirsty for, and we both know it. If you keep drinking, you're going to throw up, and I don't think you want to deal with that on top of fighting the transition." I covered her with the comforter.

The transition was the only way to become one of the Made, one of the two breeds of Vampire that plagued this world. The Vampires we'd run into were the Born, with eyes tinted black like the demons I'd slain. It was only fitting, really, since they hailed from the same beasts that haunted my nightmares. What I *didn't* know was why Vampires, or said demons, had hunted me in the first place. I glanced at Tori, her eyes wide as a child's and dilated.

"You saved me."

"Yes. Did you think I wouldn't?" I asked, my lips twitching as I bit down on my grin.

She cracked a smile. "Not really, but...I was worried you'd be too late."

I nodded, looking away. What I didn't tell her was that I'd thought I would be too. The Born weren't something to mess with. Luckily for us, there were only two, and it was daylight. They could walk in the sun, but it wasn't kind to their senses. That was the only reason we'd gotten away so easily, relatively speaking.

"You're going to be okay. Just don't die in the next twenty-four hours." I couldn't imagine what I would've done if she'd died, especially in the transition. That would've... The only message I would've sent to whoever was hunting me was their messenger's heads on a pike. The thought was more appealing every time it crossed my mind.

Tori's shaking started again, and I moved to grab her a blanket, but she shot her hand out, grabbing mine with a surprising strength.

"I know you're keepin' secrets again. Someone sent them after you. I was just the collateral damage." I opened my mouth to refute it, but she didn't give me the chance. "You saved my life, though, so we're even. I'll keep your secret."

I loosed a shaky breath and pulled her into a tight embrace. "I'm sorry about what happened to you. I'm going to find whoever's doing this and put an end to it. I promise," I whispered.

She winced, and I instantly released her. "I didn't know 'sorry' was in your vocabulary," she teased with a weary smile and tired eyes.

I appreciated her attempt to lighten the conversation but seeing the bite mark on her only fueled my anger. "I mean it, Tori. Someone's going to pay for what they did to you."

She took my hand and traced the scars. "Make them pay, but not for me. Make them pay for what they did to *you*." She looked up with startling intensity.

I gripped her hand in mine, and nodded once. It wasn't enough for all this girl had done for me, but it would have to do. For now.

Quiet footsteps came from the stairs that I recognized as Lucas's. "Help my sister get dressed and go upstairs. Alec is here," he said from the bottom of the stairs. His voice sounded strained, but I didn't ask.

Tori squeaked and tried to climb around me.

"Wait," I ordered, forcing her to sit. I walked over to the long dresser and pulled drawers open. All the clothes were way too big for her, but I grabbed a pair of sweats with an elastic waistband and a baggy shirt. After rolling the sweats a few times, I gave up on getting them tight. At least she was covered.

"Thanks," she mumbled when I put an arm around her waist and leaned down to pick her up.

"I got it," Lucas said, coming around the corner.

"It's really no—"

"I got it," he repeated. Meeting my eyes, he scooped her up and cradled her to his chest. "After you," he insisted, and waited for me to go first.

Why's he acting so bizarre this morning? I waited, staring at him suspiciously. *What's he playing at?*

He smiled smugly with that stupid half-grin on his face, while Tori hurried me along. "Selena, I want to see my brother. Hurry up!"

I gave him a distrustful glare as I turned to the stairs. Light was coming from the top, and I could make out his parents' voices.

"I don't know what's taking so—"

"Good morning, Mr. and Mrs. Hunter." I smiled brightly, and turned to the blond-haired stranger. "You must be Alec. I'm Selena," I said, but made no move to extend my hand.

"I've heard so much about you. Speaking of which, where's my darling sister?" His golden eyes assessed my closed posture and fake smile.

There were footsteps behind me, and I moved out of the doorway to give them room. Alec's expression lit up with actual joy when he saw Tori, but it was short-lived. When Lucas set her down, she stumbled two steps before Alec caught her.

"I haven't seen you since Christmas. What have you been doing?" Tori asked, sighing in contentment when he picked her up.

"I've been busy, little sister. My mistress has had a lot on her plate these past few months, and so I've been sent to deal with the other Councils in the meantime." His answer was both vague and intriguing.

"But—"

"Please, Victoria. I'll be here for a few days, so we can catch up soon. I promise. Right now, I need to find out what happened yesterday. The Council sent me here to gather information, and we need to know how you survived."

She went still in his arms, as if it had only just occurred to her that he was here on Council business. "Of course," she said sourly, pursing her lips.

He sighed. "Why don't we take a seat and get this figured out, and then I'm yours for the rest of my time here." He made it sound like an offer, like she had a choice as he carried her into the living room. She huffed softly when he laid her down on the couch.

"I'm not any happier about this than you, but the Council has forced my mistress's hand, and I must obey." His words were so formal for a brother reuniting with his sister. If this was the sibling who liked him, I could only imagine how strained it must be between him and Lucas. Something in what he said bothered me, though. I turned it over in my mind and picked up on the word obey. It was a word used for dogs and slaves. What the hell did he do for the Council?

"Who exactly is your mistress?"

"Anastasia Fortescue, Heir to the Fortescue name and Member of Court."

I'd known he served the Fortescues, but it didn't stop the pen on the end table from rattling as I took a tight breath. "You serve Anastasia?"

His gaze flicked to the pen. "Yes. Is that going to be a problem?"

"Of course not," I lied through gritted teeth.

Mrs. Hunter smiled like a predator closing in on her prey. Alec took the chair next to me, and Lucas sat with his father on the loveseat, back straight as a board. Only when Mrs. Hunter took a seat at Tori's feet did Alec begin.

"Can you please tell me what happened yesterday afternoon?"

I stared at him for a moment, knowing the part I had to play, the part I'd rehearsed when I'd sifted through it all late last night, and then I gave him the lie. I wove a beautiful, fast-paced story, complete with descriptions. I told him what they'd looked like, what they'd done, how I'd punished them. I offered every gory detail, down to the word "break." I told him how their bones snapped, and that they'd been in too much pain to explain why they were sent, or by whom. I ended with realizing Tori had been bitten, and that her safety was the priority, not my revenge.

Alec seemed bored, and he definitely didn't revel in the gory details like I'd hoped he would when I chose how to spin this tale. What could he possibly do for the Fortescues that made torture boring? I had a feeling I didn't want to find out.

"Well, you have quite a spectacular memory for details. Very impressive. Most victims have difficulty recounting what happened and what their attackers looked like. My mistress will be very pleased, but…" He sighed.

I knew what was coming, and braced myself.

"I need to see everything that happened, and make sure your memory is as good as it seems to be." He looked at his mother expectantly, and she leaped to her feet.

"No."

"Excuse me?" Mrs. Hunter hissed.

"Pardon me if that answer was too quick for you to catch. No. You may not enter my mind or touch me under any pretext." Sarcasm dripped from my voice, but the venom was clear. They would not touch me.

"Selena—"

"It's Ms. Foster to you. I don't give a damn who your mistress is," I spat. The lamp next to me shattered. My breath hissed through my teeth.

Calm…calm yourself. My internal dialogue did nothing for me, as the shadows started to whisper amongst themselves.

"Let me help you," Alec said soothingly. There was a pressure against my shield, but nothing I couldn't block. His intrusion only pissed me off more.

"You all think you're so clever. So powerful," I said. My voice wasn't entirely my own. Something cold and unyielding had slipped in there. Or someone.

"Selena, why don't you—"

"Why don't I what, Lucas? Why don't I show them real

power?" I twisted a lock of my hair, smiling coldly into Alec's gold eyes. "Now there's an idea," I mused. Whatever was inside me, it was both something of me and something entirely different. The room shifted, and the lights flickered. I was losing my shit, but in the most controlled way I ever had. The only problem was that it wasn't me controlling it.

"Selena." The voice entered my mind without invitation. I whipped my head around to glare at Lucas, and the door to my mind slammed shut. He flinched, but didn't back down.

"I need to get her out of here." The words registered, but I was so close to the edge, and power was welling up to greet me.

Release. It wants release.

Mrs. Hunter's harpy screech brought my attention back to her. "This is an interrogation! You will not—" Her mouth snapped shut with a glance.

She was abhorrent. She didn't deserve to be a mother.

"What the—" Mr. Hunter started, but Lucas silenced him.

I stood, and cocked my head as I examined her. My gaze flicked to the ground, expectantly. Her knees hit the floor so hard it sent a *crack* through the air.

Tori gasped, staring at me wide-eyed. None of them knew the darkness that lived among them like a friend. It was good at hiding, until it snapped.

"Selena," Lucas said again, with new urgency. He stood slowly, carefully. Like he knew just how far to push me before I either fled or killed someone. "She can't hurt you, Selena. Let it go." He took a step toward me, but I only watched, like a hunter examining its prey.

"Selena, your eyes..." Tori whispered.

My eyes? The shaking in her voice was enough to pull me forward. My body was my own again, but my mind was still trapped in some space in between. I numbly bent and picked up a piece of glass. Violet eyes stared back at me.

The glass shattered.

CHAPTER 7

My hands shook as I stumbled back.

"No. This can't be happening," I murmured.

I'm turning into her. The other. My other.

The front door slammed open as if it knew what I sought. Out. I needed out. I needed release.

Without a second thought, I bolted through the door.

"Selena!" The cries followed me, but I was faster, and then I was gone.

I raced out the front door and headed for the woods. The wind in my hair, I became a streak of black in the early afternoon light.

"Selena!" The sound rattled through me, and I didn't know whether it was spoken or if I only heard it in my mind. Lucas's rage carried through the air with such clarity, but I wouldn't slow. I needed to get out.

I raced down the slope, gaining speed until my feet barely touched the grass. The glistening surface of the lake registered a moment too late. My feet planted in the dirt as I threw up a wall to stop my body from entering the murky water. I slammed into the wall of purple energy so tall it almost touched the top of the trees…and gasped when the energy collapsed, flooding back into me and leaving nothing behind.

I walked to the edge of the murky brown water, my feet sinking into the cold dirt. They were bloodied and bruised from the impact of my stop, but healing rapidly. The wind tickled my midriff where my tank top had ridden up, and I sighed. I knew he was there before he spoke.

"Look at me."

I did no such thing.

I stopped at the water's edge and peered down. Eyes as gray as the water looked back, surrounded by a mane of black hair and debris. I loosed a breath.

"How bad did that look?"

"We can fix it." I didn't like that answer.

"We?" I asked. His smell hit me, pairing wonderfully with the outdoors. I ground my teeth, because I already saw where this train wreck was headed, and didn't have the self control I needed to stop it. I was drawn to him by something inexplicably animalistic. It didn't have a name, but I wouldn't have called it love. Lucas was my friend, but he wanted to be more.

"We." He insisted, fingertips ghosting my lower back.

Not this again…

"You're playing a dangerous game," I said.

"That's the thing, Selena. This isn't a game to me at all."

I maneuvered out of his range and started walking back through the forest. I needed to fix this, and playing with him in the woods wasn't going to get me anywhere.

He snatched me back by my arm, pinning me to a pine tree.

"You do realize how easily I can take you down and walk away, don't you?"

His green eyes met mine, burning like the seventh circle of hell. He gripped my waist in a way that probably would've been painful to a lesser being. "You can, but I know you won't, because if you're being honest with yourself, this is exactly where you want to be." His words sent a shiver down my spine.

Damn him and those burning eyes. But maybe I did want to taste the fire. Just once.

"What about your tit for tat, and talk of choices?" I said ruefully... I would've crossed my arms, but there wasn't even room to breathe between us.

He cocked his head and moved his hands from my waist to the tree stump on either side of me. "The choice is yours. It always has been, but after what just happened, you should think really hard about what you want and *need* right now."

The fog in my brain was getting worse, clouding over logic.

He was so close.

Too close.

I closed the distance.

Meeting his lips, I moved my hands to grip his arms as he wrapped them around me. Hard, corded muscle trembled beneath my fingertips, and I ran my nails down them. He groaned, pulling the end of my hair to tilt my head back further. A moment before, I'd wanted to kiss him until my lips bruised, but now... Something was *off*, and it wasn't just a little voice inside my head anymore.

He released my mouth and trailed his lips along my jaw. "What's wrong?" he murmured, letting his teeth tug on my earlobe.

I gasped in pleasure. Falling back into the moment, I leaned into him, but he stepped back and released me. I looked up to see him smirking as he stared down at me, hand extended. I rolled my eyes, wanting to forget the lapse in control more than anything.

"Tit for tat. We need to talk." He waited patiently for me to take his hand.

I swatted his hand aside and started through the forest on my own. "And what would you like to talk about?" I said, maneuvering under the lower branches.

"You."

"What about me?" I huffed, and threw a glare over my shoulder.

He raised an eyebrow. "I have a list. What would you like to start with?" he said sarcastically.

I sighed. "What are we going to do about your family? Your mom already hated me. Now Tori's afraid of me, and I can only imagine what Alec's already reported back to that bitch." I clenched my fists at the thought of Anastasia Fortescue.

"Leave my family to me. Tori will get over it. She's seen worse," he said vaguely, and I narrowed my eyes.

"And your brother? It's not like he's going to forget about what he saw," I snapped.

Lucas came up to my side as I continued to trudge

forward. The adrenaline was gone, leaving me all too aware of him, both intimately and not. I missed him as my best friend. They said distance made the heart grow fonder, but kissing him didn't make me weak in the knees—it only confused things even more. Whatever I was craving, it wasn't him. His hands were a Band-Aid on a bruise. They covered it, but didn't fix it. Not really. Sure, he was attractive, and kissing him was nice, more than nice, even...but he wasn't right, and all I wanted was my best friend back. I wanted the easy, careless touches, without being overwhelmed.

I must've slipped farther into my mind than I realized, when his voice startled me back to the question at hand.

"My mother already went through Victoria's mind. Your story checks out, and the Council has no reason to continue their interrogation. Yes, Anastasia will hear about this, but they shouldn't feel the need to prosecute you." He eyes shifted guiltily.

I lifted the branch in front of us with a wave of my hand. "What did you do?"

He'd implied as much yesterday when he'd said he would take care of it. For my story to check out, though...

"I wiped her memory and filled in the holes."

"You...can do that?" I stared at him, not sure whether to be thrilled or pissed.

"You're not the only one with secrets, Selena," he said, glancing up at the suspended branch.

I continued walking, and with a flick of my wrist, it came crashing down behind us. "Can all telepaths mess with people's memories?" The thought of Anastasia being able to do that...

"Powerful ones can," he said.

We fell into an awkward silence, as my mind drifted through the last year. How much my life had changed. This time a year ago I was dreading a plane trip to meet an aunt I didn't know and expecting foster care at the next turn...and instead I'd had the craziest year of my life. The strange reality where I had friends I trusted and cared for enough to fight for, or in Lucas's case, fight with. "A lot has changed in the past year," I murmured to myself.

"You have no idea," he agreed.

"It'll never be as simple as it was again, will it?" I was asking so much in that one question, but if he knew it, his gaze gave away nothing.

"Probably not. The world is on the brink of war, and with the first telekinetic in a millennium, people are scared. Desperate. Things are only going to get worse before they get better."

I appreciated his honesty. It was the reason we'd even been friends to begin with, before all...well, *this*.

"I need you to know something, Lucas," I said. Taking a deep breath, I launched into what I should've told him four months ago. "I lead a complicated life, and I can't give you what you deserve. I can take, I'm very good at that, but I can't promise you sweet nothings." I glanced at him before I continued. "My demons are getting worse, and if I'm not battling one form of madness, it's the other. I walk a tightrope, and anything you have with me...won't be fair to you. Do you understand?" The house was in sight now, and any semblance of deep conversation was coming to an end.

"I'm not asking for sweet nothings. I'm not asking for a promise of the future, or even your love. Whatever this is, I'm asking that we just go with it, because whenever you need something, I'll be there. Whether it's erasing some-one's memory, or taking the edge off—I want to be the person you go to for *everything*."

I stared at him, and shook my head in disbelief. "I've thought a lot about this. I want to be your friend, and I won't lie that I've been confused, but for both our sakes, stop pushing this. Stop tempting me just because you can. I'm going through a lot right now, and I need to figure that out first." He opened his mouth to say something, but I cut him off before he could get a word in. "I can't even promise to tell you the truth most of the time. Asking for more... you're going to get hurt. Do you get that?" Some part of me was attracted to him, that much was clear, but I had far too many commitments to add his undying love to my list of burdens.

"I'm not scared of you," he whispered.

I shook my head, almost sadly. I wished I could reverse time. Go back to every stolen kiss and turn away. Never let anything grow. Never unleash my power. Never crave touch the same way I craved death.

"Let it go, and give me time to figure my life out. That's what I *need* right now." My voice was too impassive to be anguished, but there was an undercurrent of desperation that I think spoke to him more than heated gazes or trav-eling hands.

"Okay," he finally said. "But will you promise me something?"

"I'll think about it," I said. It was almost friendly, but there was a hint of finality to it on my part, because my mind was finally made up, and I wasn't torn anymore. I'd thought about him for months, agonizing over whether what I'd done was right, and what I would do when this moment came. I shouldn't have kissed him back last April, but that was a lesson learned on what it meant to get caught up in the moment.

"What's that supposed to mean?" For the first time in three months, I heard playfulness in his voice again. He didn't like it—his eyes were sad—but some part of him seemed to accept my answer, at least for now.

"It depends on what you want."

He chuckled, and his hand brushed mine, but he made no attempt to take it. "Promise me that— Goddammit," Lucas swore, stopping before we entered the house.

"What?"

He hesitated, his eyes growing harder by the second.

"Will you spit it out already?"

He swallowed hard, and I turned for the house. If he wouldn't tell me, someone else would.

"There's been another attack," he croaked. I went still as I waited for him to continue. "The Council has declared a state of emergency. We have to return to Daizlei."

My heart hammered in my chest. Sweat slicked my palms, and the sunny-morning mountain breeze turned cold.

"Who?"

"Aldric Fortescue is dead."

CHAPTER 8

Three phone calls, a cold shower, and forty-seven minutes later, Lucas, Alec, and I stood in a circle around Tori. She was still in the midst of the transition, but with no other teleporter at hand, we were out of options. All fake manners and real hostility were let go of temporarily as we made a reckless plan to get from one side of the country to the other. Tori had to get us to Denver International Airport in one shot, where we would take a plane for the final stretch to Daizlei. Never mind that she'd never teleported with this many people before, or this far.

I tried not to let her cautious glances bother me too much. I was Selena Foster, after all, and she'd known what she was getting into before she chose to be my friend—in a way. That didn't make it any easier, though. While her mom may've been a bitch and unworthy of her affection, that didn't mean she'd wanted to see the other side of me lash out. She'd been giving me sad, almost scared looks for a little while now, and as much as I wanted to be unconcerned by it, I wasn't.

"We should talk. Get us through this, and maybe we'll get a chance some time next year," I said.

Her lips twitched as she took my hand, but my joke fell flat. "I'll get us there, one way or another." She reached out, taking Alec's hand in her other, and Lucas sealed the circle.

"You ready for this?" Lucas asked.

"She doesn't have a choice," Alec said dryly.

I wanted to respond, but lost my nerve when she took a steadying breath. She looked from one person to the next, as if committing our faces to memory.

Can she really do this?

The dark circles under her eyes didn't help my confidence. She sucked in one last breath of air, and my world went black.

I squeezed my eyes shut as the nausea rolled through me, putting all my strength into gripping the two hands I was holding.

"Agh!" Someone yelled as the ground rushed in too fast.

In a split second, I'd twisted underneath Tori to take the brunt of the impact. Nothing had prepared me for the searing pain in my head when bathroom tile greeted us. Time stood still for a moment, everything slowing to a crawl. I couldn't make out the shapes in front of me, but the ringing in my ears wasn't good. As the black receded, the world came back into focus, and Lucas was saying my name over and over again, along with something about dying.

"Holy fuck, that hurt." I groaned and pushed off the tile floor. My fingers scraped across jagged cracks where my body had left an indent.

"We need to move. The cops are going to be here any minute." Alec hoisted Tori into his arms. She was passed out, with even darker circles under her eyes. Her cheek-bones were far too prominent, but at least she was alive. That was something.

"Take Victoria and go, but I'm not leaving her."

"Then pick her up, goddammit, but—"

"I can walk. I've felt worse," I said.

My body betrayed me when my legs shook so violently I could hardly hold myself up. Clutching the bathroom counter, I looked at where we'd landed. Given the indent in the floor where my head had hit, I was lucky to be conscious. Thank god it wasn't Tori; I didn't think she could've survived that impact. Not to mention being in the throes of the transition. She would have been a Made Vampire before sunset. As it was, she already looked feverish again. If I'd had the strength, I would've insisted on carrying her.

I tugged my arm loose from my jacket to remove the small knife I'd put there not even an hour ago. A small splotch of blood was smeared against my skin, but the cut had already healed. I cursed, shoving it into the holder on my hip. Rushed footsteps sounded less than a hundred yards away, and with Tori unconscious, there was no way to get out unseen.

"We need to leave," Alec insisted. He walked out of the bathroom before I could yell for him not to. They were coming.

Lucas wrapped an arm around my waist and moved me along.

"They're going to see us—"

"He's got it covered. Just keep walking," Lucas urged silently, pulling me along.

My legs quaked, but kept moving. As we rounded the corner of the bathroom, he flattened me to the wall as men and women in police uniforms rushed by. Not a single one of them glanced in our direction. How the...?

"They only see what he wants them to," Lucas whispered as we stepped out into the terminal.

The airport was bustling with people, and I had no idea how many were friend or foe, not to mention human. We followed Alec, steadily gaining speed as my legs strengthened. My hearing and eyesight were already back to normal, and the pain was fading fast. As we rounded the next corner, I slipped from his grip, and picked up the pace.

"Lily," I said, raising my voice just enough to be heard several hundred yards away.

Her head whipped around, eyes searching for me. Her left hand trembled violently as the filthy tissue she clutched slipped from her fingers.

"Selena?" she croaked. Her gaze flicked to the men on either side of me, widening when she saw my unconscious roommate.

"We ran into some complications, but everyone's fine." I pulled her to my side and kissed her forehead. Alec made an impatient noise next to me, but he needn't have bothered. I was completely aware of the time crunch. "Where's Blair?"

"Attempting to feed the hollow leg left in my care." I turned to see my cousin holding a corn dog with mustard. Her light blond hair was pulled back in a braid, making the tiny scars that covered her all the more visible. She silently held the corn dog out to my sister and stepped back. She was more tense than usual, but I chalked it up to our situation. "We need to board. The first flight is leaving any second, but she refused to get on without you." She thumbed at Lily and turned to the 'flight attendant,' who was glaring at us. I doubted she was actually a flight attendant, given that Daizlei didn't let humans into our school. Probably just a normal Supernatural who worked for the Council or the school.

"We can't leave. Not without Alexandra!" Lily yelled, suddenly pissed and panicking. Mustard flew everywhere, and her eyes turned dark. Oh fuck, we didn't have time for her mood swings.

"Lily, get on the plane or so help me god—" I started.

"What took you so long?" she said suddenly, sighing in relief. She ran to the empty air and threw her arms around herself. What the...?

"She sees what he wants her to." Lucas grimaced.

My sister walked to the flight attendant, now placated, and entered the hallway that led to the plane. I stood, staring in horror. Whatever small slice of peace we'd found in all the chaos of leaving was going to be lost the moment my sister realized she'd been lied to and manipulated.

"Stop." My voice cracked with emotion that I couldn't contain.

Alec was already pushing past me when he slammed into an invisible wall. He cursed, turning to me. This boy had done nothing but piss me off since I'd met him. I could see why Lucas found him insufferable.

"We don't have time for this. We need to get out of here, and she wasn't going to leave without the redhead." His eyes turned predatory before shifting to Blair.

She stiffened, her hands not so subtly moving to the blade on her belt, and he deflated instantly.

I cocked my head to the side.

"How do you know what my sister looks like?" I asked pointedly.

"It's my job to know things." He turned his glare back on me, and Blair sighed. She already knew what the issue was. Anyone who'd been with Lily for ten minutes could tell.

"Then you should have known that she's already half gone, and when she loses her fucking marbles because she finds out what you did, she's going to start throwing them at you, and not even your precious mistress will save you then." I wanted to say more, to let the impact of what he'd just done fully hit him. Lily was in the worst place she'd been since my parents' deaths, and he'd just screwed with her mind to get her to cooperate. It was unforgivable, because she already couldn't tell the difference between nightmares and reality.

Blair grabbed my arm and tugged me toward the plane doors. "Leave it. As much as I would love to see you kick his ass, your roommate isn't looking so hot, and your sister's going to unleash hell on that plane as soon as she figures out what just happened."

I glanced at Tori. Her face was drawn. She had at least another twelve hours before the transition faded. She could hold out that long, though. Lily couldn't. I needed to get her back in a secure environment where I could start working with her to calm the madness. Otherwise, someone would pay.

I loved Alexandra dearly, and I would worry until I saw

her, but Lily was running out of time before she snapped again. I had to trust that my headstrong sister would keep her word and make it back to Daizlei by nightfall. She was unpredictable at times, but she wasn't dumb. If Vampires had killed Aldric Fortescue and the Council had declared a state of emergency, then we weren't safe. No one was.

Alexandra knew that. She had to.

"Let's go."

I ENDED up giving Lily enough Xanax to knock out a horse, hoping she would sleep for the rest of the flight. She was now drooling contently against the blanket I'd squished into the corner where her chair met the wall. Blair had taken up my other side along the aisle, effectively keeping the others away and giving us room.

I tugged on the neck of my shirt, sweat rolling down my temple. What was it about tight spaces that bothered me? I could've blamed it on the warehouse, but that wouldn't be true. The lack of escape or maneuverability had always agitated me, long before I'd even heard of Daizlei. It just got worse every time. I wasn't the only one struggling in the stale air of the airplane, though. Blair fidgeted right and left, her back straight as a board against the seat. The last flight we'd taken had nearly caused a panic, but this time she was prepared. We'd done enough drills over the summer for her to know how to handle her own claustrophobia.

"When she wakes up, there's going to be hell to pay," I whispered.

"I don't agree with that bastard's methods, but at least she's on the plane." Her jaw clenched and unclenched.

I narrowed my eyes. "You know him. How?"

She continued staring at the seat in front of her. Her eyes glazed over. She got like this when we talked about the warehouse, but never anything else. There was history between them, but not the good kind.

"Alec Hunter was a senior the year I entered high school. Our paths crossed, and he burned me. That's all you need to know."

I turned forward, giving her a moment before speaking. "If there's an issue, we'll take care of it. One way or another." It was a promise, and one I didn't make often. She was the exception to all my rules, though, because she was like me.

Blair nodded once, and I let it be.

The amount of shit that had hit the fan in the last twenty-four hours was unbelievable. I hadn't been any closer to finding out who'd sent the demons when the Vampires showed up, Tori was bitten, Aldric Fortescue was killed, and now, to make matters worse, Lucas was involved. I didn't really care one way or another about Aldric, but I was probably the least happy to see Anastasia ascend to the throne early. I could only imagine the frenzy the Council had fallen into, but all anyone knew were rumors at this point. Apart from Alec, and he wasn't spilling his mistress's secrets anytime soon.

With the heat of several hundred bodies pressing in on me, I was feeling pulled in too many directions, and needed something to ground me among the madness. I settled for blaming Mariana for keeping us out of the loop when the attacks had gotten worse. If she'd at least told us, this might not have come as a surprise, and I sure as hell wouldn't have wanted Alexandra to leave the States.

"Your mother didn't say anything about this the entire three months I was there. She never mentioned the attacks —or that people were being taken. I've walked into a world at war nearly blind. If it weren't for Daizlei and the whispers I heard, I wouldn't even have known that tensions were running high when the summer began," I said under my breath.

Blair sighed. "She's changed since your mom died. She's distant now, afraid of the Supernatural and our world. She avoids it, even though she tries to come across like she doesn't," Blair said, staring at nothing in particular.

I knew her well enough now to know she did that when she was uncomfortable. "When I met her, she was the spitting image of Supernatural wealth and sophistication. You were too," I said.

Her mouth tightened, and her lips pursed ever so slightly. "We all wear a mask, Selena. My mother is no different." She paused and looked at me. "After Elizabeth…I don't think she knows what to do with herself. You may have walked into this world blind, but you're not alone. Every break, she calls me back to that godforsaken house and cuts me off from the world. If it weren't for Daizlei, I wouldn't have seen any farther than her garden."

I wasn't the greatest at knowing what to say when people were vulnerable. I settled for nodding and changing the subject. "Anastasia's going to call for war, and the Council is too divided to have a chance of standing up to her. We need to be prepared." When she just continued to stare at the back of the seat, I assumed she was lost in her own brilliant and terrifying thoughts.

"We've lived through worse. We will make it through this."

I nodded in agreement.

The scars on my palms prickled, and I thought of the other me.

The one with glowing violet eyes.

One of us would be here to see it through.

For the world's sake, I prayed it was me, because she would shatter what was left of it when the Council was done.

CHAPTER 9

"Where are we?" Lily yawned, rubbing the sleep from her eyes.

"Touching down. We should be there any minute now." I pulled my hair back in a ponytail, already gearing up for a fight. Her volatile moodswings had been the only thing predictable about her these past months.

"Right..." She drawled it out, frowning to herself.

I took a deep breath and kept my eyes focused on the back of the seat. I needed to keep her calm until we landed.

"I was so worried about you and Alexandra making it back in time— Where is she?" she asked, so innocently... except that there was nothing innocent about her. Not anymore. If she knew what they'd done, and that I'd gone along with it, she would tear this plane apart. She wasn't stable anymore, now that the killing gene was active, and only time would tell if she harbored my particular brand of damning urges and destructive tendencies. Better not to find out here, though.

"She's in the bathroom," I said carefully, considering my words.

She nodded and turned to look out the window. Daizlei rose up to greet us as the plane descended well within the school's walls.

"She's been in there a long time. Maybe I should go check on her." She picked at the broken stubs that passed for her nails, glancing back at the bathroom anxiously.

"She's fine, Lily. Just grab your stuff, and we can meet her at dinner tonight." I tried hard to keep my voice nonchalant as I stood and swung my bag over my shoulder then held out a hand to help her. Blair stood next to me, collected as ever. My silent shadow.

"I really think I should check. Even for her, this is a little abnormal—" She tried to step around me.

"Come on, Lily." I grabbed her hand and pulled her before she could process what was happening. Blair followed along with her bag and came up on her other side.

"What— Selena, stop. What are you doing?" she stammered, panic rising.

I had to get her out of here. *Move,* I thought, and the crowd parted. I walked quickly, leaving before people could realize their feet hadn't moved of their own accord.

"Oh my god," she whispered, head flipping back and forth between Blair and me. Ten feet. That was all we had to clear, and then we would be outside.

"She's not here, is she?" Her voice was rising. I knew the shift was coming before I saw it.

"Blair, let go of her," I murmured, descending the stairs. The crowd only thickened, but Blair stayed a few steps behind us to keep people back.

"Where is she?" she yelled.

"*Selena?*" Lucas probed, but I didn't have time for him.

"She's coming, but I need you to take a deep breath and try to think about this rationally."

Her feet slammed into the ground, unmovable. "You told me she was here. I *saw* her get on the plane. *Where is she?*" she screamed, consumed by emotions too strong for her to temper.

I stood facing her with one hand curled around her arm as I contemplated throwing Alec under the bus. "She's not here, Lily. She's in Italy, where she's been the entire summer. She's coming back, though, as soon as it's safe for her to leave," I said calmly, not looking away from her frightened brown eyes. It killed me to see the madness there, both the killing gene and the other. She thought she'd been hallucinating.

"I-I saw her though. I saw her, Selena. She walked right up to me..." Her voice trailed off as the hurt turned inward.

I grabbed her other arm and shook it.

"You weren't going to leave, and we needed to get out of there. I didn't want to lie to you, but I didn't have another choice." I spoke slowly, watching her eyes change as she realized what had actually happened.

"You always have a choice, and you chose to lie to me. There was no discussion. You just played me." The anger was rising again, building to crescendo so strong she wouldn't be able to control it. Her eyes turned black, and the ink crept through her veins. The darkness was coming.

"She didn't play you, I did."

I whipped around to see Alec standing on the edge of the circle that separated us from *them*—the normals, the

Supernaturals who didn't have the gene or great power. "What the hell are you doing?"

"My sister was attacked by a Vampire yesterday, and your sister," he pointed to me, "saved her." Lily watched him with a strange fascination. "She's going through the transition, which is why I was carrying her in the airport. Do you remember that?" He waited, we both did, to see what she would do.

"I saw my sister there. She hugged me and walked with me onto the airplane," she said, unable to separate real from imagined.

"You saw her because I wanted you to see her." His golden eyes were fixed on her.

"Why? Why would you show me my sister if she wasn't there?" Her voice sounded small, childlike. It killed me to see her this way, so broken, the damage more than I was sure she could bear.

"My sister was hurting, and I needed to get her back here. So she was safe. Do you understand that, Lily? That she was hurt and needed help?" He was telling her the truth in the most basic and manipulative way. He was the Fortescues' servant, though, and I suppose that was the entirety of his job on a good day.

"But you lied to me. You made me see someone who wasn't there. Someone who may never make it back here, or be safe again." Her eyes hardened. I felt the power rise up within her as she glared at him. "I don't care who was hurt, you had no right to do what you did. You had no right!"

I gripped her arms in an iron hold as she tried to take a step forward. Her dark eyes swiveled from him to me, and the black tendrils of her power reached out. I threw a wall up around us to keep anyone from intervening.

"Get out of my way!" she snarled.

"Not happening. You're two seconds from killing someone. You need to rein it in. Control the darkness." I ground my teeth as the tendrils wrapped around me.

"It's so heavy. The pain just weighs on me, Selena. It's a suffering I can't see past, no matter what I do. I need someone to understand. To hurt like I hurt," she whispered, continuing to take from me, but I wouldn't falter. I wouldn't fail. I'd already failed once, when the demons took her. I wouldn't let their ghosts take her again.

"I know you do, Lily, better than anyone. You have to control it, though. Control the monster. I can teach you to give and take pain in moderation, to never sink this low again. You have to control it, though, otherwise someone's going to die."

She sighed in almost contentment, and then...I felt her shift. Something went wrong, and the black energy that had been reaching toward me was suddenly writhing to return to her, but she didn't seem to know how to stop as she screamed. "Oh my god, it hurts! Take it back! Please. Please! I'll do anything, just make it end."

I tried to pull away, to cut off her feeding, but I couldn't break the link. She sobbed, hot tears rolling down her face.

"I can't break it, Lily. You need to control it. Control the pain. Let it go."

She paused, her unseeing eyes staring into nothing as she gripped my wrists.

"Let it go," I whispered.

She took a step back and dropped her hands. Releasing the hold.

Black tendrils swarmed her. Crawling up her arms and back under her skin, they dissipated until no trace remained but her coal-colored eyes.

"I thought I knew darkness," she murmured. Her knees shook so badly she fell to the ground, kneeling before me.

I crouched down in front of her, but kept my hands to myself. She was calming the storm. She was putting her own fire out. She was learning she could do it.

"I thought I knew terror. Thought my pain was too great." Her eyes focused on mine, and I didn't back down. She needed to know that I was here, that I wasn't afraid. "I know nothing." Her eyes cleared, back to the dark, unwavering brown they were supposed to be. "How do you keep it at bay?" she asked earnestly, looking at me like I was the very god she'd been waiting for, the one with the answers, the one who could free her. "How can you laugh with such dark thoughts? How can you smile?"

"I'll teach you." I held out my hand, giving her the opportunity to decide, to weigh her options.

"You can teach me to do that? You can free me?" Her fear of being disappointed was almost tangible, but for the first time in months, she had hope. If I could stop myself from killing people because of guilt, she could save herself with hope.

"No. I can only show you how." I paused, tilting her chin up to make her look at me when her eyes fell. "Because you can free yourself."

She wrapped her arms around my neck as I dropped the wall separating us from the rest of the world. Cold eyes stared at me over Lily's shoulder. Professor Vonlowsky stood proud and arrogant next to Alec Hunter, clearly waiting for me.

"What do you want?"

"Pleasant as always, Foster. Headmaster Daizlei and his *guests* would like to have a word with you. Privately." He motioned to the mess of a girl in my arms. I turned to where Blair had been moments before I'd cut off the world. Lucas stood next to her, his hard gaze unflinching as he stared down the messenger, even with his sister curled up in his arms. Blair was wearing her bored, prep-school expression, but she cocked her eyebrow at me, a silent question.

"Take her back to her room and sit with her until I'm done, please. I'd rather she not be left alone." I stood, pulling Lily up with me.

Both she and Blair glared at Alec as my cousin led her back to Building Two. Professor Vonlowsky tapped his watch impatiently.

"Lucas, please just take Tori back to my room, and I'll come find you when this is over." I wanted to push him. To tell him to go, because I didn't even know why he was here in the first place. His sister was going through the transition. She was his priority. I could take care of me and mine.

His eyes flashed, and I remembered his little discovery about reading my mind.

"That's what you get for listening uninvited. Not always so pleasant, is it?"

He turned and walked away before I could continue mentally berating him.

"What are you waiting for? We both know that this is a

summons and not a request. May as well get it over with." I motioned for Vonlowsky and Alec to lead the way.

"You may want to drop the attitude, Foster. Council Member Fortescue is even less forgiving than I." He smirked, holding open the door to the clock tower where Headmaster Daizlei's office was.

"Fortescue?" I asked, turning to Alec. "Your mistress is here, and you neglected to mention this because…?"

"Because what she chooses to do or where she goes is none of your business." The harshness in his features returned. With the way he held himself, the tightness in his jaw, I couldn't help but wonder how fond he really was of her. Maybe a little too fond.

Vonlowsky gave the giant oak three sharp knocks, and the doors swung open. Someone was expecting us.

"Selena, darling, it's been far too long."

CHAPTER 10

"ANASTASIA."

"How dare you—"

"It's fine, Hunter. Selena is here as my guest, after all." She silenced Alec with a glare and motioned to the chair in front of her.

I glanced at Headmaster Daizlei, sitting behind his long oak desk— the desk Anastasia was currently leaning against. Her guards were stationed throughout the room, melding into the shadows, neither seen nor heard. Daizlei's face was stoic, an unreadable mask. This couldn't be good.

"Guest?" I repeated, plopping into the chair with exaggerated ease.

Her eyebrow rose, but there was no amusement in her eyes. "Guest."

"To what do I owe this pleasure, Council Member Fortescue?" I worked to keep my tone light, friendly.

She smirked at the change in title, but I played the humble commoner well. I couldn't afford to show worry. Anxiety clawed up my throat with every passing moment that she stared at me with those unwavering, cold blue eyes. Being summoned so soon for a visit after her grandfather's death and my interrogation wasn't a good sign. Something was wrong. It was the only reason she would travel halfway around the world in person. She either wanted something, or this was my execution.

"I'm sure you've heard what's transpired over the last twelve hours."

"My condolences for your grandfather. He'll be dearly missed." They were pretty words. Respectful words. The very words people had offered me when my parents died. If I'd had time to pretend, I would've looked for different ones, because, judging by the clenching of her fists and shuddering breath, she felt the same way about them I had. They weren't enough, and they never would be.

"He will be," she murmured, taking a breath to steady herself. "But that's not why I'm here." She pushed off the desk, and walked away. Her steps were measured as she approached the massive stained-glass clock that towered over campus. I glanced at Daizlei now that her back was to us, but he remained a statue as ageless as time.

"The Council is calling for war. The Vampires have been testing the boundary for the last half a century, and some members view my grandfather's death as the final straw." Her voice carried.

"I was under the impression that the table was divided. Which leaves you."

Her back straightened, and the clock chimed. "Publically, I'll support the war because my grandfather just died, and that's what's expected."

I crossed my ankles and rested my hands in a steeple. "And outside the public eye?"

She turned to meet my eyes. "I'll be putting together a group of exceptionally gifted Supernaturals to end this war before it even starts. A group you'll be leading."

I stared at her, mouth hanging open, unable to form a coherent response. "You— I— What?" I spluttered, dropping the nonchalant façade.

"I don't want to go to war, Selena. Millions will die, and there's a high risk of exposure. The Council is proposing a draft, and taking those soldiers to Veliky Novgorod before winter hits. They want to strike now...however, they understand my concerns. Therefore, they're willing to postpone any declaration of war if they start seeing results. Results I think you can deliver."

I weighed my response. Results. Such a diplomatic way of saying murder, like assassination was just marking off a to-do list. "Let me get this straight. The Council wants to attack the Vampire capital of the world, and you want to stop it?"

"Correct." Her response was stiff, but her actions seemed sincere.

"And you want me to lead some band of misfit servants to god knows where and hunt down those *things*? Don't you have anyone better suited for this?" I wanted to ask why the hell she wanted me, but I knew why. I'm a telekinetic. Which put a price on my head, but also made me valuable, because I would be able to do things they couldn't dream of, if my powers continued to grow.

"Not quite. I want you to lead a team of soldiers I've personally chosen to accompany you to hunt down

Vampires. And they are not my servants. They volunteered." She tapped her heel impatiently, oblivious to the flaws in this grand plan of hers.

"I have several issues with that statement. First and foremost, I don't know where you got this idea that I'm the girl for your mission. Second, even if I was—which I'm not —I pick my team, not you." I stood, turning to walk out the door.

"I think you'll want to reconsider."

I paused, glancing over my shoulder. "And what's that supposed to mean?"

Her blue eyes pierced me as the overwhelming presence of her mind pushed down on mine in a battle of wills. "Victoria Hunter's memory of your attack was tampered with, which is, by law, a crime I could have you put on trial for. Instead, I want to make you an offer." Her shark grin widened. "You fight for me for the duration of the war, and in the end, you go free, and can use my team to hunt down whoever sent the Vampires after you."

Silence ticked by like the hand of a clock that never stopped.

"How do you know what happened if Victoria's memories were altered? How do you know I even had anything to do with it?" I asked, trying to carefully dance around accepting the blame even though I *wasn't* the one to blame for this. If anything, Lucas was the idiot who hadn't covered his tracks well enough, and now the Head of the Council had enough dirt on me to get me killed if I didn't do what she asked.

"Because when her memory was re-evaluated, we found these interesting inconsistencies between what she thought had transpired, and the little message you sent." She paused, giving me a moment to weigh my options. Or maybe just taking the time to enjoy her victory. If she really was able to break through whatever Lucas had done...I was in deep shit. Like, mounds of it.

"Why do you want me in the first place? Why not just dole out your punishment and be done with it?" I asked, knowing full well she didn't need the Council to take action against me. She was drawing this out, playing with me, and for what? A flippin war I wanted nothing to do with.

"Because you don't have a problem killing, and that makes you useful. I'm making you an offer for freedom and a chance at vengeance. Don't be stupid, Selena. Take it, before I change my mind and kill you instead." Her abrupt switch wasn't surprising, but at least she wasn't pretending to be anything more than the monster she was beneath that face.

She was playing a dangerous game threatening me, but I wasn't a fool. Anastasia Fortescue had nothing to lose but the respect of her people. Whereas I...I had everything now. I had a sister I needed to live for, and a promise to keep. I had friends...well, kind of. I didn't know where Lucas and I stood. Given his role in putting me in the middle of this shitstorm, I wasn't exactly his biggest fan at the moment. Then there was the whole matter of promising Tori that I would get revenge—for her, for Lily, and myself.

Anastasia's deal was the best shot I was going to get, even if being her assassin stripped whatever remaining morals I had left. Something still didn't sit right, though, and the inexplicable sense of wrongness hit me strongly enough that I knew I needed to bargain for one more thing

—because I was selfish, and that was what selfish people did. "Okay, but I want something."

"I'm listening," she said.

I stared at the glass clock behind her, wondering how hard it would be to shatter it and kill them all. Wondering how my life had become a bargaining chip. How I'd ended up here. That one was a little easier, though.

Lucas.

I was here because of him, and how he'd *fixed* things. I'd been right not to get tangled up in his so-called love. It had made him a damned fool, and now I was paying the price.

"I want to choose my team. At least part of it. Supernaturals working for the Council tend to lead inexplicably short lives, and I want people I trust guarding my back." I paused, waiting for her answer. I really had no room to be arguing here. No leverage. All I had was the gut instinct that she'd give me what I wanted, because she didn't want me dead—at least not yet.

"Why would I do that? They're children, only just coming into their own powers, and while a good number of them will end up on the front lines anyway if the draft is called in, they aren't strong enough for this. I will only have the best representing the Council."

I didn't know what to say, because she wasn't wrong. But...for the first time in my life, I didn't want to go it alone. Not completely. Lily wasn't coming anywhere near this—she would be safer here—but the others...I wanted them. I would need them when the time came, to remember what living felt like. To drag me out of the darkness kicking and screaming. I needed them, because now that I knew what it was like to live, I didn't want to die inside again—but I wasn't strong enough to save myself.

I couldn't say that, though, because that was weak. So, I would approach it from a different angle, one powerful people could understand.

"I'm no older than them, and yet you don't seem to mind asking for my freedom. If you truly want a team that's strong and can end a war, you'll give them the choice, because I can guarantee that they're stronger than any band of reject royals you'll give me."

It wasn't a lie, but it also definitely wasn't the truth. I had no idea if they'd be stronger—all I knew was that the people she was bound to give me probably wouldn't care one way or another what we killed or if I died. My friends would, though. They would be my humanity and give me a reason to fight when the killing gene overwhelmed me.

"Stronger? You've killed demons, survived a Vampire attack, and I've seen you massacre a number of young men for underestimating you. You have no mercy. You told me that yourself. It's the only reason you're here." She paused, stepping forward to meet me eye-to-eye. "And you're telling me they can do the same? That they are stronger than even heirs to the Council?" Her smile was cool, and vicious.

I should've thrown myself on the pyre and just accepted her offer at face value. I shouldn't have tried to think long game, because I was pretty sure she was going to give me what I asked for. But not without a price.

Swallowing the bile in my throat, I couldn't stop myself from sealing their fate when I said, "Yes."

She missed nothing. The clock chimed behind her, like a warning bell I should've heeded.

"You have a month to train with the nine soldiers I've chosen. I'll allow you to choose six of your own, who will also train. You have twenty-four hours to get me their names and await further instructions."

What I'd just done made me want to vomit, because it was far too easy. And if I knew anything about the Fortescues, it was that nothing came easy where they were involved. Her response had been too quick. Too planned. I didn't like it.

"This is an honor, and you will treat it as such. Some people give their firstborn child for the chance to serve my family, and you get the privilege of serving as penance for *your* crimes." Her words were mocking, condescending. After the last couple of days I'd had, though, I couldn't give two shits what she thought of me. Only how this little game we were playing turned out.

"Is that all?" I asked, feeling both tired and out of control. Her patience was running thin, and I knew I shouldn't push my luck any more than I already had, but the urge to remind her who she was talking to was very tempting.

"For now," she said dismissively. "Do we have a deal?"

Deal. For some reason, the word felt off—maybe because what she was doing wasn't a deal. It was blackmail.

She held out her hand, pale white and identical in every way to my own.

At least she isn't pretending I'm a guest anymore, I thought bitterly.

I forced myself to place my palm in hers. If I played my cards right, no one would set foot in the Vampire capital, and I would get to keep every promise I'd made.

Her ice-cold fingers wrapped around mine as she whispered her final command.

I nodded once.

What have I done?

CHAPTER II

THE SECOND THE OFFICE DOORS CLOSED BEHIND ME, I bolted for Building Two. Mind racing, I couldn't even begin to process everything that had just occurred. What I'd just done. My sisters were going to be pissed. Lucas was going to be furious.

I'd just signed my life away, and, thanks to Anastasia's last demand, I couldn't even tell them why. She would come down like a hammer on us all if I told them the truth, because, unlike me, they wouldn't keep silent, and she knew that. That bitch knew that what she was doing wasn't right, and she wouldn't risk the Council's reputation on one of them running their mouths that the Head of the Council had had to blackmail me into this.

The reality of it hit me as I stood in front of my door, lost in myself, not knowing what to say to the people I would find on the other side. The door swung open, and his shadow loomed over me as Lucas stared down. I couldn't find the words to tell him that there would be no school for me, no boxing. That my old life was gone.

His eyes went wide as he reached for me, but now wasn't the time for comfort. I sidestepped him and ducked under his arm. My gaze fell on the redhead standing before me, tall and regal, boasting a slight tan from the summer sun.

"Alexandra?" After everything I'd seen in the last two days, I couldn't trust my eyes. "How did you get—?"

"You're not the only resourceful one here." She wrapped her arms around me.

Over her shoulder, I saw what she meant by resourceful. Standing only a few feet from us was her boyfriend Aaron White, the pain-in-my-ass boxer who burned with too much intensity for comfort. If I'd thought she was tanned, he was brown. His eyes settled on me with the same tension as always, black as coal and darker than I'd ever seen them. A shiver ran through me.

"What is he doing here?" I didn't even bother to take the edge out of my voice, and Alexandra tensed.

"He's with me," she said, as if that were a real answer.

I released her and stepped back, suddenly aware of how many people were in this room. Lily sat in the far corner on my bed, with her arms wrapped around her legs, watching Tori as she slept under the pile of blankets thrown on top of her. The chills must've returned, but she was looking better. The transition must be coming to an end.

Blair leaned against my window with her hip angled in such a way that silver gleamed. She wore the knife on display; little did they know she actually knew how to use it now. Blair looked at me, arms across her chest and head held high. Her eyebrow arched as she motioned to my sister's boyfriend.

"What the hell is going on?" Alexandra asked. Always the charmer.

"He needs to leave. We have a lot to discuss." I moved to Tori's side and swept the hair from her forehead. She was cold as ice, and didn't even shift under my touch. I sighed.

The room tensed as Aaron took a step toward us. In less than a second, the metal at Blair's hip was released and in her hand. Heat flared as Alexandra ignited her hands, stepping up to the plate. I turned and glared in both their directions.

"Out," I said to him. His eyes were so dark, almost like demons'. That didn't help his chances.

"No! He goes where I go," Alexandra declared. She kept her eyes on Blair, but her words were for me and me alone.

I looked at her, the way she held herself. The way she was standing in front of him, protecting him. I cocked my head, and narrowed my eyes. "We have things to discuss, Alexandra. I'm not going to ask twice. He leaves *now*." I growled the last words.

"No," she said defiantly.

Silence fell between us, but for the life of me, I couldn't understand why the sight of her with him infuriated me. *He can't be trusted,* I reminded myself.

"Alexandra—"

"I'm back!" Amber called as my bedroom door flew open. Six pairs of eyes fell on her.

Goddammit, could I not even have a discussion in peace? I had to figure out how to break it to them and ask for help, but I couldn't even clear a room.

"Amber—"

"What's going on here?" she asked, gaze darting around the room at an impossible speed.

"Nothing. Can we have the room please?" I asked, trying my damndest to be polite. We'd come a long way in the last year, and she knew more about me than a lot of the people in this room.

"You're evading," she said simply, walking around the small space. Her gaze landed on Tori. "What happened to her?"

Ah hell.

"She was bitten by a Vampire. The transition should be phasing out soon. You can ask her more when she wakes up," I said.

She stilled, staring down at her best friend with a wistful look. Her expression went blank before I could read any more into it.

"Can we get back to the matter at hand?" Blair said unceremoniously.

Alexandra rolled her eyes, keeping herself between Aaron and the rest of us.

"Matter at hand?" Amber asked. She moved to Tori's side, brushing her hair back from her face.

"Do I need to take this somewhere else, Amber?"

"On the contrary, don't stop on my behalf," she purred, but her heart wasn't in it.

I rolled my eyes and returned my attention to the two girls locked in a stare-down. "Blair, put the knife away." She stared warily at my sister and her boyfriend, but sheathed the knife.

Alexandra's gaze flipped between us, as if she couldn't believe what she was seeing, and a cackle escaped her. "I leave for one summer, and she becomes your guard dog?" She turned to me, and met my gaze with a challenge.

"Leave it, sister," I murmured. As I paced the room to collect my thoughts, the knife in my boot flew to my hand, and I spun it over and over. Its blade danced across my palm, too fast for anyone to keep track of.

"Selena." A deep voice brought me to a halt as he grazed my forearm with his fingers. My gaze flew to his, and the blade stilled. I turned my back on him and focused on the people before me.

"You're going to tell him what I say, regardless of whether he's here or not. Aren't you?"

Alexandra nodded, still standing protectively in front of him. The funny thing was that he didn't need protecting, and the look he gave me said so.

I walked to the window and stared out into the wide expanse of the sunset. I couldn't even say it was my last moment of freedom. That had already gone the moment Lucas tried to help me.

"Anastasia Fortescue met with me to inform me that I've been chosen for the *honor* of serving the Council, to try to end the war before it begins." The word *honor* tasted vile in my mouth, but I told them of my task and what I was being asked to do, and what they would do if they chose to join me. I told them of the coming war, and what the Council intended. I never told them what she'd promised in return, though, or that I'd been blackmailed to begin with. I didn't mention how I'd bargained for them, because my pride wasn't ready to admit that I needed their help, despite the great disservice I'd done to them as my friends.

I was a coward, and I deserved the sentence given to me, but they didn't.

The silence stretched on for what felt like an endless moment.

"What did they promise you?"

I turned to my wisp of sister, the first to speak, and the first to ask something I couldn't answer. Not yet. Not until the war was over, Anastasia had said, so I did the only thing I could do. "I'm sorry," I whispered.

"What did they promise you, Selena?" she repeated. Her eyes were terrified. Lost.

"Something precious." I ran a shaky hand through my hair and pulled the ponytail loose. I turned to walk out, unable to handle the weight of their eyes, but a burning hand wrapped around my bicep, catching me.

"I know that look, Selena. What did you do?" Alexandra said, her eyes burning with rage, but not at me. I couldn't tell her the truth, but maybe I could tell her something else. A half-truth.

I swallowed the bile and averted my eyes. "I was asked to serve because I have a particular skill set the Council wants. I said yes, because when Anastasia Fortescue goes out of her way to ask you for something, you don't exactly say no. It was the right thing to do. Please just trust that."

Lily's sob broke the silence, and Alexandra wrapped her arms around me. I didn't want the comfort, though—I didn't deserve it for lying.

"I volunteer."

My head whipped around.

"I volunteer," Aaron repeated. There was a certain huskiness in his voice, and something in the way he stared at me that had Alexandra's arms tensing.

"Me too," Alexandra said.

"No." It was out of my mouth before I even had time to think.

"What?" She pulled away to glare at me.

"Selena, you should consider it." His voice hit me, quiet but firm.

I stared at him, and raised an eyebrow. Accepting the intrusion for the sake of brevity. *"I don't want to put her in danger,"* I said.

"Selena, that's so fucking typical—" she continued to rant, but I was no longer watching or listening.

"You need six people, Selena, and she's not going to sit by while you leave again. She still feels guilty about the last time. You're better off protecting her, and bringing him with."

"Can he be trusted?" I asked.

Lucas glanced at the other man, whose gaze had never left me, and nodded once.

I grimaced, but accepted the truth. If anyone could save me when the time came, it was her. She knew what to do, the words to say—and I would make sure nothing touched her.

"Fine," I said.

"Fine?" she asked, mid-rant.

I simply nodded, refusing to look at the man behind her. I could keep her safe, I had to believe that, but I had someone else who could help me. Someone I wanted by my side every step of the way.

"Blair?"

"You didn't even have to ask." My cousin grinned viciously.

"I'm going too," Amber chimed in.

"What?"

"I hate school, Selena." Amber said, her eyes locking on Lucas like a cat with a mouse. "Don't look so shocked. Besides...if there's eye candy coming with, it's a win-win." She smirked.

That was terrible reasoning, and I almost said as much until I caught her face when she glanced down at Tori. Not quite lost in thought, but there was more to this than she was saying, and I could accept that.

That was four down.

"Five."

I looked up at him and bit my lip. He deserved to serve at my side for putting me here to begin with, but that didn't lessen my gut reaction: to tell him no as I'd told Alexandra. But he'd brought this down on me, and like her, he would be there to bring me back when the time came. *It's only fair,* my inner demons whispered. I nodded once then turned to my crying sister. Her tears were silent now, apart from her breath hitching. I ran a steady hand down her spine, trying to ease the pain.

"You promised me," she whispered.

"I know."

"You promised me you would teach me how to control it!" she snapped, rocking herself back and forth. Shadows danced in her eyes.

I grabbed her chin, pulling her face up. "Yes, and do I break my promises?"

"But you're leaving—"

"Do I break my promises?" I demanded, knowing that my control would soothe her.

"No," she whispered meekly, lowering her eyes as if she couldn't take the weight of my gaze.

"Then trust me," I said. Kissing the crown of her head, I wrapped my arms around her. I was just happy she wasn't trying to come. I could protect Alexandra, but Lily...she was too far-gone to be that close to anything that bit. I couldn't risk it, and I think she knew that. Sadness swallowed me whole, like hitting a nerve so vital that death would've been kinder.

This is his fault. I couldn't stop the biting thought, and knew that I needed to keep him out for good, because Anastasia wouldn't be kind if he meddled a second time.

"Selena!" he called as I slammed the bricks down and resurrected the walls in my mind. Piling them higher and higher, I enclosed myself in a prison of my own making. His body shifted backward and shuddered, but I only held Lily harder.

He'd said I'd let him into my mind, and if I'd let him in, I could keep him out.

"What's wrong with him?" Alexandra asked, looking back and forth between the two of us.

"I'm fine," he growled.

He'd recovered from being mentally chopped out of my mind faster than I'd expected. He was angry again, and I didn't—couldn't—even entertain the thought that he knew where my mind had been going. Anastasia had made her demands clear.

His presence stalked toward me, and I released my sister to turn on the giant of a man standing over me.

"What the hell was that?" he nearly snarled. His rage was unacceptable, and I glared back to tell him so. He gripped my upper arms and shook me, and I didn't know if it was rage or desperation—maybe both—but I didn't care.

Blair backed away, cleaning her nails with a knife I'd already told her to put away once.

"Hey!" Alexandra yelled, stepping up with fiery fists.

A growl ripped through the room as someone punched him in the face, and knocked him out cold on the floor below me.

I turned on the person who'd intervened.

Aaron's eyes were boiling with contempt as he stared down at Lucas. His chest heaved as he tried to rein himself in. "He doesn't touch you," he said, his words hardly more than whisper.

"You don't get to decide who does or doesn't touch me, asshole," I spat at him, working to contain my own rage at seeing Lucas knocked out, and not by me. I turned on Alexandra. "Leash your dog. I'm not dealing with this bullshit again."

"He was only trying to help—"

"With all due respect, Alexandra, we both know she didn't need anyone's help," Blair cut in, throwing her an icy look.

Alexandra's mouth snapped shut as she looked away.

I sighed, dragging a hand through my hair. This hadn't gone at all as planned. I had five people who couldn't stand to be in the same room, an unconscious body, and a broken sister.

"So...what do we do with the body?" Amber asked, a wicked glint in her eye. Given her delight at seeing him like this, I had to wonder about her pointed man candy comments.

"He's unconscious, not dead, and judging by the bruise on his jaw, he should heal just fine." I rolled my eyes at her sigh of disappointment.

"Do we want to focus on the topic at hand now? We still need a sixth person, preferably someone who's good at getting out of situations. We already have enough..." Blair trailed off at the sound of Tori's yawn. "Muscle," she finished, looking at the other girl peculiarly.

"How are you feeling?" I asked the fragile girl, stepping over her unconscious brother.

She gave me a knowing look and glanced at her brother. "Better," she said tentatively, her gaze sweeping over the room. "So, is anyone goin' to tell me why my brother is passed out on the floor?"

Both Blair and Amber chuckled, and I rolled my eyes.

"You know him, always sticking his head where it doesn't belong," I said nonchalantly, leaning down to turn his face from side to side. Aaron had given him quite the shiner, but Lucas must've been really pissed off not to see it coming.

"You sure you didn't mean hands?" Amber said under her breath.

"Amber," I warned.

"What? She's going to find out anyway," she huffed.

"Find out what?"

"Oh, just how rough he—"

"Amber!" I yelled, but I wasn't the only one who responded. A soft growl rumbled behind me, distinctly male—and since the other one was knocked out, that left only one person to blame. I turned, ready to snap at the audacity of this boy.

"What about her?" Blair said.

"What?" I asked, swinging my glare away from him to focus on my cousin.

"What about Tori? We need a sixth person, and she can teleport." Blair thrust her hand in the girl's direction and raised her eyebrows at me.

"Lucas won't be happy. Neither will Alec."

"It's not their choice," Blair said.

"I agree, and she'll be good for keeping the eye candy in line too." Amber smirked, but her words were serious.

"What are y'all talkin' about?" Tori asked, throwing her covers aside and sitting up with less effort than I'd expected.

I looked at one of my best friends and weighed my options. There were few I trusted more than Tori, and they were all in this room. If the whole point of choosing my own team was to have those I trusted with me, then why was I hesitating?

Shaking the remaining guilt out of my head, I made my choice.

"How would you like to get revenge on the bastard who bit you?"

CHAPTER 12

I stared at the names of the six people I'd lied to and then condemned. Bringing them on was little more than saving my own skin. Last night, after Tori had agreed, I'd sent Aaron and Alexandra away, and had Blair carry Lucas back to his dorm before he woke. Supernatural strengths had its perks sometimes, like getting rid of domineering asshats who'd gotten themselves knocked out for being idiotic. As pissed as I was at Aaron for pulling that, I was even more upset with Lucas. He should've known better.

The body next to mine moved. I glanced over at my sister, squished into my twin bed with me like we were still children, her long blond hair scattered across my pillow. I would've thought she was still sleeping had her breathing not changed.

"Good morning," I said slowly. Throwing my legs off the bed, I yawned. Then walked to the bathroom and prepared for the day.

"Thank you," she whispered. My roommates were still

asleep, but nothing short of Tori's foghorn alarm would've woken them.

"What for?" I asked, brushing my hair out. It was even longer than before, falling past my butt. I really needed to cut it, but somehow could never bring myself to do it.

"Letting me stay. Our time is limited now." Her heart picked up again. She was still so tied to her emotions. I needed to fix that. There was peace in ambivalence; her pain came from feeling.

"I thought we would spend the day together," I said. Her eyes went wide. "If you'd like," I quickly amended, trying to leave the choice to her. She was big on that now—choice—and Alec's little stunt had only exacerbated the need.

"I would like that," she said softly.

I pulled my hair into a tight ponytail, and shed yester-day's clothes. Pulling on a pair of yoga pants and a sports bra was second nature to me. Just going through the motions. I went to strap on the knives.

"What are you doing?" Lily asked.

My hand stilled. "Forgetting myself," I said. "You should get dressed. I have a long day planned for us."

"Really?" She looked up brightly, no sign of the dark-ness. *Yet.*

"Really."

She dressed quickly in clothes similar to mine, but opted for the more modest route with a t-shirt. I smirked, holding the door open for her as we left. Campus was still quiet, but not quite dead. People scurried by on the side-walk. I heard every word as they stared at the scars lining my body. I'd chosen my clothing to make a statement, and a statement I made.

"Where would you feel most comfortable training?" I asked, and Lily shot me a curious look.

"Away from prying eyes," she said eventually.

Good choice.

I veered left and off the path, breaking into an easy run. She was slow, and her surprise made her slower, but eventually she started catching up. I kept my pace moderate, remembering how long it'd been since she'd done anything aside from cry or mope, with the occasional thrown kitchen knife. She hadn't trained with Blair and me over the summer, but I couldn't cut her too much slack now. Not with how powerful she was. I couldn't let her continue to go unchecked and untrained—not when I wasn't going to be here to clean up after her anymore.

Miles passed, and when we reached the farthest point from campus, I stopped. The woods were wild and untamed in this part of the grounds. I led her deeper into them and away from the path we'd taken to get here. Her panting was an assault on my ears in the morning silence. We were far enough out that no other soul would hear us.

"We'll train here every morning until I leave." Her head shot up, and hope blossomed in her eyes.

"You're keeping your promise." It wasn't a question, so I only nodded.

"You have a lot to learn, and I don't have very long to teach you," I said.

The wind swept through the woods, lifting her damp hair away from her eyes. "I'll train harder than anyone you've ever taught before, even Blair," she insisted.

A smirk touched my lips. That was a high bar she was setting for herself. Blair was my protégée. Even more than Lucas, the girl had enough ice in her to keep those emotions locked down. To stay in control. She found solace in neutrality, and it made her the perfect soldier. In three months, she'd mastered something a year hadn't taught Lucas, and a lifetime hadn't taught my sisters.

"We'll see."

I swept my foot underneath her. She moved quickly, though, and jumped to recover.

"Good. Your reflexes aren't bad. It's a start," I said, moving in to grapple.

She dodged my hands and ducked to go under my arm. I spun and locked my arm around her throat, pulling her into a chokehold.

"Stop," she gasped.

I didn't, instead applying more and more pressure as I pushed her to her limits. She had them, but they were farther than she believed. I needed her to see that she was in control of what happened to her, and her emotions, her powers.

"Se-Selena," she choked out. The tendrils started down her arm, reaching into the air for me like wisps of smoke.

"Control it, Lily," I whispered into her ear, easing up ever so slightly.

The black faded as she struggled to pull my arms away. Only when I saw my blood under her nails did I stop. I expected her to drop to her knees and weep. I thought she was going to feel sorry for herself.

When she came back swinging, it was one of the proudest moments of my life. Her form was good, and I watched in slow motion as her fist steadily approached my face. She needed this; she needed the power.

I took the punch.

The darkness in her eyes receded as my pain washed over her. She moved in to strike again, the killing gene taking control. The neverending madness had gotten a taste of blood, and wanted more.

"Control."

She blinked, and her fist stilled not even inches from my face. I stared down at her, blood and snot dripping from my face. Making her take in the sight. If she was going to survive the gene, she needed to live with the consequences.

"Control," she repeated. She stepped back, her knees wobbling. Her eyes betrayed the worry seeping into her expression.

"Stop that," I reprimanded. "Your emotions will get the best of you, and that's something you can't afford. Not anymore."

She clicked her tongue in dismissal, but her eyes changed as she watched me in fascination. "Your nose..."

"It's nothing." I stepped away, hastily wiping the blood and guck from my already healed face.

"That's not nothing. That's imposs—"

"Yes, it is. Just as it should've been impossible for you to manifest a second ability four months ago, but here we are."

Her mouth snapped shut, as she turned away. "What's wrong with me?" Her voice was thick with some unnamable emotion. This was the meltdown I'd been waiting for, and I suspected we'd do it another hundred times before she even started to understand.

"Control," I repeated.

"That's not an answer, Selena! I don't even know what you mean—"

"But you will. One day it will click, and until then, we train. You told me you'd train harder than anyone before you. It hasn't even been twenty minutes, and you're falling into yourself. Into the abyss."

My words pulled her back, as she frowned at me.

"You think I can't tell when you're falling into it? You think everyone else can't see you falling apart?"

Her eyes pricked with tears that betrayed the thin line of anger that was her mouth.

"You must have *control* in all things. I gave you the summer to feel bad for yourself, and what happened in the warehouse. You've had three months to get better, and you can't even control your emotions."

Tears now rolled freely down her cheeks. "I'm sorry—"

"I don't want your apologies, Lily! I need you to be better. I-I am leaving, Lily, and I won't be able to take care of you. So, I need you to take care of yourself for me, until I get back. Can you do that?" My voice softened, but I clenched my fists. How did I make her see this? How did I make her better? I didn't know, and the impossibility of this situation had me desperate.

Lily looked at me, and the tears stopped. Her eyes were like glass, fragile but clear. She closed them, and the girl who opened them again wasn't brittle and crumbling apart. She was stronger, because she had to be.

"Again," she said.

I didn't question it, and we went round after round.

Sweat trickled down my back, and she flung droplets off her face with every shake of her head. The sun climbed higher into the sky, but true to her word, she trained as hard as Blair. I was impressed by her strength, and any would-be wound on her body healed in minutes. She had the potential to be great, but it wasn't greatness that pushed her forward. It was an insatiable urge to cause pain, because it was the one thing that would quiet her own, if only for a moment.

"Enough," I said eventually.

The sun had reached its apex hours ago, and the world would be looking for me. I held out a hand and pulled her to her feet.

"You think you can run?" I asked, walking back to the worn path by the wall.

She nodded, trudging after me.

"You did good today, but you're slow and your endurance isn't there. You need to run every day. I'll meet you here at six every morning." I didn't wait for her response as I took off down the path. My blood pounded like a battle cry through my veins, urging me forward.

"Wait!" she called, and I slowed to a stop.

"What, Lily?"

"You didn't teach me how to keep the darkness away. If anything, I just want to kill—"

"I did, but *control* takes time, and you have to learn moderation," I reminded her, already turning away.

"But—"

"You need to shut the emotions out. Don't allow your-self to feel, because feeling is dangerous for people like us. Feeling is how someone dies. Your mind is what will save you, and as long as you don't let your heart get in the way, the clarity will come."

I left her with those words, and hoped I was right. Rome may not have been built in a day, but it also wasn't built in a month. Like it or not, time was of the essence, and the clock wasn't on our side.

CHAPTER 13

"Where have you been?" Lucas snarled the second I rounded the corner of the stairs.

Standing in front of my room, he looked every bit as pissed off as I'd expected he would. The sleep had done him good, and the bruise was already looking better, but definitely not gone. His eyes were practically feral.

"Good afternoon to you too," I said sarcastically, stepping around him. I opened the door to find my room empty, and the clock on Tori's nightstand read a quarter after four in the afternoon. The bedroom door clicked shut.

"We need to talk," he said. He was doing a better job at controlling the anger, but his eyes betrayed him.

"No," I said.

Yanking my hand through my hair, I freed it from the hair tie and walked to the bathroom. I kicked the door shut, but he caught it before it could lock.

Fine, you want to play this game?

I turned my back to him and stripped out of the sports bra then hooked my thumbs in the waistband of my pants and shimmied them down slowly. I knew his eyes were on me, as his heart sped up, so much louder than it ever was before. His breath hitched, and I cast him a coy look over my shoulder. The fire in his eyes turned icy as I continued to strip.

"See something you like?" I smirked.

Whatever obsession I'd had with him over the summer was long gone, replaced by a cold, almost cruel indifference because of what he'd done—or really, failed to do. I wanted to be friends, but I needed time to figure it out. Time to not hate him.

"You really want to play this game? Because twenty-four hours ago you were telling me—"

"Get out, and close the door behind you," I snapped. I didn't need a reminder of what I'd told him, or that I shouldn't be screwing with him like this just because I was in a pissy mood.

"I'll be in your room." The door slammed behind him, and I let my pants drop.

Not even bothering to wait for the water to warm, I stepped into the cold shower and welcomed the chill as my emotions washed down the drain.

What are you doing, Selena?

I'd cut him loose because he cared too much, and I cared too little. That was the honest thing to do. The right thing.

I scrubbed the shampoo into my scalp even harder, until the water ran pink. Sigh...

You need to stop screwing with his head. You don't want him? Fine, but don't rub it in. That's just bitchy.

Crack. Without thinking, I'd squeezed the conditioner

bottle too tightly, and it had exploded everywhere.

"Selena?" Even through the door, his voice was terse.

"I'm fine. Give me a sec." Groaning, I rinsed under the water and did my best to wipe off the walls and shower curtain. I flipped the shower off then paused before the door with a towel wrapped under my arms. I'd forgotten clothes, but thankfully my sweatpants and tank top from last night were still on the floor.

Welp. I guess I'm going commando.

My own movements in the mirror distracted me, drawing my attention to the scars, which nearly glowed. I pretended not to be bothered by the violet in my eyes that took longer to fade every time this happened, but I worried that, eventually, it wouldn't fade at all. I turned away from the mirror, brushing my hair out slowly, until I was unable to delay any further. I opened the door and stepped out of the bathroom to face him. His back was to me as he stared out the only window in the room.

"Why are you here, Lucas?" I said. There was no point beating around the bush, and the longer he stuck around, the more likely I was to get pissed again.

"I only have a few hours of freedom left before you give Anastasia our names, and I'd like to spend them with you," he said slowly. His words were sweet, but felt...off somehow. Too caring. Too kind, for the expression he wore and way he acted. Something wasn't adding up.

"You said we needed to talk. I'm here, so talk," I said.

"You want to have this conversation where they can hear?" he asked. His eyes never left mine, making his meaning abundantly clear. He wanted back into my mind. Where he could listen to every thought and figure out how to play me like a fiddle. After all, who was better at mind games than the boy who'd erased his own sister's memory?

For you!

Did it matter?

Either way, I had to keep him out of my mind, because Anastasia held my leash. Funny how him attempting to save me from her was how she'd managed to rope me in. If there was anything I could rely on in this world, it was that karma and irony were never far where I was concerned.

"I'm not letting you back in, so either spit it out or leave," I said.

"Fine. You want to be like this? Have it your way." He closed his eyes, taking a deep breath. "Why did you agree to do this?"

Without realizing it, I'd frozen instinctively. I'd given them a reason. It might not have been a good reason, but why did he have to question it? Why couldn't he just take it at face value?

"I told you guys everything. You're being paranoid," I said lazily.

His gaze never left me as he lifted an eyebrow. "Really?" It was only a single word, but it was a challenge. Nosy bastard could take his challenge and shove it up—

"Really," I repeated, cutting my own rant short.

He blew out a breath, shaking his head in frustration. "Why do you lie to me at every fucking turn—"

"Because you can't accept the truth when I tell you to stay out of it!" I yelled over him. I sighed and turned away, running both hands through my hair.

"But lying to me fixes nothing," he said.

The anger that filled me quickly fizzled into nothing

more than bitterness and resentment. Lovely. At least I understood these feelings. The familiarity was comforting, the cold a welcome reprieve from all the heat.

"If you don't like how I do things, you shouldn't have signed up to work with me," I said.

"You know why I did," he whispered.

I closed my eyes, wanting this to end already. Why must he care like this? Why couldn't he accept my boundaries like everyone else?

Because you already let him past them once.

And it was one time too many.

I turned to leave, but he grabbed my arm—one last ditch effort.

"I don't want you in my mind. Some things are better left alone," I said, tearing my arm from his grip.

"You're keeping secrets. Why? You know what happens when you do this!" He raised his voice, near desperation.

"It's my choice what I do and do not tell you. Just like it's your choices that led you here. You once called me heartless. Maybe you should've heeded your own warning."

He laughed, a sad, sardonic sound. "Maybe I should have," he murmured.

Finally! Finally, he was getting it—that this chase wouldn't repair whatever was broken inside me. He wouldn't be the one to fix me, if anyone even could. I needed to fix myself, and the only way I could do that was with space.

Throwing the door open, I came face-to-face with Blair.

"Do I even want to know why you're here?" I sighed.

She looked over my shoulder. "I was just going to get

dinner and wanted to see if you were busy, but if you have *company*—"

"Oh, for the— There's nothing— Ugh, nevermind. Let's just go," I snapped.

A smirk ghosted her lips, but she said nothing as she turned on her heel down the hallway. I followed her without looking back once. I'd made that mistake last time I walked away, and I wouldn't make it again. The cool air hit my skin pleasantly, and I twisted my hair up into a bun, pulling it tight with my own long black ends in the absence of a hair tie.

"Am I supposed to ask what that was about?" Blair asked. She had excellent conversational skills—the girl could schmooze with the best of them—but we both knew that wasn't her. Not anymore, anyway.

"No, you've got enough to worry about. I can handle another..." I paused, not sure what to call Lucas. "Boy."

"Boy? That's what they call eighteen-year-olds with abs like that now?" She pursed her lips, trying to hide the smile and failing.

"Boy. Man. What's the difference?"

"The way he looks at you." Her smile faltered as she looked away.

"You sound like you know something about that," I prodded. The summer air kissed my cheeks as we strolled across Daizlei.

"I'm not dumb enough to tell you to stay away. Just be careful with him," she said, her braid blowing behind her in the wind.

"What makes you say that? Did he do something to you?" I wasn't sure if it was curiousity that fueled my interest, or this dying need to know if there was something dark and twisted in him too. Maybe then it would be easier to blame him, maybe then I could chalk this all up to karma.

"Lucas has always been kind, but so was his brother once. All I'm saying is be careful."

"So much for dark and twisted," I grumbled.

"Hm?" she asked.

"Nothing." I shrugged.

Campus was still quiet as we made our way across the grass. Fireflies twinkled against the dying sun, and when the light was gone, six people's freedom would be too.

"Do you hate me? For dragging you into this?" I blurted out the question that had been at the back of my mind since last night.

"You didn't do this. You were just the messenger, and to be honest, there are worse things in life than fighting Vampires who would enslave us all. If we win, we save millions, and if we lose, I'm either dead or hiding. Besides," she paused, resting her arm over my shoulder, "there's no way to know how good I really am now until we put it to the test. Vampires are just a step below demons."

I laughed with her, but, truthfully, I didn't even want to think about that statement. If Vampires were just a test, what would stop her from going after the real monsters when this was all over? Then again, was I really any different?

"This must be strange for you, being back here and knowing you won't be staying. Have you told Elizabeth?"

Blair stiffened at the mention of her sister, who'd betrayed us all. She'd apparently gotten here early this morning, but no one had seen her since.

After the incident last year, she'd been moved to a different dorm on the other end of campus and banned from any and all outings. Technically, I was too for beating the shit out of her, but it hardly mattered anymore.

"No. Telling my mom was hard enough. I haven't seen her, and I don't plan to," she said.

I nodded in understanding. "I don't know what I would do if one of my sisters betrayed me like that."

"Hopefully, you'll never have to find out," she said grimly.

I pushed the cafeteria door open, and tried to ignore the whispers as we passed by.

"Do you see her scars?"

"I heard she got them fighting Vampires."

"I heard it was demons."

"Does it really matter? She may as well be one. I saw what she did to that girl last year."

"Aren't they related?"

"Didn't she kill her?"

"I thought she died."

The words continued to flow like vomit from their mouths. Hundreds of whispers, and I was the subject of them all. I hated it, but said nothing. What was the point, when all they saw was the monster? May as well let them fear it.

"They sure love to talk, don't they?" Blair muttered, as they began to speculate about her own scars.

It was funny, in a way, that a year ago I'd stepped out as a stranger to this world and they'd challenged me. Now they knew me, but in my quest to protect my sisters, I'd become a villain overnight. Typical.

"Let's just get our food and get out of here," Blair said.

The line was short, and it only took us a few moments to get to the counter. We collected our dinner and hurried to leave the cafeteria whispers behind.

"Selena."

I looked up sharply at the blond-haired, golden-eyed manservant. Alec took up most of the door, blocking our exit.

"What do you want?" Blair snapped.

His jaw tightened, but he didn't even glance her way.

"I've been sent to collect the names for my *mistress*," he said tersely. The way he avoided Blair's glare would've been amusing for almost any other reason.

"It's not even six," I replied coolly.

"It was an order, Selena, not a request," he said.

Blair ground her teeth, and her fingertips turned blue.

I fished the paper out of my pocket and handed it over. "Luckily for you, I always come prepared." I smirked.

He rolled his eyes, but I got the distinct impression he knew the effect he was having on her. "Training starts tomorrow morning. Be in the Battle Simulation room by nine and bring your...friends." He turned to leave.

"Alec." I paused. He stopped a few feet away but didn't turn back. "Do you think she'll keep her end of the deal?"

He didn't ask who I was talking about. We both knew. He turned back a fraction, looking at Blair. She turned icy under his glare, and any sadness in his eyes disappeared behind a cool mask of indifference.

"Goodnight, Selena. Get some rest."

That wasn't reassuring.

CHAPTER 14

The night passed quickly enough, though sleep was hard to come by. My violet-eyed other paid me a visit in the dead forest, causing me to wake in a cold sweat as the shakes set in. Training with Lily didn't go much better.

Now, after sitting at this cold desk for the last twenty minutes while Vonlowsky prattled on, I couldn't help the irritation that was setting in.

Why is he even talking?

My inner demons agreed. He'd been appointed the 'trainer' to head this unofficial gathering every day, and the one to enforce the Council's will.

Anastasia's nine sat amongst us in the classroom-like setting outside the simulation chamber. It still reminded me of the isolation rooms in a psych ward; I guess some things never changed—like how much I couldn't stand my arrogant ex-Battle Simulation professor.

"Ms. Foster, I asked you a question."

I snapped my head up to look at him. "What?" I asked blankly.

Blair kicked the back of my desk.

"Ms. Foster, is there a reason you've shown up here three minutes late and half-asleep? You've been *honored* by the Council—"

That was my undoing. "What. Do. You. Want?" I said through gritted teeth. What I meant to say was *leave me the fuck alone.*

The feeling of his breath in my face made me tense, as he leaned down to be eye level with me. My demons roared.

Too close. He's too close.

I could hardly breathe because every hair on my body shot up. The need for pain filled me, begging for release.

"Excuse me? Until you leave the grounds, I am still your instructor, and I expect to be treated as such." He pinned me with a heavy glare, demanding my silence before he continued. "For the next month, you'll be training twelve hours a day in this building. You will eat, sleep, and fight together. After today's session, you'll find your things already moved to your new bunks on the level below, where all sixteen of you will stay. When you're not in session or with the group, you're free to roam the grounds, but you may not leave the school. Do I make myself clear?"

Mumbles of yes and nodding heads followed his statement. He stared down at me, waiting for confirmation.

"Crystal." Even as I said it, the dread set in. How was I going to be around this many people and *not* lose my shit in such close quarters? It was last year all over again.

"Good. Council Member Fortescue has instructed me to hone both your bodies and minds, in preparation for what you'll face beyond these walls. While Ms. Foster will lead you in your *excursions*, I'm here to ensure that those of you who make it past the eliminations are adequately prepared for what you'll face. Sixteen is too large a group not to become discombobulated, therefore periodic cuts will be made based on performance, amongst other *things...*" he said slyly.

Vonlowsky continued to drone on for a few more minutes about the importance of his role in this, but I couldn't focus. I couldn't think. The pounding in my head came to a crescendo as the situation I had on my hands overwhelmed me and opened the gate for my demons. My heartbeat slowed, like a drum on the dawn of an execution. The killing calm had me, and something needed to sate it.

"Selena?" Something touched my shoulder.

I snapped.

I jumped out of my seat, pulled my knife, and pressed the blade against her throat before she could move.

"Selena, put the knife down. There'll be time enough for that." I recognized that voice.

As I looked into the face staring up at me, reality came back. Blair. This was Blair. I lowered my knife slowly and stepped away. "Blair."

She nodded slowly, watching me for sudden changes. She tried to play it off, to look nonchalant, but we both knew what was really going on here. She'd seen it enough this summer, every time my self-control ran thin and the demons pounced. My violet-eyed other cackled wildly in the back of my mind.

"Ms. Foster!" Vonlowsky shouted, approaching me too fast.

I whirled, and ducked under his arm.

"What the—?"

"Don't touch me," I murmured.

Panic was seizing me as I backed away from the stares, from him. I looked from one person to another, lost in a sea of people. One dark-eyed gaze stood out. Aaron White, once again watching me with an intensity that gave Lucas a run for his money. I hadn't seen the boy in months, and I was struck by how much he'd changed since last year. His dark gaze shifted to a glimmer of gold and back so fast I had to be hallucinating. He cocked his head, arching an eyebrow in a way that was *too* familiar.

Vonlowsky moved, pulling me out of the moment. "Ms. Foster, this is preposterous. What is going on with—?"

He reached.

Glass shattered.

The double-paned window cracked and blew apart, halting his approach.

I sucked in a deep breath, trying to rein it in—but the power was like a dam, and once you broke it, the flood of power was too great to hold in.

"Selena!" Lucas shouted.

The world was a kaleidoscope of colors.

"I said, do not touch me."

This time, Vonlowsky heeded my warning. Closing my eyes, I focused on the glass and forced it back into the window, one piece at a time. Perspiration dotted my fore-head as I sealed the cracks—manipulating matter itself. Telekinesis was such a droll name for what I could do. Moving objects with my mind was just the tip of the iceberg.

A popping in my ears pulled me out of the vacuum I'd created. I focused on the man in front of me.

"As you wish, Ms. Foster," Vonlowsky said slowly. His eyes betrayed nothing as he examined me like a puzzle he couldn't piece together.

"I think we should let off some steam," Alexandra announced. She strode toward me with purpose and a flounce in her hips.

"Sit down." Vonlowsky glared.

"It's been a long few days, and no offense to you, *Professor*, but some of us have to work harder to contain our gifts in high-stress situations with no *release*." Alexandra put on a big front, and I had no doubt who it was for. She knew what this was about, and turning it into a power play would've been smart under other circumstances. It would've made me look strong, not insane, but here, now, it made me look defiant. The word *release* echoed in my mind, like a Ping-Pong ball going berserk in a box.

"Direct as usual, Ms. Foster." He rolled his eyes, pausing as if actually considering her request. "But perhaps, given the state of things, we should begin training, and I can continue going over the more tedious aspects after lunch?" He phrased it like a question. Every head in the room nodded in agreement, but it was me he looked to.

"Please." I lowered my eyes to quiet the demons urging me forward.

"Very well. Break into pairs and get in the simulator. I don't want anything else broken," he said.

I turned from the room and fled to the white room. Where was a straitjacket when I needed one?

"I'm her sister. I know what she needs," Alexandra said, walking into the room with Blair on her heels.

"She's not going to want you, because she doesn't want

to hurt you. She needs someone she doesn't have to hold back with," Blair insisted, and she wasn't wrong.

"Find someone else, Blair." Alexandra came to a stop in front of me with Blair.

"Selena?" Blair asked me expectantly.

I turned away, unable to look at either of them.

"Selena—" Lucas tried to butt in, but I silenced him with a hand. The room was filling quickly as the nine entered with Tori and Amber on their heels.

"I'm not fighting any of you."

"What—?"

"Selena, you know this isn't a good idea—"

Selena this. Selena that. *Why couldn't people leave me alone?*

"Quiet," I snapped.

Rubbing my temples, I looked over the entire group. If I was going to lead, I needed to get my shit together and lead. The war wouldn't stop because of nightmares and insatiable urges. My penance, as Anastasia called it, wouldn't be paid.

"Blair and Alexandra, you'll practice together. Tori and Amber split off to the side. Lucas and Aaron..." My voice faltered.

That left me without anyone, and I sure as hell didn't want to accidentally kill one of the royal rejects Anastasia had under her thumb. I needed someone I could hit, without feeling bad. A punching bag that could take the pain without me giving a damn.

"Use Aaron," Blair said quietly.

"Are you kidding me? Do you know what she'll do to him?" Alexandra nearly screeched.

"Yes, which is why I know that if she won't use you or me, she won't use *him* either." She thrust her chin toward Lucas and crossed her arms.

She had a point. As pissed as I was with him, some part of me didn't want to beat him to a pulp. Yet. I needed time.

"I can take it." Aaron stepped up, getting closer than anyone else had dared. He was either the bravest man alive, or the dumbest.

I stripped off my jacket and tossed it to Blair.

"Ugh, whatever. Don't ruin his face," Alexandra muttered.

The absurdity of that made me snort.

"Go train with your cousin, Alex. I can handle her." His assuredness was startling, and it made the hunter in me purr at the thought of a challenge. Something tickled at the back of my mind, though.

Alex? No one called her Alex. No one but our father. I didn't like it.

"And me?" Lucas demanded, like I was a bad person for *not* picking him.

I still hadn't gotten our confrontation yesterday out of my mind, though, and didn't have the energy to waste on coddling him right now. I was far enough down this rabbit hole that I couldn't wait to blow off steam, and he pushed my buttons.

"You're with Alec. Make me proud," I said, trying to lighten the blow to his ego, but he just stormed off toward his brother, who was watching us from the side.

I kept my eyes on Aaron.

He was just as tall as Lucas, but bigger. Bulkier.

He must've been training over the summer.

Not that that explained the golden eye shift. I reached for the knife holder strapped around my waist, and threw it to the side. Aaron never wavered as he slowly approached. Only a breath away, I inhaled once and struck.

I moved for his chest, but stopped an inch short as he closed his fingers around my fist. I flipped myself, pressing my back into him as I brought my other hand up and grasped his wrist. He shifted his body, almost as if he'd predicted I was going to throw him, and wrapped his other arm around my neck. Switching to a chokehold. He lured me in, pulling me close. I waited him out as he leaned into me, not releasing but not actively cutting off my airway either. Bringing my foot up over my shoulder, I kicked him in the face.

He stumbled, loosening his grip just enough that I slipped free and twisted to snap his arm. He closed his other hand around my wrist. We fell into a gridlock. Both unwilling to be bested by the other, but so evenly matched that it was going to take a lot more to win.

I glared up at him, and his black eyes swallowed me whole. So I did the only thing I could—I went low, and brought my knee up to mash his junk. A smirk crossed his lips as he pivoted and released me. We moved as one, two people lost in the dance of our lives. I kicked; he blocked. I punched; he pivoted. Time wore on, and I fell into a trance-like state.

It was kind of amazing that he could keep up—even with his enhanced senses, I'd expected him to falter, but he never missed a beat, and he never looked away from me. Unlike last year, when he'd lost a fight because I'd walked by, his eyes never strayed. Then we started landing blows.

Thud.

The power in my fist boomed through the room as he flew back, landing on his butt. I smirked, contorting my body to crack my neck. *That'll keep him down.*

Thack!

"Ugh," I exhaled, the fist in my gut bringing me to my knees. *How did he do that?*

"Didn't think you could keep me down so easily, did you?" He grinned.

I spat blood on the floor and picked myself back up. "Wouldn't dream of it," I snapped.

We continued back and forth for a while yet, but no matter how hard either of us hit, the other got back up. I couldn't keep him down, and it infuriated me. What had changed?

I stepped back and dropped. Kicking my leg out to sweep his feet out from under him, I waited for him to grab it as he had the last two times I'd tried this. He smirked to himself as he latched onto my foot.

Got you now.

Releasing myself to gravity, I fell to the ground and threw my strength into flinging him over me. He let go after he realized I intended to turn his own strength against him —but not soon enough. I brought the other leg up and hooked it around his neck, crushing him to me. Unable to hold himself up, he came down between my thighs and found his head trapped as I flipped. I straddled his chest, forcing his head between my knees as I used my weight to hold him down.

The world faded the moment our eyes met. His were so black, but not cold. Unlike the demons that haunted and hunted me. Now was my moment. This was when I was supposed to punch him—to bloody his face to a pulp. I should've slammed his head into the floor, as I'd done to so many others before him. He stared up at me, though, unafraid. If anything, he looked far too pleased with himself.

"Do it," he said. His voice was husky and dark. Something in me squirmed, like a door trying to open. I had this bizarre feeling of *him*. That if I only reached, I could unlock the door.

No.

I ground my teeth and punched him.

Red flowed beneath my fingers as the pressure left me. His nose was broken, smashed in at an odd angle. I pulled my arm back, ready to strike again.

Until his nose started knitting itself back together.

That's...

"Impossible," I whispered.

Not quite, a small voice said. My own bones healing rapidly came to mind.

"I told you I could take it. Again."

I looked at him like he'd grown a second head. He was asking for more?

"Again," he urged.

A tingle ran up my spine. Something like déjà vu...or that feeling you got after being blackout drunk. Either way, it didn't sit well. One second, I'd wanted blood and pain, and the next, I wanted to take a really long nap and forget this day had ever happened. Clarity hit me like a shot of adrenaline, and I was back. The demons would be sated for another day.

I let go and pulled myself up. Stumbling forward, I tried to ignore Alexandra's pissed off glare. Whether it was jealousy or anger, I didn't really care. I hadn't picked him as the punching bag because I cared for him, but because I didn't. Someone had needed to hurt, and I'd picked the person I cared the least about. She knew that, but I was still the bad guy. Some days, the cure is worse than the disease...

Lucas wouldn't even look at me as he sulked off to the other side of the room to train with his brother. Part of me wanted to tell him to shove it for being petty and jealous, but the rest of me said to leave it. He'd figure it out on his own. He had to.

"Why are you all just standing here? Get back to training," I said.

I left the room to take an unsteady breath. The white walls of the simulator were already splotched red, and the nine didn't need to be told twice. I liked that.

"You're stronger than you've let everyone believe." Vonlowsky stood, stoic as ever, next to me, watching my team.

"Strength doesn't come from power. It comes from control, Professor. The mind is a powerful thing, but one is only as strong as their weakest link."

I felt his eyes on me for a moment. "Truer words have never been spoken, Ms. Foster," he said.

Was that a compliment?

"Perhaps the reason they never win isn't because they underestimate my power but my mind." I paused. "Just food for thought."

I could've sworn a smile formed on his lips, but knowing Vonlowsky, it was probably a trick of the light.

CHAPTER 15

The nine, as I called them, weren't what I'd expected. They were nearly as ragtag a group as my own team, albeit a more gifted bunch. Every one of them was talented in some form or fashion, and some had gifts I'd never even heard of. For the better part of that morning, they sparred separately and wouldn't interact with us. One girl in particular caught my interest, though. Her golden eyes flashed every time she looked at us, and there was something strange behind her quiet demeanor. I shook my head and looked away.

You're paranoid.

Lunch was just a continuation of their indifference. Two floors down from the Battle Simulation Building there was a small lunchroom with one long table that reminded me of middle school. Had this been here before all this happened with Anastasia and the Council? If so, why could they possibly need a lunchroom that looked like it was out of a juvenile detention center? Wedged between Blair and Tori, I took a slow bite of my burger and glanced across the table.

"What's your name?" I asked the guy opposite me. He was massive, nearly seven feet tall, and built so thick that three-foot wide oak trees looked small in comparison. His skin was so black it looked almost blue. He was beautiful in an odd, exotic way. He glanced up at me with golden eyes, flecked with green. It was fitting that he looked like carved stone—given what I'd seen of his ability this morning.

"Constantine," he rumbled.

"You're an earth user." It wasn't really a question, but I waited for a response.

He gave me an odd look. "Yes."

"Excellent. When we're done with lunch, you'll be fighting with Alexandra." I kept my eyes on him, all too aware of the stare I was getting from Alexandra.

"The fire user?" He glanced at my red-headed sister.

"Yes, I want to see how you compare."

He frowned slightly but kept quiet.

Lunch went on, but the only conversations were held in hushed whispers.

As we headed back upstairs, Blair grabbed my arm and pulled me aside. "Do you really think it's a good idea to put Alexandra against one of them?"

"It needs to happen sooner rather than later, and he's more even-tempered than the others," I said quietly, watching the door for the stairwell close.

"He could be a pacifist and I'd be concerned. Do you think she's ready?"

"She was born ready. The girl has fire in her veins. You just have to know how to unleash it." Blair cut me a questioning look, and I sighed. "You forget that she's my sister.

She's trained with me since we were children. You may not see her control, but it is there." I started walking away.

"But—"

"I can't say more, Blair, not right now."

Flashbacks of fire and blood rooted me to the spot for a moment. I reached out, steadying myself against the wall.

That was a long time ago, I berated myself.

Exactly. Which is why you shouldn't dabble with it now.

I stepped through the doorway into the classroom outside the simulator. Vonlowsky was waiting with the group right outside, and he didn't look pleased. I marched over to him with my shoulders back, hand resting cockily on the dagger at my hip. Daggers had become my weapon of choice; the irony was amusing. He watched me warily as I approached the group, but made no move to piss me off after this morning.

That's what you get for biting off more than you can chew.

"Alexandra, Constantine. Get in the simulator." I kept my voice steady, eyes not leaving Vonlowsky. "I hope you don't mind, Professor, but I wanted to mix it up a little." It was an olive branch, the most I could force myself to give at the moment. He'd given me breathing room, and I didn't want to be smothered again.

"Very well. But after your trial, we have work to do."

I nodded once and motioned for them to enter the simulator. The door snapped shut behind them, and I took a deep breath before facing the window.

"Begin the match," I said.

Vonlowsky pressed a button, and a horn sounded.

Alexandra moved first, trying to dive in for a quick shot at his solar plexus, but she wasn't fast enough to get out. It didn't take long before Constantine had her pinned. I grimaced. Flames shot up as she ignited, and his arms shook as he struggled to keep his hold on her, despite the fire that rose up to greet him. His skin changed, darkening to onyx. He was made of solid stone.

"Can we be done with this?" Vonlowsky sighed, reaching for the button.

"No."

He stopped and gave me an incredulous look.

I kept my eyes on the burning girl.

Please forgive me.

"Hotter," I said.

Her head twitched, and even though she couldn't see me, her eyes made contact. Fire raced down her body, scorching away her clothes. The flames were spreading, burning even the white-tiled floors. Still, Constantine held her.

"Hotter," I repeated.

Her body surged again as the lines of her skin blurred. I couldn't tell where the fire stopped and she started. Bodies pressed in around me to get a better look, and Vonlowsky regarded me curiously. His gaze flipped between the burning girl and me.

"Selena, I don't think she can—" Blair started.

"Hotter, Alexandra. Now," I commanded coldly.

It was the first time in almost seven years that I'd pushed her. Instead of trying to hold the fire back—as we had in the human world—I wanted to unleash it. I wanted to make a statement: that it wasn't only me they needed to fear. I wasn't the only threat.

Her body glowed bright, nearly white, as she lost her

human form entirely. Constantine shifted, unable to hold her any longer as she burned even stone. He moved away, but she was faster. She was living flame. Alexandra pushed onward, forcing him back, but everywhere he turned there was fire. She consumed the world.

Her control was starting to slip, though. She hadn't held this form in many years, and her body didn't know how to handle it. Her energy was falling, and Constantine saw it. The ground beneath them shook, forcing her to retreat from the mountain man. Flames exploded as the room burned. Unable to hold back any longer, Vonlowsky hit the button to signal them to stop. The siren blared, and like a phoenix meeting her end, Alexandra blinked out—collapsing on the ruined floor, unconscious and exhausted.

Fire alarms rang out, as the simulator flooded, flowing into the classroom as the door opened. I pushed through the group and headed straight for my sister's unconscious body. The floor was burned away, and rocks jutted through like onyx crystals. Deadly and beautiful. I stayed wide of Constantine, who was sagging against the opposite wall, not completely conscious yet. She'd given him a run for his money, and that was all I'd needed.

I approached her naked body, and slipped my jacket off to cover her. Her head lolled to the side when I picked her up, locking my arms around her back and under her legs, somewhat awkwardly because of the size difference. Avoiding the rocks on my way back was slightly harder with her cumbersome body, but we managed.

Constantine hadn't fared much better. The golden-eyed girl from earlier murmured words of reassurance in his ear while she simultaneously tried to treat the burns and keep him from falling into the hole in the ground two feet to his left. Another boy rushed onto the scene to help their shaken friend, and it stirred an unwanted feeling of guilt in my chest. I kept walking, disinclined to give my apologies. Relatively speaking, apart from the destroyed room and unconscious body, it was a success.

"What did I say about breaking things?" Vonlowsky asked, rolling his eyes.

I shot him a glare, nodding to the girl in my arms.

He pressed his lips together in a slight grimace. "The bunks are one floor down. Your things haven't been moved yet, but I'll see that hers are brought over first," he said, pausing as phantom hands opened the stairwell. "We'll break for the rest of this afternoon until the simulator is fixed. We'll have our evening lecture during dinner tonight."

I mentally shut the door behind me as I traveled down, into the underground of Daizlei. Not even one day back, and I already had an unconscious body.

Was it karma that it was my very own sister this time? I hadn't even laid a finger on Alexandra, but I was still at fault for pushing her. For breaking her.

I glanced over the room, feeling more than ever like an enlisted soldier. A simple room, it had concrete floors and walls, ten twin-sized bunks, and doors on either end labeled men's and women's bathrooms. I carried Alexandra to one of the bunks in the corner. I threw the threadbare sheet over her, hoping it would be enough. Water leaked from her hair all over the mattress as I pulled it to the side and wrung it out on the concrete floor before braiding it away from her face.

*I shouldn't have done that...*but I knew why I had.

She was being thrown into this just as much as I was, and like Lily, she only had so much time to get ready for whatever was to come. Blair was a mile ahead of them, both in attitude and ability, at this point. Tori and Amber were in a different category altogether with their abilities, but it didn't make my job any easier. They needed to train more, all of them. I fell into troubled thoughts, backing away from her bunk toward the people now milling around the room. The nine had moved their stuff to the other side of the concrete prison, where Constantine was passed out on the bottom cot. The golden-eyed girl examined me cautiously from her bed, with eyes that glowed more than I was comfortable with. It had been a long day, and it wasn't half over.

I turned to my soldiers, the team of misfits.

"Two of you are to be with her at all times until she wakes up. I'll be back," I said hastily, not even bothering with my jacket as I turned to walk out.

"Where are you going?" Tori asked.

"For a run," I said.

"I'm coming with," Amber said, moving to my side in a second.

I rolled my eyes. "Whatever."

We took the stairs back up into the classroom and paused. Vonlowsky was on the phone with someone, while technopaths worked to put the simulator back together. Most of the water had already been removed.

"Is there something you need, Ms. Foster?" he asked crossly, not even bothering to address Amber's presence.

"Nope, we were just on our way, Professor," I said

quickly, hurrying out the door before he could comment further.

"So…are we going to talk about what happened today? Or why tall, dark, and handsome is pissed at you?" Amber asked, nudging me with her elbow as we walked outside of main campus.

I groaned. "Seriously, Amber? I'm not in the mood."

"Oh please, I know you, and I know the Hunters. The boy has it bad for you, and as amusing as it is that he picked you, of all people, I kind of get the impression that it's not one way," she mused, pulling her brown curls into a pom-pom on top of her head.

"Honestly, Amber, it's none of your business," I said steadily, taking off in a run.

It didn't take her any time at all to catch up. "Touchy-touchy. He's the same way about you." She smirked.

I rolled my eyes. "I don't know what you're talking about," I said. The lie fell flat, though, even to me.

"Just keep telling yourself that. Before you know it, the whole world's going to implode with your drama. Those boys are about to have a throwdown." She laughed, even as we ran.

"Boys?" I asked, hoping that, for once in my miserable life, I'd heard wrong.

"Oh my god! Don't tell me you have no idea what I'm talking about. Lucas was two seconds from kicking his ass after you walked out of the simulator this morning." She cackled.

My heart raced in my chest, and it had nothing to do with the run.

"Aaron is nothing. He's no one. The only reason he's

even here is because Alexandra was going to throw a fucking temper tantrum if he wasn't."

Amber sobered and looked me over. "Do you really believe that?"

"Yes."

"Really? From where I stand, you yielded and brought him on. Alexandra's just an excuse," she said flatly, cocking an eyebrow in challenge.

"That's bull. I can't stand Aaron. It's the reason I picked him this morning. Not because I *care*," I said, like it was dirty.

"I don't think it's as simple as you're telling yourself." She scrunched her nose the way she did when she was thinking.

"I think you're reading something into it that's not there. Lucas, Aaron...hell, next you're going to say Alec has it for me." I laughed at the thought, but her smile fell away.

She dropped her gaze to the ground darkly. "Not quite."

"Oh what? No Chatty Cathy now?" I smirked, but deep down I knew something was up.

"Lucas is a different kind of devil than Alec. His morals are loose, but he has a heart. He just needed someone like you to make him feel it. Make him settle," she said ominously.

"So I've heard. I'm not sure whether to be pissed or ask why you keep coming back to him *settling* on me," I said.

She snorted and picked up the speed as we raced through the forest's edge. "You're a shade of gray, Selena. You're not good, and you never were—even before you met Lucas. You're just as likely to stomp on his heart as you are to throw a punch. That's what I find amusing. He had girls pining after him before you…still does. His player days are over, though. They were the second he met you." She shrugged and kept silent.

"It's not going to happen. He needs to move on," The words popped out before I could take them back.

"It sounds like you've made up your mind," she said.

"I have, because it won't work. There was a time when I thought maybe…but he's not what I want. Not mentally at least." I muttered the last part more to myself than her.

"And what's that supposed to mean?" Amber asked, like I'd said something scandalous. Or maybe she just found it amusing.

"It's nothing," I said, not sure I really wanted to get into this with her.

"Doesn't sound like nothing." She smirked.

"Lucas is my friend, a very attractive friend who sometimes makes me want to push those boundaries, but…I don't feel the same way he does. Even when he kisses me, there's something holding me back."

And then there's the whole wiping Tori's memory and getting caught thing. Not that Anastasia bothered to go after him, when he'd given her all the ammunition she needed to get me. Hateful harpy.

"That's oddly thoughtful of you," she said quietly.

I shrugged, cracking my neck while I did. "Don't give me too much credit there. I haven't been the kindest where his heart is concerned."

In fact, I didn't think I'd ever been great where matters of the heart were concerned, even when those affections weren't aimed at me. Alexandra had had many boyfriends, and I'd detested each and every one. Love made people blind. It made them weak. Alexandra was strong when she played the game and usually never cared about who she hurt, but with Aaron...she was changing, and love was to blame for it. Stupid sentimental love. I shook my head to try to scatter those intense dark eyes far from my thoughts... and it didn't work.

"You look like you're running from something. He get under your skin?" Amber asked.

"What...who are you—"

"Well, I was talking about Lucas, but now I've gotta wonder where your mind went. Your other suitor?" She snickered even though her eyes weren't in it. How right she was about who was bothering me, but not for the reasons she thought.

"Aaron's nothing to me," I insisted. I was beginning to feel like a broken record.

"Okay, if he's nothing to you, answer me this: what's so wrong with him that you just brush off his obvious attraction to you?" she asked, bringing me to a gradual stop.

This was...deep. Deeper than I wanted to go where men were concerned, but we were already here, so it seemed I had to answer.

"He's dating my sis—"

"Other than that," she said, brushing her thumb across her bottom lip. The wheels were turning behind those eyes.

"He's a pig. Seriously. The first day I met him, he was going on and on about banging his girlfriend the night before, saying the most— Ugh, he deserves to have his balls chopped off for what he was saying." My fists clenched at the thought of it.

"That's all?" she asked, making a face like she was weighing her next words carefully.

"I've spent most of my life being ogled by men and watching them abuse my sister. I have no interest in dogs," I said. Aaron would have my scorn as long as he lived.

"I just find it amusing, because Lucas wasn't any better. Until you. And Aaron...well, we all have our faults. You're judgmental and have probably done worse things than I care to know, and he likes pretty women." She shrugged. "The whole lot of you had your issues. Still do, if you ask me." She muttered the last bit under her breath.

"Hey!" I said, slapping her arm while she laughed so hard she snorted. Amber collapsed against the wall in a fit of laughter that was infectious.

"This is nice. Not so...heavy. Not complicated. Why can't life be like this all the time?" I said absentmindedly.

She regarded me slowly, her gold eyes glowing. *Gold?* I was about to ask what the deal was when she spoke. "Some of us are destined for more, and with greatness, life gets complicated. Things aren't always simple, because the world isn't always black or white. There's a lot of gray." That was pretty wise coming from Amber, who was almost as shallow as Alexandra. At least, I'd always thought she was. "Like you and your...man friends," she continued, cracking herself up.

Yep, there it is.

I groaned again. "You do realize that Aaron's my sister's boyfriend, and Lucas is Tori's brother. They're going to kick both our asses if you bring this up in front of them, even if it's hogwash." I leaned against the wall with her. This was the lightest I'd felt in days, and I wanted to relish the sun on my face.

"There's a grain of truth even in the most blasphemous lies. Remember that?" she said, pulling herself up off the wall.

"Sure. Just keep those lies to yourself, and I'll do whatever you want," I muttered.

She chuckled to herself. "If those are your bargaining skills, no wonder that Fortescue bitch screwed you."

It wasn't funny, and I really shouldn't have laughed, but I did. "You're the one who signed up for this. You screwed yourself," I pointed out.

"I suppose I did." She shrugged. "If the world's going to hell anyway, I may as well get to see it before it burns. Don't you think?" she asked. Her eyes had that wistful, hopeful look I'd been seeing so much of lately.

Everyone was hoping for something, but the odds weren't in our favor. No matter how much I laughed it off, it didn't change the fact that the Council had screwed us all. Or really, Lucas had screwed me, and I'd screwed them.

Instead of saying that, I kept up the light banter. It was easier this way, having friends who were close but not close enough. Friends who had hope, and gave me hope that even though the world was gray, there would still be a world left when this was all over.

CHAPTER 16

"Tʜᴇʀᴇ ᴀʀᴇ ᴛᴡᴏ ᴅɪғғᴇʀᴇɴᴛ ᴛʏᴘᴇs ᴏғ Vᴀᴍᴘɪʀᴇs ʏᴏᴜ'ʟʟ ᴄᴏᴍᴇ across in your assignments—the Made and the Born. It's critical that you identify which you're dealing with. Not only your life, but your comrades' lives will depend on it." Vonlowsky was just firing up his speech as we sat down for dinner. Someone had set up a projector after lunch, in the "cafeteria." The slide flipped to a picture of a man with silver hair and ivory skin. His eyes were the darkest navy blue I'd ever seen. So close to black that humans would've thought they were bottomless.

"The Born, ladies and gentlemen," he said. Flipping the slides, he showed more pictures of silver or white-haired men and women with ghastly pale skin and dark eyes.

"Born Vampires pride themselves on their lineage as a bastard breed between Supernaturals and demons. For them, immortality is worth more than anything, even at the cost of creating a stronger race—the Made. If the one they're feeding on dies in the weakened state of the transition, the victim comes back as the Made—an enslaved race of those unlucky enough to find themselves undead."

I kept an eye on Tori as he went through his little fear-mongering presentation. She shivered, but didn't cringe at the slide.

"The Born are dangerous because they have the ability to create a zombie race out of every other species on the planet. The Made are controlled by the Born who bit them, but don't let that fool you into thinking they're weaker. Magical species that are turned are often the first and only line of defense the Born ever need, because of how much stronger they are. The Made have been known to turn on any who are not their sires, which makes them unpredictable and dangerous—even to the Born." He flipped the page again, and I found myself face-to-face with the essence of evil. The Made were unnatural, even in appearance. Their eyes were tinted red, giving them a feral look. I didn't question the zombie reference any further.

"What makes the Made so much stronger?" Alexandra was the first to speak, drawing everyone's attention from the glaring red eyes. "The Borns' age alone makes them nearly undefeatable, both faster and stronger than us because most of them have been around for hundreds, if not thousands, of years." While I was impressed that she'd done her homework and researched Vampires, after sleeping for so long, there was a vital piece of information she was missing.

"Because the Made were once one of us and now have all the strength and speed of the Born as well as their abilities from when they were living," the strange girl from earlier answered. Her voice was grave, like she knew from experience.

"Ms. Kozak is correct. The Made retain everything from their mortal lives, and are stronger in every aspect for it. Their abilities become magnified, and they are frozen eternally. Never to bear children or grow old, the Made are more dangerous than any other race in existence." He paused before proceeding. "Council Member Fortescue has given explicit instructions that any who are bitten during a mission are to be killed on the spot." He glanced at Tori, and my blood ran cold.

"What?" I snarled.

He sighed and turned his attention to me. "You heard me the first time, Foster. You should know by now just how cruel this world can be. Look at this as a mercy killing," he said.

"There's no way in hell I'm murdering someone who has another option," I said, slamming my fists on the metal table. The sound ricocheted through the tiny space as heavy silence fell.

"Then have someone else do it," he said, turning to go on.

"No."

"No?" he asked, his eyes narrowing.

"That wasn't part of my agreement, and I'm not pushing it onto someone else." I glared at him.

"You would risk the lives of your team, for one?" he asked, and for once I had no answer. His laughter felt like a slap in the face, but I couldn't back down.

"It isn't everyone for one, Professor, just like it's not a

mercy killing. Don't exaggerate." I spat the words at him, and the look on his face almost made me regret it.

"Ms. Foster, you are out of line. The terms of your agreement with Council Member Fortescue were binding. You took an oath to serve and be her right hand, ending the war before it begins. Don't let foolish notions of sentimentality corrupt your judgment."

I gritted my teeth against the urge to obliterate him into dust...because in a way he was right. I was the property of the Council.

"It is a mercy killing, Ms. Foster. We've all done things we're not proud of. Grow up. Don't risk it. Council Member Fortescue will not be pleased. Do you understand?"

His threat was clear. I couldn't act, though, because I was property, and I knew my job. I was to be the assassin, the Vampire hunter, the death bringer, and now a mercy killer. Mercy. I once told Anastasia I had none. Maybe I was right. If I went through with this, surely I was merciless.

"Do you understand, Ms. Foster? I will not repeat myself again."

I swallowed my pride and nodded, keeping my head down for the rest of dinner. A stone had settled in my stomach, and the pressure wasn't welcome. When he dismissed us for the evening, it couldn't have come soon enough.

"A word, Ms. Foster," he called.

I sighed, debating whether to listen or disobey him outright. Blair squeezed my hand as she walked by, and against my better judgment, I turned and walked back into the lunchroom. It didn't take long for the room to clear out, and I stood brooding in the doorway while Vonlowsky disassembled the projector.

"Please close the door," he said quietly.

I stepped inside, and the door clicked behind me.

He glanced up, but didn't say a word. Silence stretched before us.

"Selena, it's only day one of training, and I'm concerned," he said.

My mouth popped open. That wasn't how I'd been expecting this conversation to go. I kept silent, waiting for him to continue.

"Would you be making the same argument if it was one of the other soldiers on the line, and not one of yours?"

I blanched, the stone in my stomach like a bowling ball. I couldn't answer.

"I didn't think so," he murmured.

"I want to say yes. I want to say I would," I said hastily.

"But you can't," he summed up for me.

As much as I hated it, I only nodded.

"Make no mistake, Selena, about what's on the line here. If you don't carry out Council Member Fortescue's orders, they'll see to it that you cease to exist. You've already shown that your power is great. Don't give them any reason to see you as a *threat*. If you aren't with the Council, you're against it. Do you understand?" The threat wasn't his own, but it still burned like whiskey in my throat. Anastasia wasn't to be trusted. None of them were.

"I understand, *Professor*," I said, my voice steeped in sarcasm. He sighed deeply, aging ten years in five minutes. "Is that all?"

"You're excused," he said, dismissing me.

When I left the room quietly, the voices of my team carried from the floor above.

"I'm not sharing a bunk with her," Alexandra was saying.

I sighed deeply, feeling like I'd aged ten years myself.

"I don't know how you two are even related," Blair muttered as she stormed toward the door I was walking in.

"Is there a problem here?"

The room went silent.

"I asked if there's a problem here."

Blair was the first to speak. "There are only five bunks on our side. Amber and Tori said they'll take one, but Alexandra doesn't want to share a bunk with anyone other than Aaron, and Aaron thinks it's not appropriate even though there are two beds. We all kind of assumed you'd want your own because—"

Oh my god. Were they seriously arguing about sharing bunk beds? Seriously? We weren't at summer camp; this was boot camp—and I didn't really give a damn who shared what. We had ten beds and seven people, why this was even a discussion was...ludricous.

"You and I can share. The boys and Alexandra can have their own. Problem solved," I said, walking over to my trunk sitting haphazardly in the middle of the small corridors.

"Are you sure?" she asked skeptically.

I grabbed the trunk handle with one hand and tossed it to the bunk in the corner opposite Alexandra's bed.

"I'll take the top," I said. Opening the trunk with phantom hands, I simultaneously made the bed and stored my things underneath.

The room fell silent again, and this was the crux of the matter. Even simple telekinesis threw them off, because they didn't know how deep the power ran. Would I simply move things with my mind, or would I do more and become the demon of legend? The one my father had warned me about. The one my mother had feared. The one I was well on my way to becoming.

"Oh, for the love of— Yes, I'm telekinetic. If you all are going to be on *my* team, you'd better get used to it. Are there any other issues that need to be taken care of before I get some sleep?" I rubbed my temples and glanced over the room. The nine were pretending to be busy, twiddling their thumbs and not bothering to comment.

"No?" I asked, turning to my group.

They all stared at me like I'd grown a third eye, apart from Aaron. He was lying on the lower bunk next to mine, absorbed in whatever he was reading. Wait...what? Reading? I didn't know he read. Amber's comments about being judgmental came to mind, but then again, I'd seen him every day, in both my classes and my life, for a year. I knew enough.

"Excellent. I'm exhausted." I looked over at the strange girl the nine seemed to answer to. "You. What's your name?" I asked.

She glanced my way, apparently unperturbed by my straightforwardness. Her golden eyes resembled a cat's, with their slit-like irises. "Johanna." Her voice wasn't soft, but hard like stone—forged by whatever burden she carried.

We've all done things we're not proud of...

Did I even want to know what she'd done that had landed her here?

"So tell me, Johanna, did you volunteer for this?"

Her lips twitched into an almost-grin. If I was being honest with myself, I didn't know what the hell I was doing here past the bullshit Anastasia was feeding me. Maybe Johanna did.

"Not quite," she said.

Alec was throwing dagger-like glares at both of us. His *mistress* would've crapped herself if she'd heard how we talked about her, and this mission. And on our first day.

She said I had to serve and couldn't tell them why. She never said I had to like it.

Maybe it was the same with Johanna. Or maybe she was a liar. It was hard to tell these days.

"If anyone needs anything, you go to her. I'm turning in for the night," I said. My goal for today was done. The demons were locked in their cages, and everyone was still breathing. Maybe if I played nice with the strange girl, I could learn a thing or two about the rest of my so-called team—like, if they wanted to slit my throat while I slept.

"Me?" she asked, just as I reached my bed.

"You seem intelligent enough, and they trust you. That's worth more than my pride, Johanna."

I kicked my leg up to get enough leverage to pull myself over the railing and roll onto the bed. They milled around a bit more, speculating about what happened between me and Vonlowsky while I pretended to be asleep. Both Lucas and Aaron said nothing all evening, and I thought back to my conversation with Amber. Whatever was going on with either of them, it wasn't my priority. Lucas had his own shit to work through, and Aaron was just an attractive punching bag. I needed to be on top of my game to make it through the next month. One slip up, a single misstep, and the

Council would see me as a threat that needed to be removed. If I was going to survive this, I needed to become the monster.

I needed to be merciless, and figure out why someone kept sending their own monsters after me. But...I needed my friends too. This wasn't going to be an easy line to walk. That much was already clear.

CHAPTER 17

Dreamland was different this time. Not the dank, dark forest I was used to, but a place I'd thought I'd wiped from my memory altogether—my childhood home. Next to me, my nightmare self with violet eyes was leaning back against the roof. She lounged against it, basking in the pretend sun of what was surely going to turn into another nightmare.

"Not this again," my other said dryly.

Below us, a child-me was sparring with our father.

"What are you talking about? What is this?" I asked, bristling at her comment.

"You tell me," she quipped, throwing a hand over her eyes in a more human show of exasperation than I was used to from her. This wasn't like our other encounters. Something was different here.

A sharp crack jerked my attention back to the scene below. I was huddled in a ball, my father standing above me.

"You're going to have to do better than that, Selena," he said coldly.

No, that couldn't be right. He wasn't cold. He was kind.

Child-me looked up, eyes fractured by hurt, but already recovering. He walked away, not making it five feet before the little girl's hand shot out.

My father slammed into a wall then turned slowly to face his daughter. I—she—didn't say anything as her hand tightened into a fist, and phantom hands lifted my father off the ground by an unbreakable grip around his neck.

"Now we're talking," other me said. She looked down at the child with a smug grin, and something almost like affection. This most definitely wasn't a memory. I'd never used my ability again after I manifested, and that was years before the little scene playing out before me.

My father struggled, and a booming voice rattled my mind, but I wasn't the only one who heard it—or even the one it was directed at.

"Harder, Selena!"

The silent command was the child's undoing. She dropped her hand, folding in on herself as my father fell to the ground before her. It took him no time at all to recover.

"Selena, look at me," he said.

The girl pulled herself in tighter. The darkness was coming, already... I was so young.

"That wasn't a request," he snapped.

Child-me looked up, her eyes shining with a faint violet hue.

"Come." He held out a hand that she took shakily. They started walking hand-in-hand to the old alpine larch that guarded our property.

I jumped from the roof to follow them.

"What are you doing?" the other-me asked.

I looked back at the roof. Yes, it was different here, more terrifying in its own way. As if she'd heard me, my thoughts, she grinned down at me with razor-like teeth. I turned and kept walking, trying to keep up with my dream-father and child-me.

"Do you know why I make you train like this?" he was asking her. They both sat on a boulder, watching the sunrise. This seemed more like him, like the father I remembered.

"Because they're scared of me," she said.

"They are. Do you know why?"

I frowned, and the little girl echoed the expression. That wasn't how this was supposed to go. This was where my father was supposed to ask who'd told me that then dissuade me from all the bad thoughts that my sister tormented me with. I liked this dream less and less. Where was the surreal train station when you wanted it? Or the creepy-ass forest where shark-me liked to prowl?

"Because I'm stronger than the rest of them," she said fiercely.

I almost smiled. The orange sunrise painted my childhood home an egg-yolk color, instead of the pale yellow it actually was. Our white picket fence cast shadows across the rocky land.

"Yes, but it's not really you they're afraid of, my dear. Not yet," he said softly.

Shivers went down my spine as I recalled a similar conversation between us. I was only seven at the time.

Surely the girl sitting here was older, though. Her eyes were already so haunted.

"Why not?" she asked.

"Because you haven't come into your full power, yet. One day you will, though, and when you do, even the telekinetics of legend won't compare," he whispered reverently, petting my head affectionately. While the mannerism wasn't odd for him, I didn't remember his reverence in my memories. If anything, I remembered him telling me to shut the power down and never let it get that far.

"You're talking about the matter manipulators?" she asked, her head perking up.

"Where did you hear that?" he asked, cocking his head. This man was my whole world; he hung the moon as far as I was concerned—but here in dreamland, he wasn't the same.

"Lily told me about it, said Mama was looking for answers in the past," she said. Oblivious to the darkening of our father's eyes, she babbled on about our mother.

"Did she tell you who they were?" he asked, playing this game a little longer while child-me shook her head. He sighed deeply.

Drawing her arms around her knees, the little girl relaxed just enough for her father to tell her a story of the telekinetics of old.

"The matter manipulators lived a long time ago, Selena, longer than most of the world can remember. They were the strongest of the Supernaturals, so powerful it was said that Nyx herself had to bless those who became one, because only the strongest would survive." He paused, his eyes darkening again—but this time for a very different reason. I knew what was coming.

"Your mother is killing herself, traveling through the realm of the dead to find answers, because she doesn't like the truth. The matter manipulators were wiped out by their own minds, Selena, just like you'll be if you don't learn to control it now." He fell silent, and she followed suit for a moment, but my—her—curiosity wouldn't be silenced.

"Does that mean I'm a matter manipulator?" she asked, her eyes wide in awe of something she didn't understand yet.

"The matter manipulators are dead, Selena. I just told you that."

"So are the telekinetics, but here I am."

He went quiet, watching his small daughter, who was too observant for her own good. The whole interaction was wrong, as if a filter had been placed over my childhood memories—but part of the scene was still the same.

"Not all telekinetics become matter manipulators—only the strongest. Just like not all matter manipulators survive their gift. It isn't me who'll decide what you become, Selena, but you." His words felt both inspiring and ominous.

My father stood, walking back to the house.

"Wait, Dad…I have one more question!" she called, sprinting after him.

I waited where I was, a pit settling in my stomach.

"What is it?" he asked, not bothering to stop. My mother's voice carried from within the house, humming a melody I recognized but couldn't place. I was tempted to follow them just to see where that led. Would I see her again too? Would she be the same?

"They're all dead. The telekinetics and the matter manipulators," the little girl said. I saw the clocks turning in her mind even if my father didn't.

"Yes, I already said that." He pinched the bridge of his nose in frustration.

She was persistent, though, like a dog with a bone. "Then how am I here? How is that possible?"

My father stopped, swallowing hard. He placed a large hand on my shoulder and leaned down until we were face-to-face. "I don't know."

"But how—" she protested.

"I said I don't know, Selena. Let it go." He dropped his hand and kept walking, sweeping both my sisters up in his arms at the door. I may have only been a child at the time, but I knew a lie when I heard it.

My mother smiled from the doorway, calling child-me inside. Her white-blond hair was already gray...even though she wasn't old enough for gray hair.

It's just a dream, I told myself, even as I watched my small, dark head duck inside my childhood home. There was more to this dreamland, even if I didn't want to admit it.

CHAPTER 18

THE FOLLOWING DAY DRAGGED ON, AND THE ONES THAT CAME after it. A routine formed. Wake up. Train with Lily. Eat. Train with the team. Eat. Train again with the team. Eat. Study with the team. Sleep. Repeat.

It was a grueling pace. After six days of it, every single one of us was ready to drop dead. Staring into the mirror before me, I felt like the ghost of Selena's past. Dark circles lined my eyes, the telltale sign that the killing gene was rearing its head again. I bent and washed my face with water for the third time, attempting to clear the barest smudge of violet from behind the gray. My other had visited every night since that dream, but none of the dreams took me through distorted memories. I preferred it that way.

"You look tired this morning," Johanna said.

I glanced sideways across the long bathroom mirror at the amber-eyed girl. Her simple linen pajamas fit right in with the prison-like atmosphere. "I haven't been sleeping well," I mumbled.

"It's hard to be at peace these days. We live in dangerous times," she said.

I frowned into the water. Something seemed off about her words. Almost rebellious.

"That we do," I said slowly, wanting to gauge her reaction.

She continued splashing her face with cold water. Silence stretched before us, and I turned back to my sink.

"I would be careful letting yourself get too tired. You never know when the next elimination will be," she continued.

I stilled again. I definitely wasn't imagining it this time. She was trying to tell me something.

"I can't really be eliminated," I said tightly. We locked eyes in the mirror. The rest of our cohorts were still sleeping, completely oblivious to the silent exchange.

"No, but you could fall out of favor with the Council, and Her Highness by extension." Her words were soft and deceptive, but that simple statement said so much.

Johanna was sending me a message: elimination day was here. The real question was why. What point was she trying to make? Even if we were having one today, why risk herself?

"Why are you telling me this?" I asked.

She took a deep breath, turning her body a fraction. "Do you kowtow to the Fortescues?" she asked, blunter than most dared to be with me. I liked it.

"No."

"Then you have your answer." Johanna walked by me, her mouth too grim for the wink she gave me before she left.

Her words replayed in my mind as I flipped the shower on.

That was weird.

I continued my morning routine before heading out to train with Lily at dawn. Chirping crickets greeted me at the door as the morning dew seeped into my cotton tank top. My legs carried me quickly from one end of the campus to the other. Elimination day. Was she telling the truth? Why would she? I shook my head, glaring at the horizon in the distance.

"Why so gloomy?" Lily asked, bringing me back to the ground in front of me.

"You're one to talk," I muttered.

She let out a short laugh in agreement, and I arched my eyebrows.

"What?" she asked, already retreating into herself. Too soon.

"Nothing. It's just nice to hear you laugh."

Her lips quirked up as we fell into our warmup—tree climbing. It was amateur in some ways, but it did her good to start off with something reminiscent of our childhood in the alpine larch. It was happier—for her, at least.

"You're getting better," I said.

Swinging from branch to branch, Lily pulled herself up, still two branches below.

"It does seem that way," she said, hauling herself up another branch as I moved on to the top. Up here, the branches were thinner, more precarious. Balancing was as much a necessity as a skill, but the sunrise was worth it.

"Well, how about that? You finally made it before the

sun came up," I said, giving her a second to catch her breath before I nudged her shoulder and pointed east.

"Whoa..." she said, letting out a breath. Her awe lasted about two and a half seconds before she slipped, losing her grip on the branches. She only fell five feet before invisible hands plucked her out of the air and deposited her on a branch a few feet below me.

I was getting used to practicing with it for little things like making my bed, or turning light switches on. Her writhing body required more control, though, and more power. Adrenaline hit my system almost instantly, because now that I was using the power, I already needed my next fix. It was the two days I'd spent in Nashville with Tori and Lucas all over again. My body craved something my mind didn't want to give it, and a low growl escaped my throat. I scrambled down the branches, not caring what they scraped or how much I bled. Lily fumbled in her attempt to keep up, but she didn't fall again.

"Selena, what's going on?" she called.

The moment my feet hit the ground, I paced back and forth, trying to calm myself. The sticky tendrils of madness clawed up my arms and into my brain, but I couldn't lose it. Not with Lily.

"Selena—"

"Just give me a sec." I held up a hand to ward her off as my blood cooled. The key seemed to be sensing it before the episodes came on, and making sure nothing prodded the cage too much until the monster settled.

Lily waited quietly by the pine tree as the clawing receded, and I no longer felt something crawling under my skin.

"It's getting worse," she said.

I didn't even try to deny it. "Some days are worse than others…" I muttered, my voice trailing off. There was no room for excuses. Not anymore.

"And today?" she asked, her voice brittle.

"Elimination day," I said, as if that explained everything.

"Already? How do you know?" she asked, unconvinced. One eyebrow went up as she pursed her lips.

I sighed, leaning back against a tree. "Johanna," I muttered into the wind.

"Who?"

"A Supernatural girl Anastasia brought in. She's odd…" Something about this whole thing grated at me. Why would she tell me? Me and mine passing meant one of hers didn't.

"You sure she wasn't lying?" Lily asked. She kicked a rock hard enough that it stuck in the tree ten feet away. When she reached her potential, she was really going to be something.

"I don't think so." I shook my head, running a hand over my hair.

"Okay…are you ready? Are they ready?" she asked, seeing my train of thought as if it were her own.

"Yes and no," I said, playing with a piece of my hair.

"You are, but they aren't?" she guessed.

I nodded, throwing my hair over my shoulder, then rocked forward and turned to leave.

"What's wrong? I thought you picked them because they could handle this kind of thing," she said. Her footsteps trailed me, even as I took off down the path.

"I underestimated how strong the Supernaturals she brought in would be. Tori isn't keeping up well, and Alexandra's still exhausted from coming so close to burnout." The monster inside was locked in its cage, but pawing at the latch. I needed to ditch some energy and fast, or someone was going to get hurt.

"Then what are you going to do?" she asked, picking up speed to stay even with me.

"I have no idea. If Johanna's wrong then it doesn't matter, but if not... I have no idea what they have in store today." I clenched and unclenched my hands in an effort to calm myself. It failed miserably.

"What if I can help you all?" she asked. There was a lilt to her voice I hadn't heard in a long time. It set me on edge. She was planning something.

"What did you have in mind?" I asked, intrigued but fighting the urge to shut her down. We didn't need a repeat of the warehouse, but I had to stop leading with an iron fist when it came to her.

"I can transfer your energy to them," she said smugly. She had an air of confidence about her that hadn't been there since the warehouse. It was nice to see, but I still didn't buy it.

"How?" I asked skeptically.

"Think about it. I can heal people...or kill them, depending on whether I'm giving or taking energy. Maybe I can act as a conduit and take your energy, but give it to them instead of absorbing it," she said. Something about the way she phrased it made it sound like she already knew she could do this.

I slowed to a walking pace, and we weren't even halfway back yet.

"What's wrong?" she asked, slowing as well.

"Have you done this before?" I asked bluntly. She looked away, playing with a piece of hair. "You have, haven't you?" I demanded.

She looked up to me, her brown eyes watering. "It was an accident."

"An accident?" I asked icily. The wind whipped around us, stronger than was natural.

"It happened this summer, but I covered it up because I didn't put together what was going on..." Her voice trailed off under my stony glare.

"What happened?"

"I tried to hurt Elizabeth, but her energy just went from me to Blair, making Blair stronger. She pulled me off Elizabeth before I could tell for sure, but..." She continued mumbling to herself, and it was seriously starting to get on my nerves.

"But what?"

"Our first day back at Daizlei I attacked you, and I took something from you when I did. It hurt, though, because I took too much. I couldn't hold it, and then...I kind of—accidentally—sent some of it into Tori when I bumped into her and Lucas on the way back to the dorm. I tripped—it all happened so fast. I know what I felt, though, and I know I passed your energy into her. At least some of it. If I can control how much I take, I think I can siphon enough to take the edge off for you, and help them—like I did with Tori." She looked away guiltily, and as pissed as I was for her not telling me, I couldn't exactly blame her. It wasn't like I was the most forthcoming.

"Well, that answers that question," I muttered, running my slick hands over my damp tank top.

"What question?"

"Can you actually transfer anything without hurting someone—including yourself," I added. Her eyes lit up. I really shouldn't have been entertaining this idea, even if she could do it.

"I can!" The dumb grin on her face said it all. This was how she wanted to contribute.

"Lily..." I started, already knowing we couldn't go down this road. Maybe if we had a few more months of practice and she was stable, but this—this was ludicrous.

"I can do it. I know I can. I won't let you down. I prom—"

"It's not happening. I'll find another way." I walked past her as I headed back to main campus.

"Wait a minute. Since when do you get to decide for me?" she called, like this had only now occurred to her.

"I'm not deciding for you. I'm deciding for me. You won't do it, because without me, you have no energy to give."

It wasn't really a lie, but in deciding for me, I was deciding for both of us. Sure, she could try with someone else, but she wouldn't, because she didn't trust herself, and that was all I needed to know not to trust her doing it either. So, she could gape at me all she wanted, but I wasn't taking chances. Not with the killing gene, and not with her.

CHAPTER 19

Johanna wasn't lying, and while that was good to know, I couldn't piece together why she'd told me in the first place. I couldn't exactly stop and ask her, though, because the evaluation kicked off as soon as I got back. Despite all the sparring we'd done in the last week, Vonlowsky wasn't testing tactics or brawn. Instead, he wanted to see who could get out of sticky situations the fastest. With the simulator running at full power, he gave them five minutes each to find their way out of an ivory maze he'd created from the white tiles of the simulator floors. The padded room concept took on a whole new level when I stared at the tight corridors. This was going to be a claustrophobic's worst nightmare, and Blair was already panting.

Tori and Amber volunteered to go first and were walking through the open door in seconds, effectively disabling the traps that were too slow to catch them. Tori was swaying on her feet, though, and that jump hadn't even been a hundred meters, from one end of the maze to the other. That didn't bode well.

Next came the Graeme twins, a brother and sister from Germany who had abilities based on changing their own density. While Sebastian could pass through the walls, Scarlett simply brute-forced the matter and made herself impenetrable. I'd never seen anything like the way she obliterated walls by stepping through them. Bombs went off right and left, hitting her, but she kept walking, completely unharmed. She was going to be one to watch in the upcoming weeks.

The clock ticked on as, one by one, every soldier stepped up to show their worth. Alexandra did better than expected, and Blair did worse, even given our training for situations like this. She panicked when one of the walls tried to close in, and ended up freezing then having to use her daggers as ice picks to climb out. Both of their times were sufficient, though, and that was all we needed. They didn't have to be the fastest, just fast enough.

Worry itched at me when Lucas stumbled through the door in last place with a time of three and a half minutes. His ability had failed him more than anyone else, because his opponent was a machine and not capable of thinking. With only four people left, I held my tongue and kept my jaw tight to keep from growling or grinding my teeth. Aaron was next.

His dark hair was slicked back from running his hands through it too many times. The muscles of his chest were prominent, even under the damp black t-shirt. He was strong, and not a single bruise marred his skin, but dark circles ringed his black eyes. He looked like a demon, straight from the textbook. I instinctively took a step back as he passed. Alexandra wrapped her arms around his shoulders, kissing his cheek. He stared right through her, looking at me with fathomless eyes.

I grimaced, fighting the hammering of my pulse that was telling me to run. The reaction was silly, almost childish, but his eyes were too dark, too deep, too devilish... I whispered a hasty excuse to Vonlowsky and descended to the floor underneath us.

The bathroom. I'm using the bathroom, I reminded myself.

I tugged my worn leather jacket loose and dropped it on the concrete floor as I entered the bathroom. Water. I needed water to drown the fire creeping through my veins and threatening to consume my last shred of sanity. The cold hit my skin, bringing clarity with it.

Calm. You need to get a hold of yourself. There are no demons here. You're being paranoid.

My racing heart refused to still as I splashed a handful of water onto my face.

His eyes burned like the depths of hell.

More water. Water would drown the fire. Drown the demon. My own demons screamed in rage—this was different than *her*, though. These demons didn't have my face or wear my shape. Instead, they lurked in the darkest recesses of my mind, waiting for a moment of weakness. A moment when the shadows of my past turned the black of his eyes into the portals to hell.

I stumbled away from the sink, staring at the foreign creature in the mirror. Midnight hair framed a face made of bone. Her eyes held death in them. My death. The stumbling turned to shaking as my back hit the wall behind me. She stared on, zeroing in for the kill.

Please be hallucinating. Please be hallucinating.

I wanted to scream, but no sound would come. I succumbed to the fear, collapsing to the floor. Water pooled around me, flooding the bathroom, but I didn't care.

The demons were here.

They'd come for me.

I was suspended outside time as I waited for the killing blow to come, too petrified to do more than stare blankly at the water bubbles floating around me.

"Oh my god," a voice said.

I recognized the sound, but couldn't find it in me to answer.

"Selena," the voice said.

Water splashed, but fear held me in place. I'd always known I was a time bomb, ticking away until my timer ran out. For, despite the brave face I wore, the moment something triggered the demons, they came for me. Like locusts, they swarmed me, filling my head with lies until I saw what they wanted me to see.

"Selena," the voice repeated. There was a note of desperation in it as they started saying other names. "Lucas, bring Alexandra and get down here right now."

Footsteps followed, but I couldn't tell whether I was really hearing them or not. I felt the shift in energy as others entered the room, but water floated by, keeping them away, for now.

"Selena," another voice said.

I recognized this one too, but still couldn't find my voice. The demons were coming for me. It was only a matter of time. I wouldn't waste my last breath.

"What the hell happened?" one of them growled. They were angry.

"I don't know. I found her like this, and she won't respond. It's like the lights are on but no one's home," the other voice whispered.

No one. The words echoed through me.

Was I no one? The floating bubbles seemed to agree with me.

"Selena, I need you to talk to me now," the other voice said.

Green eyes filled my vision, reflecting off the bubbles. Still, I couldn't speak. but I recognized the person in front of me. I just couldn't place them. Streams of water shot toward me, though, separating us as the eyes darkened to black. The water would keep me safe. It would drown the fire.

The demon cursed in rage, and I drifted even further away.

"What's going on?" a different voice said. This was familiar, like a cup of tea on a cold day or a fire on a winter night. The voice wrapped around me, filling me with warmth.

"Get out," the demon roared.

Water would drown the demon. In a rush of power, streams of glistening liquid wrapped around me, surrounding me in a cocoon. *Safe.*

"She's losing it. What the hell is going on in her head right now, Lucas?" the first voice said.

Water. I need more water. I need to build a shield of water so deep they'll never find me.

"She's having a panic attack. I'm going to have to break her mental shields. It's the only way she'll listen," the voice said resolutely.

"No!" several of them yelled. Too many to keep track of. Too many to stave off forever.

"There isn't any other way. I have to shut her down or she's going to drown herself, and us with her."

I don't like the way he talks about me. He wants to break me. To break my shields. I need more water.

"Let me talk her down," the warm one said. The pull of this person was strong, even inside my watery prison.

"No!" the demon yelled, but other voices soon drowned his out.

"Are you sure about this—"

"Why would she—"

"Selena," he said warmly. He called to me like the moon to the waves. The water stilled as he tried to part my shield. This one was different. He wasn't a demon.

I watched in fascination as the shield fell, layer by layer.

"Listen to me, Selena. I need you to come back now. It's safe," the voice whispered.

Safe. It was safe? The shield around me continued to disintegrate, until, finally, a hand broke through the water and wrapped around my wrist.

A door appeared in my mind. Shaking violently, it threatened to burst open on the precipice of something— something I couldn't...didn't want to comprehend. Pain quaked through me as the final layer of my shield wore thin.

And I looked up.

The eyes were black and bottomless.

He was the last tether that kept me here. That made me feel safe. And when that tether snapped—so did I.

Water rose and flooded into me, rushing so quickly the

demon couldn't react. He, who was the warmth, was a fraud. With eyes as black as obsidian stone, he was my undoing. My assurance that these were no hallucinations. This wasn't like the other times. Death was coming.

"Selena!" the voice cried out, but I wouldn't fall for the false sense of security again.

The others were speaking. Faster now, more frightened.

If I knew anything about fear, it was that it made others desperate. It made me desperate, because I wasn't going to let them get me. Not this time. This time, I would do what needed to be done. This time, I would drown us all, because even death would be kinder than reliving what had happened. Never again.

"You had your chance. Now it's my turn," the dark voice said.

Water rolled, and waves flooded the bathroom at my beck and call. Protecting me, filling my lungs as it sought to bring me a release from this world.

"No," a fourth voice commanded. Light was blazing from the other side of my shield. Hell's fires were coming. "There's another way," the voice whispered. Like a sun swelling to consume a universe, the light grew brighter. The water turned to steam, and still it grew. Layer after layer was ripped from me, but the water in my lungs was already there and burned as hot as any star. I swallowed, only to be filled once more.

"She's drowning, Alexandra. You'll never reach her in time," the first voice said.

How right they are. I'll never be taken again.

The light burned through my shields in seconds as the fire surrounded me.

And then I heard the words.

"Dormi, dea, propter manicaveris."

Sleep, little goddess, for you must rise with the dawn.

Both power and water left me as I fell to the floor, eyes closing before I even hit the concrete.

CHAPTER 20

"Mᴏʀᴇ, Sᴇʟᴇɴᴀ."

It was the first thing I heard, but as I looked down at child-sized me, it didn't look like she had much more to give. Dreamland. Again.

"That was quite the little stunt we pulled back there. What do they call it? Cool? It was so cool."

I faced my violet-eyed other, groaning internally. *Of course she's here.*

"Where else would I be?" she asked.

"You can hear my thoughts?" I yelled internally. What the hell was this?

"Well, we are kind of the same person, so.,,"

"We are not," I said, turning away from my overtly creepy other.

This time she basked on the roof wearing nothing but a corset and underwear. Her pointed teeth reflected in the sunlight, and her hair was way too done up for my liking.

"Dislike me all you want. It's not going to change

anything. It's me and you for life," she said, crossing her fingers mockingly.

Bitch. We're nothing alike.

"We are in all the ways that matter," she said.

I wasted no time jumping from the roof to the scene below, ignoring my other and getting closer to child-me. I was older in this dream, harder already. My knuckles were calloused, and black energy swirled under my skin, almost like Lily's did now, in the real world. Whatever childlike curiosity I'd had was long gone. At barely five feet tall, I was already a soldier. But I wasn't the only one. On the other side of my father was Alexandra, her red hair bound tightly to her head in warrior braids. The whip in her hand already had blood on it.

What's going on here?

"Do you really want to remember?" my other said. She'd followed me off the roof.

Something about the way she said it caught me off guard. "What are you talking about?"

She snorted. I wasn't imagining it this time. She wasn't acting like the boogeyman here. She was acting...real.

"That's because I am real," she sneered.

I rolled my eyes and turned back to the scene.

"Again!" my father shouted. He had a short beard, and he was thinner than I remembered. I couldn't recall a time when he wasn't clean shaven, but Alexandra being here meant we were nine. Father hadn't let her practice with us until she'd manifested, and that was only a year before they'd died.

Not that this is real, I reminded myself.

"Just keep telling yourself that," my other said. She was the only one who seemed to be able to communicate with me here. Why was that? Rocks started rattling, drawing my attention back to the false memory.

One by one, the rocks came up, flying toward my father and sister. He was fast, though, deflecting them like they were nothing, but child-me wasn't giving up so easily. The ground beneath their feet rumbled as the earth split in two.

"Better, but not enough. I said more!" he shouted, and my head whipped around just fast enough to watch a spark of fire light in child-me's eyes.

The rumbling continued as fissures opened and the ground collapsed in on itself. My sister looked terrified, but not me. Oh no, even as a child I'd known what I was doing, and it didn't matter that my nose had started to bleed. Child-me didn't care, as long as he didn't get through. My father sent a warning shot at my shield, a silent command of pain that only a telepath could give—but this time, my shield held. I would never forget this moment, when my father watched me bleed from harnessing too much power —and did nothing. Even as a kid, I was losing myself to whatever blasted curse Nyx had given me.

But this is dreamland, I reminded myself as nine-year-old Selena battled burnout. Despite it, child-me sent a wave of darkness for him and my sister the moment they turned away. He must've sensed it coming, though, because his next command made me want to hurl.

"Now, Alexandra," he yelled.

I gave child-me credit for not wincing when the wave of fire came for me out of nowhere, only to clash with my wall of swirling energy. She didn't falter when my sister whipped her mercilessly until she collapsed. Showed no fear when my sister spoke the words he'd been teaching her for months now. The words he'd conditioned me with.

In case I ever got out of control.

It was my switch, but only two people in my life knew how to flip it.

"*Dormi, dea, propter manicaveris.*"

Sleep, little goddess, for you must rise with the dawn.

I remembered thinking even then that one day I would rise. Like the matter manipulators of legend. Like the telekinetics who'd died. I would be stronger.

I would be the strongest.

That couldn't be right, though, because this was just a dream. Even if I knew without a shadow of doubt that it was real.

I OPENED MY EYES, taking deep breaths to calm my erratic heartbeat. The bunks that lined the walls were only imperceptibly lighter than the concrete that surrounded me on all sides. My head throbbed with the realization of what had happened, as it all came back to me.

Oh fuck.

I pushed the covers aside, and silently slipped from my bed to the cold stone floors. Glancing from one bed to the next, I watched my team sleep—it seemed my six had made it past the first elimination. Even with the elation that brought me, I couldn't find peace. Not here. As the events that had caused my blackout flashed before my eyes, I fled the dark prison—leaving my claustrophobia behind. One door after another clicked shut until it was only me and the midnight sky.

Night? How much time has passed?

I reached for my pockets, where my phone should've been, but for some reason, I was wearing somebody else's sweatpants, and a cotton t-shirt that was too big.

Shit.

The door behind me opened again.

"Shouldn't you be sleeping?" I asked.

"Do you remember what happened?" Blair asked softly.

"Enough to say I'm sorry," I whispered.

She was all silver when I turned around, with eyes of iron that matched my own.

"I'm sorry?" she asked, but I couldn't tell if she was in shock or furious.

"Yes?" I asked.

Her scowl deepened. "I don't want an apology, Selena. I want to know what's going on. I want to know why you lost it in there and didn't wake up for over thirty-six hours. Was it because of what Alexandra did?" She stared at me, waiting for answer.

Shock it is, then.

"What do you know about what she did?" I asked, not knowing how much Alexandra had told her—or if she'd even told her anything at all. The safe switch wasn't something I talked about. Ever. With anyone.

"Enough," she said, her face looking impressively detached despite the very slight narrowing of her eyes.

"Then don't ask me about what she did and don't over-react. It's not like this is the first time something's happened, and it won't be the last," I said, thinking back over the summer. She'd been there everytime I went down-hill, and everytime, she'd gotten me out. Maybe that would give her hope, and she would lay off.

Or maybe my age-old excuse—that it had happened before and would happen again—was no longer sufficient anymore. "So that's it? You have a panic attack and act like nothing happened? I saw the look on your face, Selena! I watched you try to drown yourself, and you're damn lucky Alexandra was there to stop you."

Her voice cut me like a knife. What did I say to that? What could I possibly say that she might understand?

Nothing.

I sighed and turned away. "I don't know what to tell you, Blair—"

"The truth!" she demanded. This was the angriest I'd ever seen her, but it was a righteous anger.

"The truth?" I muttered to myself, playing with the words. "The truth is I don't know real from imagined. Were they demons...or hallucinations? Are you real or just another splinter of my mind that's broken off and taken a face I know? Questions, questions..." I trailed off as hysteria entered my voice.

"They weren't lying..." she murmured, her eyes soft with pity.

"What are you talking about?" I snapped. I didn't need her pity. Didn't want it.

"Lucas tried to explain to us what he was hearing, but your mind snapped. He thinks your ability's too much for you to handle. Maybe Lily can help—" she started, putting together too many pieces for me to comprehend.

"Lily? What does Lily have to do with this?" I demanded, temporarily putting aside her claims about Lucas. He and I were going to have a little chat. This was exactly what I'd meant about him meddling where he didn't belong.

"Did you think she wouldn't come looking for you when you didn't show up to train her? She told us what happened in the woods, and while I agree that she needs to train, are you even sure you can take the stress anymore? I'm starting to think they may be right. Maybe your energy is lashing out and causing hallucinations. We could always try—"

"There is no we!" I shouted.

She went silent instantly, staring me down. This wasn't a test of wills, though; it was a matter of choice. "You need to be reasonable about this, Selena. Aaron and I already said we could be the ones to take what Lily can't handle. She's already done it with me before," she added as if that argument was going to change my mind.

"Take what she can't handle?" I asked, my blood cooling instantly to something far more dangerous than the heat of the moment.

"Lily has to transfer your energy somewhere. If she can't take it, we can," Blair said.

We stared at each other for a moment, neither willing to relent—until I let out a mocking laugh. "No one's taking anything from me, and you're a damn fool to fill my sister's head with heroic notions. I can save myself," I said.

The wind howled in my ears, silencing everything but Blair's voice.

I turned to walk away when she spoke again.

"I've stood by you through all of this and not questioned you once. All of us have. You can wear whatever mask you want for the world, but don't do this. Let me help you. Let us."

I sighed deeply. I shouldn't leave things like this between us. The problem was that the deeper down the rabbit hole I went, the clearer it became that none of them could help me. Not really. Sure, they could pull me back when I snapped and tried to kill people. They could help me to a lesser extent with my other, who lurked in the shadows of my mind. The panic, though? That wasn't something they could fix. Simply being there for me wouldn't change that, and neither would trying to siphon my energy off.

"Let me ask you something," I said as I walked back to face her. Her eyes gleamed like a dagger, her skin so pale it was almost translucent. "Do you know how it works? Can you promise me my sister won't kill herself trying this?"

"She won't," Blair swore, but it wasn't a promise, and we both knew it.

"I didn't do this just to have her—"

"Do what?" she asked sharply.

"Agree to fight—just for my sister to get mixed up in it. Besides, it's not like she can come with us when we leave, and that's supposing that Lucas's *theory* is true, which I find doubtful."

Her eyes narrowed to slits. It seemed she didn't believe my story, but she let it drop this time.

"Okay, so if what Lucas says *isn't* true and Lily *can't* help you, what are you going to do about it then?" she asked. Her long pajama pants billowed in the wind and strands of her hair slipped out of her braid.

"I'll train harder, and shut myself down before I ever get there," I insisted, grasping for straws as I racked my brain for a solution. In the past, it had always been boxing, and over the summer, it was training, but now I was gearing up for the fight of my life, and somehow, it wasn't enough. Hurt wasn't enough. Pain wasn't feeding me.

"And if that doesn't work?" she asked, gentler this time but still firm. No matter how prettily she phrased it, I knew what she wanted, and I wasn't having any of it. Over my— literally—dead body.

"If that doesn't work, you can put me down yourself," I said apathetically.

She snorted, covering her mouth as the tension broke. "Don't be a drama queen."

"You're the one talking life and death, Blair. I'm simply making my opinion crystal clear. Lily isn't to be involved, and that's the end of it." I placed my own hand on her shoulder and gave a gentle squeeze.

She smiled tightly. "Can I ask you something?"

"You just did," I quipped. Like Lucas, she didn't find that line funny.

"How much of this is the warehouse?" She was too forward for my liking, but not intrusive enough to make me squirm.

"Enough."

She nodded, like she was finally putting together some puzzle she hadn't been able to solve. "I'm going to let it go this time, but I'm not messing around, Selena. If it happens again, we're going with Lucas's plan. It took a lot out of

Alexandra just to put you down, and Aaron nearly lost his shit when he saw you drop.”

“What does Aaron have to do with anything?” I asked.

Blair grimaced, falling quiet for a moment. “How much did you say you remember?” she said slowly.

“Enough,” I said. She opened her mouth and closed it, twice before she said, “You should probably know that Alexandra broke up with him.”

“What? She dumped him?”

Blair nodded.

Seriously? After how she fought to keep him here...

“I wouldn’t judge her too much for this one,” she continued, fidgeting with her hair. “They broke up yesterday, but Alexandra is still pretty pissed. And...she’s probably not going to want to be around you right now.” She scrunched her nose, another nervous tic.

“What?”

“I don’t really want to get into it, but I feel like someone should tell you. Just know that while it’s not your fault, it’s not unjustified on her part either. She’s hurting...” Blair trailed off, making me all the more curious.

“Are you going to tell me what their breakup has to do with all of this, or do I need to wait until morning when she starts the silent treatment?” I asked matter-of-factly.

What was the big deal? It wasn’t like she wasn’t pissed at me half the time anyway. And Alexandra practically had a new boyfriend every month. It was weird she’d even been with Aaron as long as she had. Something about the whole situation had rubbed me wrong from the beginning, but this breakup was even weirder.

"It's not my place to say. You need to talk to *him* though."

"Him? Why would I talk to him?"

"Just do it, Selena. The sooner this sorts itself out, the better we'll all be."

Her words stilled me. "Okay," I agreed.

She visibly relaxed a fraction before returning to the topic at hand. "You need to talk to me next time it gets bad. Okay? Maybe just having someone to talk you down would help." She neatly skated around the fact that when I was like that there wouldn't be any talking. Who was I to point out the obvious, though?

"You think you can fix me?"

"No."

That made me laugh. At least she wasn't being senti-mental about this. She knew what she was up against.

"I do think I can help you, though, for what it's worth."

"Don't make promises you can't keep," I warned, not wanting to go there. Not tonight.

"I'm not making you a promise, Selena. I don't do promises. I've lived through some pretty shitty things, though, and I think talking to someone is better than doing nothing and hoping for the best." She paused, pulling back and giving me the look that meant I wouldn't like what she was going to say. "Don't get me wrong, you try anything stupid, and I'll have both your sisters on you before you do something you'll regret—but I don't want to go there any more than you do if we don't have to."

As much as I hated to admit it, I could live with that. It was a reprieve, of sorts, and one I hoped never to need—but like most things in my life, the universe had other plans. For the umpteenth time, I looked up at the stars and asked, *Why me?*

Just like every time before, no one answered. The ancients of old were dead. Just like the matter manipulators. Just like I would be, if I didn't find a way to stop myself next time the hallucinations came.

CHAPTER 21

WIIEN I GOT UP THE NEXT MORNING, TWO THINGS BECAME PRETTY apparent. The first was that no one had been eliminated. Apparently, my meltdown had compromised the structural integrity of the roof, which was also the floor of the simulator. My friends had covered for me, but word was that Vonlowsky wasn't pleased. We now shared the only other bathroom, which had been the guys'...but everyone was so tired they didn't really care as long as they had somewhere to shower and piss.

The second, and slightly more important thing, in my mind, was that Alexandra wouldn't look at me. Never mind Aaron, or what Blair had told me would happen— from the moment she'd woken up, she'd completely and utterly ignored me. Her inner fire burned, but her eyes were distant. Every time I tried to speak with her, she would mutter some nonsense and walk away. After the third try, I was at my wits end.

"Alexandra, what's your problem?" I said, coming up beside her to sit at the lunch table.

Both Lucas and Aaron had been giving me looks all day, but the second the words were out, they found the cracks in the floor just fascinating. Assholes. This was getting stranger and more infuriating by the second. Blair had said to give her time, but they wouldn't even tell me what I'd done that was so bad that she needed space.

"Now's not the time," she said lightly.

Time. Time? *You want to talk about time? Let's talk about every time you crossed a line, and I cleaned it up.*

Her pale hands trembled as she picked up her fork and began eating her salad.

"Then when is the time? Because I've tried to talk to you all morning and still can't get a straight answer." I should've known by the settling silence that a storm was brewing within her. I should've seen the signs.

"You want to know?" she asked, setting the fork down on the metal plate with a clink. The sharp noise made me wince, but she paid it no mind. "Why don't you talk to him?" She motioned to the dark-eyed man at the far end of the table.

It occurred to me that him sitting amidst Anastasia's people probably wasn't a good sign. Something else I should've noticed.

"Do you want to tell her?" she asked him, her voice rising an octave.

What the hell happened while I was out?

"Alex, we talked about this. Can we not—"

"You do not get to call me that anymore," she said sharply. The quiet hatred was scarier than her hot-blooded anger. What had he done to make her behave like this?

"I'm sorry," he whispered. His gaze dropped to the table in front of him, as his ego deflated.

"What did you do?" I accused, and his gaze shot to mine.

His lips parted, like he wanted to say something. His black eyes traveled over every facet of my face, searching for something he would never find.

"Oh, this is rich!" Alexandra said darkly. Her wicked cackle reminded me too much of the darkness I'd seen in myself for my liking. "You know what? I'm not going to get involved." She smiled too sweetly for it to be real. "I'm going to see how this plays out for *you* when she finds out." I knew all too well that I was the unnamed 'she;' what I didn't know was what I had to do with this.

Alexandra left her tray as she stomped out of the lunchroom. I took a step toward her, wanting to help in some way.

"Don't," Tori said. She reached for my wrist and squeezed gently, rising with her and Alexandra's food in hand. "I don't know what's goin' on, but I feel like she ain't gonna want you to go after her. Let me try," she said softly.

"Let her go," Blair said. Had it been anyone else, I would've told them where to shove it.

I sighed, nodding for Tori to go instead of me.

"I told you to give her time," Blair said quietly.

"That would be easier if you told me what I was giving her time from. I haven't done anything," I snapped. I stared down Aaron, trying to will him to speak without saying it.

"You exist. It's not your fault, but he's not being the most forthcoming," Blair said sharply.

Aaron glared at her with a vengeance. "What happens

between me and her is none of *your* business, Blair," he growled.

"But it is mine," I cut in.

His gaze flipped between the two of us, like he couldn't decide whether to be angry or honest. Eventually, he settled for, "You're not ready."

Aaron got up and slammed the door behind him on the way out, not even bothering with his uneaten dinner. I had half a mind to go after him and demand to know what I wasn't ready for, but as the moments passed, I became increasingly aware that I was running out of people who knew what had happened and would talk. I bit the bullet and turned to Lucas. He watched me uneasily as I made my way to him with legs so stiff I thought I would fall over. There was no smile on his lips or in his eyes when he looked at me.

I swallowed the bile in my mouth and spoke. "We need to talk."

"Do we now?" he asked, eyebrows arching so high they disappeared under his shaggy hair. He cocked his head in a way that was oddly familiar, and almost mocking.

"Yes," I said through tight lips, walking to the door before he spoke again.

"Is that all we need to do?"

I could've throttled him right there, because I didn't understand where his sudden coy attitude was coming from. I refused to show how pissed I was and add fuel to his fire, though. Two could play this game.

"That's for me to know, and you to find out." I didn't wait for a snappy comeback, and ascended the stairs quickly. He would either follow or not, and it wouldn't take long to figure out. When the stairwell door closed two floors down, I picked up speed and left the building entirely, taking the long route around campus to the boxing gym. It was late enough in the evening that no one would be here. I opened the last door, and the smell of home enveloped me. Blood. Sweat. Tears.

And then Lucas was there, carrying the scent of the woods with him. "You said you wanted to talk?"

He was leaning against the ring I loved so dearly, looking like the prick he was becoming. Someone owed me answers, and I wasn't going to take no for an answer this time.

"Yes," I said hastily. I already wanted this to be over. I crossed the space, each heartbeat sounding louder than the last. "What happened in the bathroom?"

He looked away, running a hand through his unkempt hair. Actually...now that I really looked at him, he wasn't looking so great in general. Dark circles lined his eyes. The exhaustion was taking its toll. The glimmer I was used to seeing in those eyes was practically gone, replaced by something colder. Harder. It was no wonder my subconscious thought them all demons, especially him. The emerald was practically a forest green now, and the look he was giving me didn't help the uneasiness in my stomach.

"I don't want to go there," he muttered, uncharacteristically vague.

I grimaced. "I didn't ask if you wanted to go there, I need you to," I snapped.

His eyes glazed over, hardening to gemstones. "Need? Really, Selena? After everything that's happened, it's him you need?" he asked—demanded, really—growing louder by the second.

"You know that's not how I meant it," I said dryly. I wouldn't give into this petty jealousy. I didn't even really understand where it had come from to begin with.

"Of course, that's how you meant it, you just don't realize it." His eyes gloated with whatever he thought he knew, and it was beginning to get on my last nerve.

I moved to snap my fingers in front of his face, in the most derogatory and insulting of ways. Even though I knew his temper better than anyone, I always tested it. My fingers snapped once before he closed his fist around them and yanked me to his chest. My head hit it with a thunk. He'd caught me off guard, and it took him no time at all to grasp my hips and spin me around, seating me on the ring and wedging himself between my legs. I glared defiantly at him, folding my arms across my chest.

"Do not snap your fingers at me," he growled. He placed his arms on either side of me. This little act of dominance wasn't going to work on me. Not anymore. My intentions with him were clear, and I wasn't blurring that line again.

"Maybe you should answer my questions then," I said, not leaning back no matter how close he got. I wasn't going to cower, but I wasn't going to kiss him either.

"Tit for tat, Selena, you know how this goes," he murmured. His eyes would've been almost hypnotic, if not for how dark they were. He moved closer, his lips only a hair's breadth away from mine.

"We need to talk," I said, not a trace of coyness or passion in my voice.

"I'm not talking about *him*," he nearly sneered, and his lips crashed into mine.

The burning passion wasn't there, though, not for me. I simply froze, letting him kiss a cold, unmoving statue. Maybe then he'd get the hint.

His breath was hot as he kissed me, but it didn't take long for him to grow frustrated by my lack of—well, everything. He grabbed my shoulders and pushed me away, holding me at arm's length as he shook me for all of two seconds before I put a stop to it.

"Stop, Lucas. Goddamn it, what the hell is wrong with you? I came to talk, not for—whatever this is. So, either start talking or I'm leaving," I said, shrugging his hands off me.

"I'm not going there. But if you want to talk, let's talk. What happened to us?"

I didn't like this change of direction. It was too demanding. I leaned back on my arms to put distance between us. Not that it really helped with him wedged between my legs.

He scowled, but didn't try manhandling me again. "Ever since we got back, you've just kicked me out of your life again. You've been up and down, nearly killing yourself in the process." He ran a hand through his hair in frustration. "What happened, Selena? Where did I go wrong?"

I sighed, because this was the talk we should've had at his house. I should've told him that, no matter what happened after this, I would never be his. Not just because his kisses no longer made my head swim, or even because it was his poor decision that had put me here. I could try to get past those, but at the end of the day, I just wanted my best friend back.

"You didn't do anything, Lucas. This isn't your fault. It's mine."

And for the first time, I actually believed that. It *was* my fault—because this was what I truly wanted. He was the first real friend I'd ever had, and I didn't want to lose that because we'd both gotten caught up in the moment along the way.

"Then how do I fix this? What can I do to make it right?" I cringed at the desperation in his tone, written on his face. "What's wrong?" he asked, suddenly aware of the effect his words were having on me.

"Nothing." I pulled away, further back onto the ring until I was supporting my own weight.

Lucas moved his hands to my hips, trying in vain to regain control of the situation and swing the ball into his court. Part of me wished I could be different, that this could've...been something. That I could've loved him the way he deserved to be loved by someone. I accepted what had happened, though, and my part in it. I just needed him to see that while I might not be in love with him, I did want him. As my best friend.

"You're pulling away again. Why? What's going on with you, Selena?"

His pleading was the blow that broke the dam, and I finally told him the truth.

"I want to be friends, Lucas—and before you try to interrupt, let me tell you why," I said, cutting him off when he opened his mouth again. "When I went away for the summer,

I was confused by your feelings as much as my own. I missed you, but because I'd never had a friend before, particularly a guy friend, I was confused by what liking someone really feels like. I couldn't tell if it was just us being good friends, and enjoying your company—or if it was something more. When I saw you again, I really wasn't sure what I wanted—your sister had just been attacked and shit continued to hit the fan —but when I kissed you in the woods, I finally figured it out." I paused to catch a breath and try to read his expression.

His face was a mask, though, so I went on.

"I don't want to be your girlfriend, Lucas, and I don't want you to be my everything. I just want you to be my friend, and I'll do my best to be yours. I still need time to figure my life out, but I want you to know that I'm trying. I'm trying to fix this, and be a better friend." The words poured out of me in probably one of the most honest things I'd ever said, and he looked like I'd slapped him.

"It's because of him, isn't it?" he asked, his eyes never wavering as he stared at me.

"Lucas, I just told you—"

"I care for you, Selena, and I'm trying to keep you from getting mixed up with that...that...animal." He was frantic in his delusion of saving me. He gripped me tighter and it was like a noose tightening around my neck, because everyone wanted something from me, and no one was happy with what I had to give.

Anastasia wanted my service. My family wanted to save me. Lucas wanted my heart. Aaron wanted...something I couldn't even process at this moment as I realized the weight of the burden on my shoulders. At the end of it all, the world needed me to have my shit together. I needed me to have my shit together. Or else game over.

I'd told him I wanted to be friends. Hell, I'd stood here and poured my heart out. Tried to be honest. To be a good friend, and not just take all the time.

The noose tightened, but I refused to be a fucking possession.

I refused to feel guilty when he wasn't even thinking clearly.

And so I made a choice—he got one more shot, and then I would cut him free, because I didn't have time for this game anymore.

"I don't know what you're talking about, but you need to let me go. Right now. I don't want to play games. I don't want to hurt you, but I will if you make me." Seventeen going on eighteen, and I felt the weight of the world on my shoulders. I cared for him, but I didn't have anything left to give. "I care about you, because you're my friend. Don't throw that away on jealousy."

His face changed. His entire demeanor shifted. The hands on my waist hurt, and his eyes burned a hateful, nauseous green.

"Jealousy? That's what you are going to blame this on? Why don't you just tell the truth. That this is about *him*?" He sneered.

My mouth popped open, not sure how to take this sudden change in him. "I wouldn't know, because no one's told me a damn thing!" I shouted, my eyes pricking with tears I refused to shed. Not over this. I hadn't cried when I was tortured. I hadn't cried every time shit hit the fan growing up. Hell, dreamland seven-year-old me hadn't even cried. He didn't deserve my tears.

"Give it up, Selena. I may not be able to hear your thoughts anymore, but I can still hear his," he said darkly.

"Oh really? Because last I checked, his thoughts have nothing to do with my actions—which everyone seems to have forgotten—and even if they did, it's none of your damn business." My heart and head hammered out a dangerous melody.

"So, you admit something's going on with him?" he said haughtily.

I wanted to facepalm myself at the insanity behind his statement, and this entire conversation.

"For Christ's sake, Lucas, you're the mind reader. You tell me, since you seem to know more about my life than I do."

"You've changed. Ever since we got back here, you've been keeping secrets. Avoiding me. Fighting with him."

My mouth fell open, gaping at him in disbelief. Fighting with him? *Excuse me?*

"Well, I'm glad you've come to the same conclusion then, Lucas, because we've both changed," I spat, pushing him off me. "Ever since we've gotten back here, you've been nothing but a territorial prick. You've let jealousy of the fact that you cannot and will not be everything to me blind you." I swung my legs off the ring, prepared to pull no punches if it came to that. "For god's sake, I can hit him in the face, and you're the one fuming. At least he knows how to act. *He knows how to—*"

Crack.

The slap rang hard and clear, and I stared at him, dumb-founded. Had he actually just slapped me? The feeling was surreal. I didn't know what to think or how to feel about it. I'd barely even processed the sting coming from the left side of my face. We'd fought many times before, and a slap was nothing in comparison...except we weren't training right now. He'd hit me because he couldn't control his temper. Pulling my shoulders back, I cracked my knuckles in passive warning. I'd had enough of his manhandling for one day. I wasn't an object. He didn't own me. Apparently, he needed reminding, because this situation was so blown out of proportion at this point that there was no coming back.

"Get out," I said. I was two seconds from putting him down, quite literally, and this time it had nothing to do with the killing gene. I could forcibly remove him, and it wouldn't be pretty, but I was giving him one chance. The lights flickered, and he smiled cruelly, stepping away entirely.

"As you wish. Next time you need a fix, you can go to your half-breed signa—"

I punched him in the face.

He hit the floor with a thud, face-first, his body crum-pling. For once, I didn't give a damn. He could stay there, for all I cared. My pulse calmed very slowly.

What did he say? Something about Aaron being a half-breed?

"Maybe I should've let him finish before I knocked him out," I muttered to myself.

At least this makes us even, I thought gloomily.

Blair had warned me. Amber had warned me. I'd seen what I'd wanted to see, though, because I'd been desperate not to be lonely anymore, to have one friend. I'd wanted to escape myself and be someone else, and somehow, he'd fallen in love with that person, and it had consumed him.

I didn't know what had happened, or how we'd gotten here, but I was stronger now. I might not have known who I was yet, but I knew who I wasn't. If he'd thought I was heartless before...he was in for a very rude awakening.

CHAPTER 22

"Who crapped in your coco puffs?" Amber said crudely.

I rolled my eyes and took another bite of toast. Two days had passed since I'd done a number on Lucas, while I stewed and decided how I was going to handle this situation.

The month was halfway over, and we were growing more divided by the day.

"Don't start with me," I said around a mouthful of cereal.

She raised her eyebrows, swirling her coffee in its mug. "Touchy today, I see."

"Then keep your mouth shut and mind your own business," I said.

Amusement flitted across her features until there was a thunk under the table.

"Hey, what's your—" she said to Blair, whose gaze flicked between Lucas and me.

Realization dawned on Amber as her mouth snapped shut. She stared at her coffee like it was the most fascinating thing, never mind the insane bruising on Lucas's face or that one of his eyes was swollen shut.

Unable to stand the tension any longer, I left my half-eaten cereal and exited the room. I took the stairs two at a time on my way up to the simulator. Vonlowsky was lounging against his desk, staring into the psych-ward lookalike room.

"Am I interrupting something?"

He bristled at my comment, but let his scowl speak for itself. "And here I thought you were taking this more seriously after—"

"I am. Don't get your knickers in a twist—or whatever you call them," I said quickly before he got pissed again. The last thing I needed was one of his 'motivational speeches.'

"You are doing better. You've seemed less *distracted* this week. That mindset will serve you well in the field," he said. This was high praise coming from the man who referred to my telekinetic abilities like they were some parlor trick.

"Speaking of the field, when's the next elimination?" I asked. Unlike Blair, I didn't try to schmooze my way into getting information, and I wasn't waiting around for Johanna to tell me the day before again. Not if I could help it. Brute force always appealed the most; I didn't have the patience to beat around the bush.

"Now that my simulator is fixed, soon," he said ambiguously. His eyes cut across the room, narrowing on me with suspicion. They may have covered for me, but Vonlowsky wasn't a fool. Ceilings don't just collapse, because bathrooms don't just blow up. Yet between me and Alexandra, that was exactly what had happened.

I rolled my eyes. There wasn't much else to say. Vonlowsky wasn't much of a talker, and I preferred the silence. I had enough drama going on in my life right now without picking a fight with him.

A dark shadow crossed in front of me, and my mood plummeted again with the reminder of Lucas.

"All right, you know the drill. Everyone in the simulator," Vonlowsky said as people came through the hidden staircase.

Feet shuffled as they groggily entered the simulator, but the tension was thick.

Alexandra was hurt by something beyond my understanding. Blair wouldn't tell me what. Lucas was being a douche. Everything came back to one person—Aaron, and whatever he'd done that had made everyone hate me.

I stalked toward him, ignoring everyone else as I crossed the room. When I was only a few feet away, he looked up from the small girl in front of him. Her opaque, cloud-like eyes widened as she regarded us.

"Camilla, you'll need to spar with someone else today," he said.

She nodded, and her dark brown cornrows swung side-to-side as she ran to Johanna. The other girl, my honorary second, met my eyes and nodded once, pairing the younger girl with the Graeme twins instead.

"I'm surprised you find her a challenge," I said.

His eyes followed mine, watching the young Supernatural weave back and forth between them with expert skill. She was always a step ahead. "Someone once taught me not to judge a book by its cover." A smirk touched his lips.

I rolled my eyes and unzipped my jacket. "Hmm, let's see if you learned your lesson."

The banter flowed too easily. *You don't know him. You don't even like him.*

Stop that, I berated myself. *You have a job to do.*

"Oh please," he purred. "Like you could teach me anything." His eyes flashed gold as he took a step forward.

An almost animalist urge to growl at him went through me. I tossed my jacket to the floor and lunged.

He was quick—sidestepping just enough that I only caught his shoulder. There was a crunch, but he'd moved all the same. I didn't waste my time waiting for him to heal. He could take it. He'd said so himself.

I planted a roundhouse kick right into his rock-hard side. The snap should've been sickening. And I probably should've stopped when he started laughing and blood came up.

"What's so funny?" I demanded.

He wiped the blood away with the back of his hand, looking unperturbed as usual. "The lengths you go to to deny yourself."

What does that even mean? You know what? It doesn't matter.

His cocky grin was maddening, and I wanted nothing more than to wipe it from his face. I brought my hand up, prepared to slap him into his next life, but stopped in midair when he grabbed my hand. He held us there in a stalemate, his rough callouses brushing against my sensitive skin to the point of pain and pleasure. I yelped.

Stepping back, I suddenly found myself pinned to a wall with nowhere to go. His black eyes stared down, intense, hot, and heavy. It was as if the blinders were ripped from my eyes, and I saw the sun. They were right.

The look he was giving me wasn't just the thrill of the fight. It was the challenge of one creature claiming dominance over another. It was a mating call. This was why Alexandra wouldn't speak to me. The reason Blair wouldn't talk. Why Lucas was so jealous. Aaron had it for me; Amber hadn't been lying. The only problem, the thing all of them failed to see, was that I didn't return the sentiment.

I brought my knee up between us, forcing him to move back or lose his manhood forever. Using both hands, I shoved forward, only to find the other wrist ensnared. He had me, but this wasn't over.

The look he gave me was his undoing, as I mentally tore him from me and blasted the bastard through the only double-paned glass window in the room.

"Again?" Vonlowsky frowned from the other side, motioning to the broken window. I rolled my eyes. "The least you can do is fix it," he muttered.

I reached out with my other sense, feeling where the glass had fallen and how each piece fit together. Bringing my hands up, I traced the cracks with my eyes as I melded them shut. This was the part I enjoyed about being telekinetic. I saw a puzzle in every creation. Just as easily as I could destroy, I knew how to put it back together in a way others never would. The very essence of matter called to me. I was the master puppeteer of *everything*.

A guttural, almost wild growl alerted me. I turned from the glass to see Aaron stalking toward me. Rage mixed with something else in a deadly and heady combination. He was hunting me, but not in the way I'd imagined. I stilled, curious to see what he would do.

"Did you really think that would work on me?" His voice was deeper. Darker. Something in it told me I'd been warned. Something in it made me see his face. His eyes. Gold rimmed in black, more animalistic than demon for once.

"I certainly hoped it would." Cracking my neck, I walked right up to him.

He was pumped and pissed off. It made him sloppy as he tried to take me down.

Block left.

Block right.

Duck.

Jump.

We fell into the neverending dance of the sun and moon, always fighting for power.

Always fighting for dominance.

He landed a punch to my stomach, and I hunched forward into him. I took short, quick breaths—and instantly regretted that decision. Something about him smelled wild. Untamed, even. It was like a wildfire in the dead of winter, crisp. There was no mistaking it. Underneath it, I smelled something else too. Something I'd never noticed before. Something I couldn't name. It was almost *warm...*

"Ugh," I groaned, finding myself backed into a wall yet again. He trapped my wrists above my head, effectively holding me in place for the second time. Leaning in, he brushed his lips against the soft spot just underneath my ear.

"Pinned," he whispered.

"As long as we're here, you plan on telling me what the hell happened in that bathroom?" I shot back. His touch was far too gentle for my liking.

"You're not ready."

"Mr. White, I don't know what you're doing, but you have a bed downstairs for that. Get back to work!" Vonlowsky shouted.

The sudden intimacy of the moment hit me. Taking no time to rethink the decision, I waited for him to loosen his grip just enough...before I kicked his ass ten feet through the air.

My boot made a dull *thunk* against his chest as the bastard went sailing. I watched him land on his ass with my hands on my hips.

"Apparently you didn't get that message loud and clear the first time," I said, leaving his punk ass lying there groaning and wheezing.

"And you," I said to Vonlowsky from the other side of the window. "Keep your comments to yourself next time, *please.*"

He rolled his eyes, looking at the rest of the group. His piss-poor attitude toward me was waning the closer we got to the month ending. I could only guess he'd decided I had my act together.

"What are you looking at? What are any of you looking at? Get back to work," he said, clapping his hands together as if that would make them move faster.

I looked back at Aaron, who was dusting himself off. It was now or never. He couldn't run from me here. I walked over, standing directly in front of him. There was a glint of gold in his eyes that was coming out more every day.

"Why did Lucas call you a half-breed?" I asked.

That got his attention, as well as everyone else's in the room.

Aaron went completely still, no longer acting like this was a game. Behind him, Johanna's eyes glowed gold as she narrowed them at a slowly backing away Lucas.

"He said what?" Aaron asked, very, very quietly. It wasn't hurt that softened his voice, but fury. Why, though?

"He told me you're a half-breed. What does that mean, and why is it important?" I asked again.

"Is that all he told you?" Aaron asked. His eyes were entirely gold. The ring of black around them was so thin that, for the first time, it changed his looks completely. Before, he'd been handsome, in a pretty way, but still rugged and unrefined. When his eyes turned, it sent a shiver down my spine—the way he looked at me. Dangerous. His body rippling with a power I'd never seen in him before. Is that what Lucas had meant? Something told me telling Aaron that wasn't a good idea.

"He called you something else. My sig—" I didn't even get to finish the half-word I'd heard when Aaron roared. An all-out, animalistic, monstrous sound. His form blurred, almost like he was shaking too fast for me to see...but that couldn't be right.

"Aaron!" Amber yelled, charging him with everything she had. Her body slammed into his, but he didn't budge an inch. His eyes were wholly focused on Lucas, who was backing away faster now.

"What's going on?" I asked, but for once, no one was

paying attention to me. Really? Right now? Of all the times to ignore me...

"You need to step back, Selena," Alexandra said. For someone perfectly happy giving me the silent treatment when I'd gone to her for information first, she seemed pretty concerned about what was going down.

"No! Not until someone tells me—"

"What is going on in there?" Vonlowsky yelled over the intercom, but still no one cared.

"I'm going to kill him." Aaron growled low, his voice not entirely his.

"The boy crossed a line. One too many, it appears," Johanna said.

I wanted to pull my hair out. While that may have been an answer, it wasn't really.

"You gotta calm down, Aaron. It ain't worth it. You can't afford to provoke the Council's wrath—" Amber started.

"*What the hell?*" I yelled. That got their attention. My rage was growing more volatile by the minute, as my own monsters stirred beneath the surface. The room rattled.

"Selena. I don't have it in me to do it again. You need to calm down," Alexandra said. Very slowly, she started walking toward me, taking deliberate steps. As much as I wanted to cycle down, though, whatever was happening in me only grew.

"Aaron, you gotta chill, bud. You're getting her worked up. We can deal with the boy later, but right now, you need to help her," Amber spoke quickly and quietly, but it only angered me more.

Energy was pouring out of every orifice of my body. Covering me. Bathing me. Consuming me.

"By the dragon..." Johanna murmured, watching me like she couldn't believe her eyes.

"She's going to blow. Time for plan B," Blair said, coming up on the other side of Alexandra.

Plan B? Let my sister drain me, and hope for the best.

Not today.

I flicked my wrist, and they flew. There was a monster inside me, and they'd just woken it.

Tori disappeared from the back corner in an instant as my sister and cousin came crashing down. I clenched my hand into a fist, and every knife in my belt came alive and pointed at one thing.

Amber gasped, trying to cry out a warning, but it was too late. Something deep down inside me snapped.

I was tired of the secrets.

Tired of never having answers, and some primal part of me lost all sense of reason. The daggers went flying through the air. Aimed right for Aaron's heart.

CHAPTER 23

Aaron turned to face me, wide-eyed and determined, in less than half a second. The daggers sailed straight for him, but he plucked them out of the air like they were paper planes instead of deadly weapons.

He'd once told me his gift was enhanced senses, and so far, that was the only thing he'd done to make me believe that.

His eyes glowed with the most brilliant of golds, and again I wondered why. I cocked my head to the side, watching him through narrowed slits. Any and every sound around me came out warped, and raw. Instead of hearing words, I heard screeching and panting, but one thing stood out among it all. His breathing.

Slow and steady, it calmed me, and I didn't know why. The door in my mind was shaking violently, letting streams of golden light slip through the cracks. I wasn't quite sure what was going on, but something made me reach out. Just to touch it. The handle wiggled in my grip, warm under my palm. It wanted me to open it.

Until time sped up. A hand latched around my arm, ripping me from the surreal moment.

"No!" I didn't know who said it, but fire sprang to life in a wall around me as I turned to face my attacker... Lily.

Her eyes darkened to black as the wisps flowed from me to her. For a moment, I felt better. The world seemed lighter. Easier. Until she started screaming.

The wall of fire around us vanished just as Lily collapsed to her knees, and I remained standing. Unscathed.

"Stop! Stop! The lies. The secrets. His eyes are so dark," Lily shrieked, ranted. Those weren't her thoughts, though. They were mine.

"The world of the dead is coming. *They* are coming," she continued.

I didn't know how to stop her. I didn't know how to comfort or console, when the fears she saw were my own. No one dared to touch her or help her, and the more she took, the stronger I became. I pried her fingers from my wrist, hoping that breaking the contact would be enough.

"That's not supposed to happen," Alexandra said uneasily.

I whirled on her, the shadows swirling under my skin once more. Unlike the other people Lily had taken from, I wasn't weak. On the contrary, my power was nearly limitless, and this might kill her yet.

"I told you not to mess with things you don't understand. I told you not to do this!" I yelled. If it wasn't one form of madness, it was another. I could never escape it... Maybe it was time to give in.

"The demons are here. They live among us. They wear the mask of a friend, but you never know where evil lurks."

I snapped back around to my sister. Her eyes were no longer black. No, something much darker was in possession of her now, and it was sending me a message. Violet eyes stared up at me as her hair ran black.

"I'm watching, Selena. Our time is coming."

Lily fainted as the darkness seeped out of her skin and crawled back to me. Strong arms yanked me away, but it was no use. Like my hair or my skin, the power belonged to me and me alone. It rose from the ground, weaving around me but not hurting as it sank back under the surface.

With my sister unconscious, a familiar pair of arms wrapped around me, and more bewildered stares than I could count, my only thought as I blacked out for the second time in a week was that this wasn't how I'd planned on spending my junior year at Daizlei Academy.

"LONG TIME NO SEE." She cackled. Her glowing eyes made me uneasy, as always.

"That was quite the show you put on. Was it for my benefit or theirs?" I asked, being cheekier than I should've been with her.

She's a figment of your mind, Selena. You don't give nightmares credibility. You don't name them. You don't talk to them.

The forest was lighter tonight, not quite so dark or heavy. I should've known better than to let myself fall into a false sense of security.

"You liked that, did you?" She purred, her pointed teeth all the more menacing when I could actually see them.

The wind howled as it barreled down the rows of trees. The dirt was cold and compact, my bare feet hardly making a dent as I walked. She would follow; she always did.

"It's time to wake up," I muttered to myself again and again. It was my prayer, but no god answered. Where the hell was Nyx when you actually wanted her? There was a reason my father only ever used that name as a curse.

"You think I can't reach you when you're awake?" she asked mockingly, as she trailed along next to me. She was too polished for the forest, more polished than I'd ever seen her. In the last year, she'd gone from looking homeless to swaggering it up in my dreams with her corsets and leather jeggings. Something in the change both worried and confused me.

"I know you can't," I insisted, pushing onward.

"And yet I just did, and through your sister, no less. Her soul was too light to hold me, though. It didn't feel right. We couldn't connect. You and I...we're perfection. You're the first one who's ever been able to handle me, you know. You're the strongest. The only one worthy," she rambled.

For once, it didn't sound crazy, though. She was changing, evolving, and with it her language, her dress, even her mannerisms.

"You're just a nightmare. Part of my imagination. You don't have thoughts. You don't get a history. You may be a part of me, but I'm not a part of you."

Her wicked laugh rang through the night, as her cold fingers locked around my wrist, bringing me to a halt. Her pointed nails ran along the veins there—a silent warning of what would happen if I pulled away.

"Don't touch me," I spat, but the words didn't have the bite I was looking for, and she knew it.

Her eyes were sphinxlike spheres of glowing amethyst, set in black veined sockets. "I have no intention of hurting you. I am you, and it's only a matter of time until you see it."

Her words sent a shiver down my spine.

She dropped my wrist and backed away, her Cheshire cat smile haunting me long after she was gone.

The sudden jarring foghorn in my dream awoke me, and this time I remembered everything.

"I think it's time we all had a chat," a voice next to me said.

My eyes flashed open, and I tilted my head to the side to see who'd spoken, even though I already knew. Aaron was seated on a too-small plastic chair, next to the bunk I was lying in. Which wasn't my bunk, but Blair's. On the other side of him, my friends were all crammed together on his bed, for who knew what reason. Alexandra stifled a gasp when I opened my eyes, and I had a feeling I knew why, but didn't want a mirror to confirm my suspicion. I tried to sit up, but a gentle hand held me back.

"How are you feeling?" Aaron asked, with a surprising kindness in his voice, not the animalistic roars and growls I was getting used to hearing.

"Like I was knocked out of my body and dragged back. One of you assholes hit me like a freight train." My head pulsed, searing like it was being cleaved in two.

"Apologies. That was me," Johanna said. She came into

view from around the corner of the bed, and I glared up at her.

"What did you do?" I asked, forcing myself into a sitting position despite Aaron still trying to force me down.

Johanna smiled tightly, her eyes glowing gold briefly before it disappeared.

"And what's with the creepy glowing eyes? Why does everyone have gold eyes?" I asked, my questions bubbling to the surface, and with them my anger.

"Well, you're one to talk," she said, motioning to my own eyes.

Yep. As I'd suspected, they were still violet. It was fading less and less every day. Pretty soon, they were going to stay this way permanently, unless I figured out a way to stop it. Still, I gave her a glare and the middle finger. Kindness was never my strong suit.

Blair sighed deeply from her spot next to my sister, while Amber and Tori let out a laugh. Aaron...Aaron just watched me with his ever-intense and always-perplexed gaze.

"You weren't raised in this world, were you?" Johanna asked, more curious now. She was either ignoring me flipping her off or didn't understand that it was an insult. I suspected it was the former and she had the patience of a saint.

"No. She wasn't," Aaron said.

I turned my gaze back to him, narrowing my eyes at his audacity in answering for me.

"Do not be angry with your signasti. He means well," the girl said.

Signasti?

"Why do you call him my bound?" I said, stunning both her and Aaron into temporary silence.

"You know Latin?" Johanna asked, her eyebrows pulling together more and more the longer we talked.

"My father ensured I had the best possible education until he died. I speak Russian and Latin. I'm skilled in four different forms of combat, and can wield almost any weapon like a master. I've died and come back. I've fought demons and Vampires alike, and right now I'm getting more irritated by the second as you keep asking questions without answering mine." The bite in my tone didn't faze her in the slightest.

In fact, she laughed, as did several others I didn't really know or recognize. All part of the nine.

"Also, who are the rest of you people? We all sleep in the same goddamn room stacked on top of each other like dominoes, and I still don't know who you are."

"You are not what I expected, Selena Foster, but I think we'll hold off on introductions for now. I will answer your questions as best I can. Firstly, what you called 'knocking you out of your body' is actually quite accurate. You needed to be shut down temporarily, and so I sent you into the spirit realm to try to help your mind heal. The body doesn't always know how or when to do it for itself, so I...expedited the process. You seem more or less yourself, although the purple is still there." She frowned like something had just occurred to her.

I wanted to ask her what but stopped myself—at least someone was telling me what the hell was going on here.

"As for our creepy eyes. It's because we are what pure-blooded Supes consider half-breeds. My family, and those of your friends, were blended. Think of it as someone having a dark parent and a light one. Wouldn't the child be mixed?"

I nodded stiffly. I wasn't that dense. "I'm not an idiot. What are you mixed with? How is that even possible from a biological perspective?" I asked, for once feeling like the smart one in the room.

Johanna grinned just a little.

I'm happy you find this so amusing. I rolled my eyes.

"Certain species are more compatible than others. The theory is that far enough back, we were all one species, which over the millennia became many. My father was both part-Supernatural and part-Witch, which is one of the most common. I believe your signasti is part-Shapeshifter."

There was that term again. My signasti. My bound. I didn't even want to try to interpret that, or why they kept saying it. My lips pursed, and Johanna fell silent, probably sensing the reason.

"And no matter the combination, your eyes are always gold?" I asked.

Johanna nodded

"What are you, Amber?" I asked.

Several heads turned to her, and she blushed just a little but recovered fast enough. "My mom was a Shapeshifter and my dad's a Supernatural." I could tell she wanted to say more, but Aaron gave her a look, and she stopped short.

"And you?" I asked pointedly, drawing my legs into a cross-legged position. The sheet pooled around me. My tiny tank top was pulled down just enough to give the room an eyeful. I adjusted myself quickly and discreetly, but Aaron's gaze hadn't left me since the moment I woke up—and that was a bit unnerving.

"My father is a Shapeshifter," he said stiffly. I assumed that meant his mom was normal, but I guess you couldn't make assumptions.

Alec caught my gaze. His eyes were also gold, but that didn't make sense. Lucas's were green. Tori's were green.

"And you?" I asked him.

Tori shifted uncomfortably, and when he looked at her, she gave him a shrug.

"I know what you're thinking. I was born before my parents met, though. My birth father was a Shapeshifter, and he left my mother when I was very young. Tori and Lucas are my half-siblings." He seemed uncomfortable enough that I let it drop, but one answer led to another question.

"Where is Lucas?" I asked.

A very slight rumbling came from Aaron, but I could tell he was trying to keep himself under control.

"I don't know what your deal is, but I'm getting sick—" I started to snap again.

"The boy is lucky he's not dead. While you may not know any better, that little wanker did," Johanna said, attempting to be my voice of reason.

"Where is he?" I asked, putting more of an edge behind my tone.

"Not here," she mimicked.

I wanted to facepalm myself. *Clearly, he isn't here, Captain Obvious.* "Not here as in he's being beaten and tortured in another room, or not here as in he went to the gym?" I knew I was being dramatic, but I needed to ask, and everyone here seemed hesitant to bring him up because of the arrogant boy sitting next to me.

Johanna's lips twitched in what I thought was a smile. "He went off on his own for a while, as far as I'm aware," she added, her eyes glowing again before she nodded.

A small moan came from another bed—a voice more familiar than even my own.

"Lily," I breathed. I tore through the room and was at her side before most of them could even blink. Her body looked so tiny, curled up in a ball on Alexandra's bed. I crouched on my knees before her, and pulled the blanket back far enough that I could see her face.

"What the—" I dropped the blanket, backing away.

Her hair was as black as mine, not a strand of blond in sight. I'd dreamed of my other, which meant I'd been out for a while, but for how long?

"She's still healing, but it may never be the same again. Whatever she was trying to do to you rebounded, and she was hurt. I was concerned it would do the same when it returned, but whatever rejected her seems to cling to you." She sounded surprised, disturbed, even, by the thought.

I wasn't, though. I knew what it was. My darkness. My particular brand of evil. Like the shadows, my power clung to me—and if my other was to be believed, she did too. I reached forward to brush Lily's hair from her face.

"I would rather you not," Johanna said, catching my hand before our skin made contact.

I faced her, my mood darkening instantly.

She held up her hands in surrender. "It's not you I'm worried about. Just like you lash out in your sleep, she is too. Touching her could accidentally hurt her if she starts trying to pull from you."

I stared at her, silently weighing my options. "How much time has passed?" I murmured.

"Two days."

"Has she woken up?" I asked, but I already knew the answer.

"No."

At least she didn't sugarcoat it. There was no point asking if she would wake up. The brain was a fickle thing; maybe it would just take more time for her to get better. I had to believe that. She wasn't dead, and that was something. I just hoped she was the same Lily when she woke up, and not some sort of hybrid demon changed by whatever the other me had done to her.

"She needed more time. You have a signasti's strength to aid you, and she does not."

There was that word again. The only question she'd so very carefully danced around, but I wasn't having it. If Lily would be okay, it was time to get some more answers.

"Why do you keep referring to him like this? What does that even mean?" I asked then instantly wished I hadn't.

"Signasti animam is a soul-bonded person. Think of it like—"

"I think that's enough, Johanna," Alec said quickly.

I was already backing away. Toward the wall. Toward the darkness.

She watched me coolly, never changing her stance, never advancing. I wish Aaron had done the same.

I could handle sickness and crazy.

I could handle demons and Vampires.

I could handle all this half-breed nonsense, and the hippie vibes she gave me from time to time.

I, however, could not and would not buy into this *soul shackled* nonsense. I'd studied Latin. Signasti roughly translated to bound. Pretty vague.

Signasti animam, on the other hand, that translated to soul shackled—quite literally. And I most definitely was *not* okay with being shackled to my sister's ex-boyfriend. More chains were the last thing I needed, even as the noose tightened ever so slightly.

Aaron stood from his rickety chair, looking at me like I was everything, when all I wanted was to be nothing. Soul shackled? Not happening. It only took one look from him, and I bolted straight for the door.

CHAPTER 24

I WAS FASTER, BUT NOT BY MUCH.

While I got past Johanna and the Graemes, clearing the door proved troublesome when Amber intercepted me. I still didn't understand her role in all of this, but right now I didn't care.

"Get out of my way," I demanded.

"You're a danger to yourself and others. Not happening." Since when did she give a damn about other people?

"What I am is overwhelmed. You have two choices. Either move, or I will make you." Part of me knew this was crossing a line, that somewhere deep down I should've been more concerned by what she'd said, but I didn't want any of it.

"It's not your fault, Selena. I get it, okay? You're angry. You're confused. You don't really know what's going on, and half of us are still trying to figure out why we're all here. I get it. Your sister's in that bed because of you, though. They told you what would happen if you couldn't control it, but you still couldn't. Now, you need—"

I stopped listening after that. Not because I snapped. Not because I punched her. I didn't even run. I stopped because I knew what I needed. It was like something was pulling me as I retreated inward. Turning right around, I walked back to my bed. Hooking my hand over the post had become second nature now, as had avoiding Aaron when I swung my foot up and rolled onto the bed.

I was a danger to everyone I knew. Myself included.

I was broken.

But if I knew one thing about about being broken, it was that restarting usually fixed the problem. So, I was going to restart myself the only way I knew how.

Amber couldn't have hit it more on the nose if she'd tried. Lucas was hurting because of me. Lily was tainted because of me. Alexandra was single, and Aaron soul-shackled—whatever that meant.

I didn't have it in me to keep listening anymore, but I also didn't need to fight them. One of the first things I'd learned about having control was that while you couldn't always get rid of the situation, you could always remove yourself from it.

"What's she doing?" Amber asked.

I rolled onto my side, facing the wall. With my back to them, I could almost pretend I was alone.

"She's checking out," Alexandra said softly.

As bad as her anger had been, the pity was worse. I didn't want her pity. She'd known about all this crap and left me in the dark. Blair too.

"What does that mean?" Tori asked, her country twang nearly as sharp as Amber's condescension.

"She's here, but nobody's home," Alexandra said, and her sadness fueled me more.

My blood rushed, adrenaline spiking in my system to urge me to fight. I wasn't going to, though, not this time.

Here's the thing about being crazy. There was enough going on in my head that I could step out of reality almost at will. I hadn't done it in years, but it was nearly as useful a skill as the walls I could resurrect and crumble with mere thoughts. This wasn't something my father had taught me, though; this was all on dear old mom.

Limbo was a lot like being awake on the verge of sleep, or the other way around. I could hear them, but the words were distorted. Reality twisted as I retreated deeper and deeper into the recesses of my mind. I needed space. Time to think about what was happening. If they wouldn't give it to me, I would make it.

I would start over.

This was the ultimate panic attack, and the deepest meditation. Caught somewhere between a state of adrenaline and calm, the balance struck. I'd found it.

Peace. Control.

Weren't they the same?

"She's a bloody coward," someone cursed.

Is it the same day? Is it only moments later?

I didn't know. Nor did I care.

"She wasn't ready," Aaron murmured.

He didn't sound far away. Somehow, even here, his noose knotted around my neck. His voice was thicker than usual. Deeper. Darker. I needed to go further. Somewhere I could think. Somewhere I could be alone.

"She doesn't have a choice. None of us were ready, but

you don't see us sleeping all day. We've covered for her long enough. She needs to grow a pair."

I didn't know who it was, but the voice sounded familiar enough that I knew I'd heard it before.

"She'll come back eventually. She always does," my sister said. I could almost feel her heat, deep in my chilled bones.

I pressed further, until the only voice I could hear was my own. Inside my mind, the vast darkness expanded before me in a neverending vacuum outside of time or space. Was this why people abused drugs, or drank themselves into oblivion? Sometimes, you just needed to drown out the voices.

"Is this peace?" I asked, my voice echoing in my own ears.

"Not quite," a voice answered. I should've known she would be here. That I could never run far enough.

"What do you want? Is ruining my life not enough for you?" I yelled. My hands clenched into fists of their own accord. I was as angry as ever. Resentful as always.

My other made a *tsk* sound, her cherry red heels clicking despite the lack of a floor.

"I didn't ruin your life. You're being dramatic, always cursing at people because 'nobody understands you.' Gag." She pretend-shuddered.

Only fueling my hatred more. Deep down, I knew I should walk away. I should go back, and talk to my family, my friends. I shouldn't be making deals with the devil, but maybe that was what I'd come here for. Maybe this was how I would find peace.

"Says me to me. Okay. I have officially lost it," I deadpanned.

My other smirked, sucking a tooth obnoxiously. "This is why I like you," she said.

I blinked, raising an eyebrow. "Huh?"

"As much as you pity yourself, deep down, you and I are the same." Her eyes traveled over me lazily. Too familiar for comfort, but foreign enough to give me the creeps.

"It's hard to be the same when you're not real," I said. *Why am I wasting my time with this?*

"Not *that* again. Haven't we been over this?" She rolled her eyes, tapping her heel impatiently.

"You only recently learned to talk. I think you're over-selling yourself," I scoffed.

"I think you're underestimating how strong we really are. If you spent half the time you waste moping actually learning self-control and searching for real answers, you wouldn't have to dream about freedom. We would already have it," she said.

"What's the point in freedom when I can't even have peace? I'm angry all the time. I can't keep my temper. Any semblance of control I had is long gone..." I trailed off. Coming here was supposed to help me. It was supposed to make clear whatever I'd been missing. When I was younger and the voices got too bad, they never followed me here. When I'd been whipped bloody by my own sister, the pain had never followed me here. So why was she here?

"To help you. Isn't that what you wanted? An answer to your questions. A voice to guide you." She paused, motioning to herself like she was the lady of the hour. "Peace and freedom aren't all that different at the end of the day. What if I told you I could get you there? What if I said I could free you?"

Those were dangerous words to a drowning girl trying to find the surface. Which meant they were too good to be true.

"You're a damn liar," I said, walking back the way I'd come.

She didn't follow, but then again, maybe she didn't need to. She always seemed to be there, in the back of my mind.

"We're one and the same. You want to soothe the pain? You want peace? Then stop acting like a fool. You're the strongest one here, and yet you cower before your own gifts and try to shove them under the rug for the sake of others. If you want peace, you have to take it. Nothing is free in this world. Your gifts come with a cost, and it's time *you stopped denying yourself.*"

Those words hit a nerve. Like something deep inside me resonated with them. Where had I heard them before? A door illuminated, standing out from the blackness. Golden light peeked through the crack as it rattled violently in its frame.

I reached out to brush my fingers over the handle, feeling it come alive beneath me. The metal warmed to my touch, almost intimately, as odd as that sounded. I pulled away, not wanting to know what I would find behind it. Not wanting to face that truth quite yet.

My other had given me enough to think about without going there.

"What happened to Lily?" I asked. Time here ran differently than the real world. These minutes could feel like hours, but days could be only minutes. I never really knew how much time I'd spent in this state of in-between until I returned, but I couldn't go back without knowing this.

"She burned herself out trying to take in your energy with nowhere to send it. The little glutton doesn't know moderation, and if she's not careful, next time will end poorly." Her eyes glowed. Pure undiluted violet. Even when mine took on the hue, the color was never quite so striking. It was just as terrifying as it was beautiful.

"So you did cause it?" I demanded, but the anger wasn't there. Not anymore.

"No. You caused it. I merely took advantage of it. Her soul wasn't strong enough, though, and it's that weakness that'll get you both killed if you keep playing with gifts you don't understand." She spoke in riddles, and while I wanted to make a comment about her being crazy...she was saner than I'd given her credit for. Or I really was this far gone. Neither thought sat well with me.

"You seem to know a lot about things you shouldn't. How is it possible you know this, but I don't? Aren't we one and the same? You said so yourself," I pointed out. Something was drawing me back, like a thread that wouldn't break.

"I did, didn't I?" she mused, avoiding my question entirely.

"You're going to keep terrorizing me when I wake up, aren't you?" The thought made my skin crawl, because I was tired of fighting her. I was tired of fighting myself over the right to my mind. The one thing I was coming to realize, though, was that the more I fought, the stronger she became.

"Have you ever stopped to think that if you didn't fight it, maybe it wouldn't hurt so much? Your instincts know what you need, even if your sentimental heart doesn't."

I didn't ask any more questions. I didn't need to. Deep down, some part of me needed to hear it, and know that my pain was in my control. My anger was in my control. And maybe, even peace was in my control. She wasn't real, and I had no reason to believe her. I had no reason to trust a demon that wore my face, but I did. I'd come in here looking for answers and a way out, but the answer had been there all along.

There was no point hating myself for existing. There wasn't strength in bottling it up, just to explode on people because I couldn't control it. I wanted to protect my friends from myself. I wanted to hate them for making me care. Ultimately, I didn't really know what I wanted.

Was I Selena the protector? Or was I terror?

Maybe if I stopped holding back, I would find out. Maybe if I stopped hiding, I wouldn't have so many secrets. Maybe if I stopped caring so much about what other people did, I could control my own actions.

My eyes snapped open, but this time the gray concrete walls were a welcome sight. For once, everyone was gone. I pulled my phone from my back pocket to check the time, but the screen stayed black. An empty battery icon flashed red, and I pursed my lips.

Time to go find them. Time to fix this.

I hopped out of bed with a lightness I hadn't felt in a while. My tank top was as disheveled as before, and I had no idea how much time had passed, but I was about to find out. I looked at Lily, still curled up in bed.

I will find a way to fix this. I'll come back.

The hinge of the bunker door squeaked as I slipped through it and into the stairwell. There was no way it was nighttime, not with everyone gone.

A floor above me, I could already make out the grunts of someone falling on their ass in the simulator. Next thing I knew, an explosion sounded. *What?*

I took the stairs two at a time, throwing the door open hard enough that it stuck in the wall beside me. *Oops.*

"Well, well. Long time no see. Your friends here were just telling me how unwell you are, but I'm so happy you could make it for the next elimination."

Another shout came from inside the simulator, but all I could focus on was Anastasia Fortescue, smug and smiling as bombs went off left and right while my friends screamed. They were so royally screwed, but, judging by her grin, I was too.

CHAPTER 25

Not one person looked my way as I stood next to the master who held my leash. On one side of the double-paned glass, Anastasia and I watched silently. Vonlowsky monitored from a few feet away, stoic as ever. Silent because he knew this was wrong.

Now isn't the time to overreact, I reminded myself.

I could help them, but I needed to be smart about it. Throwing a temper tantrum like a three-year-old would get me nowhere with the Council Member.

"Look at them, running around like ants waiting for a boot."

I didn't respond and carefully kept my face blank. Maybe it was the shadows, but my doppelgänger looked like she was enjoying this a little too much.

So much for her spiel about not wanting to start a war.

Maybe she just liked putting powerful people under her thumb to see how they fared. To make sure she always came out on top as Head of the Council.

A bloodcurdling scream pierced my ears when a bomb

went off that Blair hadn't been able to diffuse, and Alec jumped in front of her. Shrapnel bounced off the glass, and the bloody shreds of his jeans told me it wasn't good.

"I thought you were supposed to be training them, Vonlowsky," she said sharply.

My teacher swallowed hard, choosing his next words wisely. For someone who had no problem telling me where it was at, his attitude was a bit more pliant when it came to the Supernatural would-be queen. "I have been, my lady, but there have been complications…"

I narrowed my eyes at his damned cowardice. Complications? He meant me. That bastard was going to throw me under the bus.

"Complications? The prison break they orchestrated was more thought out than this," she sneered.

I tucked that information away for later, as one more piece behind the nine's presence fell into place. *A prison break?* Which one of them had been the prisoner…or was that person even still alive? Now wasn't the time, though, because I wasn't getting blamed for this mess of a hit squad, even though it was kind of my fault.

"What he means to say, Council Member, is that they're unaccustomed to not having orders. How can you expect them to fight as a unit without me there to guide them?" I asked. My palms broke out in a clammy sweat, and I wiped them discreetly across my thighs, hoping she didn't notice.

"Guide them? I think you're overselling yourself, Foster. This course was designed to simulate a war, because a war is what you'll be fighting. One girl won't make a difference. You won't make a difference. Do you understand that?" she snapped, suddenly colder than ever before. Something I said must've triggered her defenses, because she seemed determined to make sure I understood how insignificant I was.

But I'm not.

"I understand, Council Member." I paused just long enough for her to settle and turn back to the glass like it was a boring TV show. I should've stopped there, but I couldn't. "But I think you're underestimating me. Aren't my skills the reason you *made* me do this?"

Unfortunately, I didn't take into account that even speaking at all would bring down her wrath like a merciless god.

Her hand twitched, like she was having to control the urge to do something, but what was beyond me. To add insult to injury, when she turned her cold eyes on me with the full weight of her fury behind them, I refused to look away and lower myself to the level of her measly, cowering servants. I didn't know what had happened between now and when we'd last spoken, but something had changed in her. Her coldness was harder, her silver tongue sharper.

"Last I checked, Foster, your skills are the only reason you're even of use to me, but if you're so desperate to demonstrate how *important* you are, show me just how you plan to save them all." For all the fury consuming her, her voice was lifeless. She didn't seem to particularly care one way or the other about what happened to them. I did, though, and she didn't like that. She didn't like that I gave a damn about what happened to them.

"By all means, Mistress. I live to serve," I hissed back through a clenched jaw.

She smashed a button on the remote in her hand,

opening the door to the simulator. Fire shot out, and I took a deep breath before plunging into the flames, feet first and headstrong as always.

If limbo had taught me anything, it was that I needed to man up and buckle down. Whoever had called me a coward wasn't wrong, but I could change that. I could save them all.

The smoke filled my lungs faster than I'd expected, but it only added to my sense of urgency. Anastasia hadn't been kidding when she said she'd turned this place into a war zone.

Concrete littered the ground, sometimes stacking up so high I couldn't see around it. There were clearly buildings in this simulation, before the bombs, but they were broken now. Demolished. Disintegrated. Desolated. That was what this simulation was: despair given life. This could've been any city, anywhere, since rubble was all that remained of the once mighty concrete jungle. Fire spread from one downed power line to the other, as explosions shook the earth.

How the simulator even worked was outside my understanding, but this scene...it was something else. Piles upon piles of smoking concrete stacked up in every direc-tion. This was madness. No, that wasn't right. This was war, and it brought out a desperation in people that could make some go crazy. But I wouldn't falter, and I wouldn't fail.

"Your leader said she could save you all. You should hope, for your sakes, that she's right." Anastasia's voice sounded over the room, but even I couldn't tell where it was coming from. No wonder no one had noticed me earlier. With all the smoke and debris, it wasn't like you could even find the damn window.

"Selena?" It was Alexandra's voice, sounding more disbelieving than anything.

A flash of metal skimmed by her, landing three feet away. Two beeps, and I knew what was coming. Swinging into motion, I crossed the twenty yards before anyone saw me and chucked the metal bomb thirty feet up as it exploded in a shower of sparks. Alexandra jumped, whirling around to stare at me. Her eyes were wide and…watering?

"I told them you'd come back," she whispered, oblivious to the second bomb that planted itself two feet behind her.

"I always do," I called as I sent it flying.

A chorus of battle cries came from over a ridge.

That had better be the rest of them, I thought grimly as I grabbed Alexandra's hand and made a run for it.

"They didn't believe me when I said you would. Can you blame them?" she yelled over the next explosion ten meters behind us.

I had to slow down so she could keep up, but I wasn't leaving her behind here. Not in a war zone. No matter how pretend it was.

We reached the top of the concrete slab just as another metal disk came flying for us—or more specifically, for our friends about thirty feet below.

Have you ever stopped to think that if you didn't fight it, maybe it wouldn't hurt so much? Your instincts know what you need, even if your sentimental heart doesn't.

This time I wasn't letting my sentimental heart get in

the way as I pushed Alexandra off the ridge, and jumped ten feet out into the air, plummeting straight down.

Cries of warning and relief rang through the air as I fell, my eyes never leaving the shiny metal disk as we met in the middle. Ten feet from the ground, I plucked the disk from its flight path and rebounded it like a shotput straight for the artificial sky.

The room rattled as the bomb exploded, right as my feet hit the ground. The clearing was soft enough that when I landed, I rolled, coming up face-to-face with most of the rest of my team.

"Where are Blair and Alec?" I asked, but all they did was stare.

Am I really so unreliable that they didn't think I'd come back? Assholes.

"We lost them when the building came down. This place is a madhouse. We need to get out of here before the smoke gets worse," Aaron said finally.

Silently, I was thankful that someone had at least addressed me. But that wasn't happening.

"Over my dead body. I'm not leaving without them," I said.

Who would've thought that would be such an unpopular opinion?

The Graeme girl spat at my feet as her brother pulled her back. "Are you bloody nuts? You're going to get us all killed!" she cried, and I had no doubt then that she was the one who'd called me a coward.

"I never said you all had to stay, but I'm not leaving without them. Now we can go back and forth about this all day, but last I checked, I'm the one who volunteered to come out here and save all your asses. So, you can follow me or not, but this isn't a debate," I said.

For once, I found myself acting like a leader and feeling like I had a choice. It was freeing, in a way, but short-lived.

As if Anastasia knew the precipice we were on, another two bombs came flying at us and a third at the base of one of the only standing power lines. I could've showed off and made a display of trying to dispatch the three with my speed and strength, but I could do one better.

I plucked them from the sky with invisible hands, and redirected them toward the simulated black sky.

"All right, we're running out of time here. Whoever's leaving needs to go now. I need to find Blair and Alec." Last I'd seen, he'd gotten himself blown up and wasn't looking so hot, but I didn't need to tell them that.

"I'm coming with you," Aaron said.

I resisted the urge to roll my eyes and instead settled for a raised eyebrow as I looked at the others.

"You're going to need me," Alexandra said. She wasn't wrong when this entire simulation was burning up—even she couldn't control this fire, though.

"We're with you," Amber said, her arm wrapped securely around Tori's waist, who walked with a slight limp.

"We will fight," Johanna said, presumably speaking for her nine as a whole.

"We will?" the Graeme girl asked, clearly disagreeing.

"Alec is in here somewhere, and we're not leaving without him." Johanna's eyes flashed with authority, but the blonde wasn't having it.

"She's a coward, Johanna. How can you—"

"The measure of a great leader is not lack of fear but how one faces that fear, Scarlett. She's made some bad choices, but haven't we all? I'm willing to give her another chance to prove you wrong. What say you, Milla?"

I followed her gaze to the twelve-year-old child Aaron had been sparring with the day I'd snapped. Her eyes were strange, not clear or gold, but a cloudy white, like cataracts. She had darker skin and frizzy brown hair. Not entirely Supernatural, but not half-breed either. What would give a child so much authority? And how had she ended up here?

"She has spoken with the Mother and her path is clear," she said.

Johanna nodded like any of that actually made sense.

I shook my head; we didn't have time for this. As if on cue, another scream drew my attention two hundred meters deeper into the room, where another explosion had just gone off.

"Time to move!" I yelled, as we took off toward the swirling cyclone of smoke and ash.

Thirteen people down. Two to go. They'd better both be in one piece when I got there, or someone was going to pay.

Hang on, Blair. I'm coming.

Mercy killing be damned. No one was getting left behind.

I wished for a moment that I hadn't spent so long moping and had actually trained with the nine like a leader. Maybe then I wouldn't worry about the Graeme girl stabbing me in the back...but that was probably wishful thinking.

Concrete grit rained down like hail with every bomb that went off. It seemed that for each disk I misdirected another landed just out of reach. It didn't help that the smoke grew thicker, and with nowhere to go, it was more likely to kill someone than the fire.

"We're not going to find anyone with all this smoke," Scarlett muttered. She wasn't wrong.

"Instead of complaining, why don't you find a way to fix it?" I asked, not really looking for an answer. We had another hundred feet of incline before we reached the next rise, and hopefully Blair and Alec.

"Oh really? And how do you bloody expect me to do that? Just wave it away?" She cut off, falling into a fit of coughing. She was being an ass, but something about what she said clicked.

"That's it," I said, stopping suddenly. Something ran into me from behind, knocking me face-first toward the concrete. I held up my hands to protect my face, but this time, I didn't need it. Mentally, I pushed back, and the earth yielded.

Invisible strands of power sprang from my fingertips as I righted myself, forcing the smoke back as I went. Telekinetics moved things with their mind, but smoke wasn't tangible. It had no form. Only the strongest telekinetics could manipulate it, because it wasn't solid. But it was matter.

I sucked the smoke into a tight, swirling orb of ash that spun like a dying globe over my palm. I grinned to myself at the simplicity of an act that should've been impossible.

"You're telling me you could've done that ten minutes ago?" the Graeme girl groaned.

"Maybe I just wanted you to choke," I snapped, drawing my lips back.

A light touch to my back made me jump, and I turned to find Aaron standing too close for comfort. Meanwhile, Lucas silently skulked toward the back of the group, his eyes dark and hooded as if he had his own thoughts about Aaron being near me. Alexandra grabbed his arm, yanking his attention away as she leaned forward to whisper something in his ear. Aaron coughed loudly, pulling my attention back to him.

"Do you have to touch me?" I asked, the orb of smoke dissipating in a shower of ash all over us.

"When you're picking fights with the heir of House Graeme, yes," he said, rolling his eyes as if I were the foolish one.

"I can—" I stopped short at what I saw coming.

Not thirty feet from me, the fire raged, burning both concrete and wood alike. It shouldn't have been possible for it to grow so quickly, or move so fast. Another zing through the air distracted me, as the bomb landed in the fire and went off with a bang.

"How the fu—"

"*Run!*"

I don't know who said it, but it was the only thing that pulled my eyes away from the terrifying blaze as I raced to the top of the ravine. The others weren't quite as fast, and I used the time to push the smoke back toward the fire, trying to squelch its flames, but it made no difference. This wasn't an ordinary fire. It was a living, breathing thing coming for us all. As I hauled myself up over the last chunk of concrete, my throat went dry at the sixty-foot drop, and the two people stuck at the bottom of it.

"I found them! We just need to get them out of there—"

"Selena, we've got a problem," Johanna panted, coming up beside me. Her footing was impeccable as she twisted on the sharp edge, and spun me around.

"What is she doing?" I asked.

Alexandra stood at the base of the rubble, her hands raised in surrender. The fire licked at her worn black boots, trying to follow us. Try as it might, though, she wouldn't let it past her. My heart dropped into my stomach.

"She can't hold it forever," Johanna said, putting words to my fears. My own panting had nothing to do with the running as my throat closed.

Calm yourself. She can hold it. She is fire.

I took a not-so-deep, steadying breath.

You're a leader. Be a leader. Trust that she can take care of herself.

"She doesn't have to hold it forever. She just has to hold it long enough."

And then, I did the dumbest and bravest thing I've ever done.

I jumped.

CHAPTER 26

Turned out six stories was a lot higher up than I'd originally thought.

The ground was coming up too fast. Throwing my arms wide, I pulled the air up to meet me, slowing myself just enough that I landed with a roll...and instantly regretted it. Rocks jutted out, shredding my back, until I came to a stop and hauled myself up.

It wasn't the safest of methods, but it had gotten me down here faster, hadn't it?

The ground was relatively flat in the clearing, but walls made of rubble surrounded it on all sides. The easiest way out was where I'd come from, but that wasn't an option a second time around—especially if Alec was hurt. I squinted through the haze, sweeping the smoke away so I could find them again. Up at the top of the cliff, I could barely make out my team, and I hoped they would find a way down... Another zing through the air had me turning to catch a bomb, but what I found was far deadlier.

"Blair."

Her eyes had a wild look to them. Something desperate lurked there, and I needed to make sure she recognized me before I made a move. The knife at my throat pressed down just enough to draw a trickle of blood, before she snapped out of it.

"Selena? Oh my— Are you okay? How did you find— Where's everyone else?" The craziness had left her eyes, but she was still wary. Dirt caked her body, and tiny pieces of debris clung to the gash on her arm where the blood had already dried. She looked like she'd been through a war zone, but for all intents and purposes, she had.

"They're at the top. We need to get out of here. Where's Alec?" The words had barely left my lips when a fit of coughing flared up behind her.

"I'm right h-here," he rasped. Just behind Blair, Alec pulled himself up, using the concrete fragments for leverage. If I'd thought she was bruised and bloody, he was a downright mess. His pants were shredded, and chunks of his legs were missing as my gaze travelled down. His foot was only half there, and I grimaced to think how we were all going to get out of this.

Think, Selena. Think.

Something landed next to me, jarring me from my thoughts. Maybe I shouldn't have been surprised, given the way everyone referred to him as my bound and soul-shackled, but when Aaron looked down at me, it wasn't the relief I'd been expecting that someone had made it down here. It was the urge to hurl, because it was *him*.

It only took a moment for Johanna to land behind him, and Amber and Tori literally popped out of nowhere. An idea slowly formed even as shouts rang out around me. I stared at Tori long enough to get her attention then flicked my chin toward Alec. I hoped she got the hint that I wanted her to teleport him up. Her eyes went big as she motioned to the rest of us with a sweep of her hand and a raised eyebrow.

"You want to teleport all of us?" I asked, giving up on the silent communication.

"I mean, I could, couldn't I?" she responded, shrugging like it was no big deal even though her hands were already trembling. Amber, who was closest to us, looked between the two of us like we were nuts.

"You're already exhausted. Be damn sure you can do this before you agree, because we don't need two bodies to haul back. You hear me?" Amber said.

Part of me almost agreed with her—the part that knew that if it wasn't this jump that pushed Tori to burnout, it would be the next. The rest of me said we all had to make sacrifices, and this was our best shot. Alexandra was running out of energy. Alec was running out of blood. We were running out of time.

"I can do this," she whispered.

That was all I needed to hear.

Linking our hands, we formed a circle around Tori, positioning Alec between Johanna and Aaron. Blair's eyes kept darting to him, but when the time had come for us to fall into line, she'd insisted on being between Tori and me. Not that I cared, really—I was more concerned about getting us out of here—but it was interesting. Blair and Alec were another puzzle to solve, if we ever got enough of a break to bother.

As if on cue, another disk landed a few feet to my right.

Tori's breath hitched, and she squeezed her eyes shut. The beeping sped up as I mentally counted down. Three. Two. One.

The bomb went off, but it was distorted. Tori sucked us through a vortex so quickly that one moment, we were waiting to die, and the next, I was sixty feet up.

Time to move.

I opened my eyes and peered through the haze. Our world was on fire, and even though everyone was together now, we weren't out of this mess yet. The group in front of me was still collapsed, but the others who hadn't followed us were fighting. Each other.

Not much time had passed, but in the minutes it had taken us to go down, get them, and come back, a fight had broken out. Lucas and the Graeme bitch were going at it, while the others were trying to separate them. Alexandra was still holding the wall, but barely. She was already on her knees, shaking as she tried to calm the fire. I'd been right to trust her, but, unfortunately for us, time had almost run out.

When we get out of here, I'm ringing Fortescue's neck.

I let my emotions burn away in the flames until all that remained was the ability to do what needed to be done. I looked out over the group who'd followed me down. They'd trusted me with their own survival, and I'd failed them.

Tori was coughing up blood, and Alec's leg was blown to bits. My sister was about to hit burnout, and even Lucas was fighting with some German chick over who knew what. Why was it that every time I started to get myself together, the world chose that moment to fall apart?

This was it. Make or break.

Are you a leader or are you coward? Pick.

We make our own peace. Don't let your sentimental heart get in the way of what you need to do.

I made my choice. After letting myself literally fall apart and hit rock bottom, there was only one way to go.

Up.

"You guys get Alec and Tori to the door. I gotta deal with this," I said.

Running like a madwoman, I tackled Lucas head-on, stopping him in mid-swing. I landed on top of him and quickly readjusted so that I straddled his chest and had the upper hand.

"Go! I'll handle him," I yelled at the Graeme girl and the boys holding her back.

"You better learn to control your mouth before you insult my house again. Next time, she won't be here to save you!" Scarlett spat at the ground and threw a look of disgust at him before letting them drag her toward the door. I hoped the others had also listened, but they weren't my concern right now.

"Get off me," Lucas growled.

I pursed my lips, looking down at him with my arms crossed over my chest. "Not until you stop acting like a prick."

He let out another growl, and I decided to do what I should've done last time we talked.

I punched him in the face.

"Ahh! What the hell, Selena?" His nose was bloody and broken, but I'd held back.

"Think of it as a wake-up call. If I can get my act together, so can you." The conversation was taking a surprisingly serious turn until Lucas flipped us and pinned me beneath him.

Welp. That's not how I was planning on doing this.

The concrete under my back scraped as it bit into the skin, but I didn't have to stay like that long before Lucas was torn off me.

"You don't get to touch her like that. Not anymore," Aaron said as he threw him aside—luckily not into the fire.

"How many times do I have to—" I started to snap at him.

"Do you want him to touch you like that?"

No. Not that I could bring myself to say it, but it was still none of his business.

Aaron crouched down, grabbing my hand to pull me to my feet. "It's been *my business* since I first set eyes on you, and that bastard knows it. We can talk about this later, though. Right now, Alex needs you."

His words left me reeling, because I hadn't answered him aloud. Somehow, he knew what I'd been thinking. He wasn't telepathic, and that was alarming. My sister did need me, though, and it was the only reason I ripped my hand from his and turned to face the fire.

Once again, she'd used too much of herself, and now all control was hanging by a thread that was going to burn to ash. The shaking had stopped, but only because her body had dematerialized into a living flame. Now, the only thing that could stop it was to put that fire out. Good thing my father had been paranoid, because I wasn't the only one he'd conditioned.

"Ignes ad cineres. Cineres ad ignes. Renascere denuō, itaque tu es incendere incendia."

Fire to ashes. Ashes to fire. Be reborn again so you can light the pyres.

Her fiery figure vanished, leaving in its place a naked Supernatural girl with flaming red hair and skin as pink as a newborn baby's. The fire bore down on us both, and I really hoped Aaron and Lucas had had the good sense to get out of here.

I turned into the wall of flame as it hit me, but didn't burn. No one knew why or how, but for as long as I could remember, the flames hadn't burned. Not really. Were they hot? Hell yes, but I'd endured worse.

Channeling anger from my core, I rooted myself to the spot where I would make my stand and bring this whole simulator down. This time, I would listen to my instincts. This time, I would not be afraid.

I reached down into myself, smashing the dam that contained my power with a mighty crack. Strands of darkness poured from the fissure, calling for me to seize them. The dam blew apart, and the world flashed from black to white with strands of darkness connecting everything. Mentally, I pushed on those strands, trying to scatter the fire with strong enough winds. It was too far out of control, though, and bombs were still going off. I needed more power. More strength.

"We can do this. Let go."

I knew who the voice belonged to, but found myself holding back, despite my burning clothes and ash-filled lungs.

"I can't lose control again. How do I know you're not just going to kill them all?"

"You don't," she whispered, pushing me from my body as she stepped in.

I reached out to hold onto something, anything, but my hands didn't move. I tumbled blindly through my mind, until there was no chance of forcing her back until she was ready. No longer in the driver's seat, I observed as she clenched and unclenched my hands.

"Fortunately for you, I'm in a helping mood today. Time to make a little noise."

My foot came down—and the ground rolled as the rubble reduced itself to nothing more than ash. With a flick of my fingertips, she summoned a wall of air so strong that it swept across the simulator, smothering the fire wherever it touched the flames. It was beautiful and terrifying to watch, as I decimated the world. A thrill ran through me when the air slammed into the walls of the simulator, creating a fissure to the outside world.

"Holy shit. Why didn't I do that?"

My other laughed and said, *"Because you don't know how to. Not yet. But soon you'll make what I can do through you look like child's play."*

I reveled in the darkness, finding peace in this kind of control. That should've scared me more than it did. Another bomb came at me, but this time, with the fire gone, I saw where it was coming from. She jumped to meet the flying metal disk in mid-air, and redirected it back to the hole it had just been ejected from. It exploded on impact, but when the dust cleared, the gaping hole in the simulator was a jarring enough sight that my other slipped out and I back in.

"I'll be watching," she said, but her parting words didn't feel as ominous as they had before.

Which meant I was in deep shit. When you trusted the voices in your mind more than you did yourself... I shook my head. The falling soot made me cough, but I was otherwise unharmed. Even my clothes had survived enough that I wasn't butt-naked. I stripped off my riddled leather jacket and approached Alexandra.

After covering her up for the second time in less than a month, I carried her out, hoping she would understand when she woke. I'd let her make her choice, just as I had the others. There wasn't always a right answer, but she and Lily were still alive, and that was enough for me. I approached the door, barely held in place by its hinges. I guess the shockwaves I'd created had done more than damage the simulator. The glass was blown out of the window where Anastasia watched me approach. Her posture was stiff, but her eyes betrayed nothing. She looked bored despite what had happened, which I found a little odd.

I picked up the pace as my blood quickened. Just as I crossed the threshold into the classroom where I'd spent most of my sophomore year, she spoke.

"I suppose you all pass this round, seeing as no one died. I'll be back in three days, and I'd better be impressed." She turned and walked out the door.

Never mind that we didn't have a working simulator to impress her with, or that I didn't give a damn what she wanted. I had half a mind to follow her and cut her limbs off piece by piece.

Let's see how much that would impress her.

I was halfway out the door, when Vonlowsky coughed

and stepped in front of me. "What are you doing?" he asked, gentler than I would've expected.

I looked down at my not-so-little sister. Alexandra was only younger than me by eight minutes, and yet I'd never looked at her as an equal. Until now.

"I'm going after—"

"No, you're not. Don't even think about it. Let it go. You did well today," he said.

Was that pride I heard in his voice? There was no mistaking it when he put his hand on my shoulder for a second, before pushing me toward the barracks.

"You all did well today. Take the rest of the day and tomorrow to get back on your feet. Alec, go see Love immediately to have her look at that leg. I've been given orders that no one can come here, but she never said I couldn't send you there." His support of us and defiance of the Council Member was startling, and a nice change of pace.

As I headed for the barracks with my head down, someone stopped me, stepping in front of the door. Probably Scarlett wanting to pick a fight for almost getting her killed in there.

"Look, I get you're not my biggest fan right now, but I need to get her to bed. Can it wait, like, five minutes?" I asked, not even bothering to look up.

"It can wait as long as you need," Johanna said. My head snapped up. "I wanted to say thank you, for what you did in there. You saved my friend." Her eyes flicked to Alec, who was being held up by another blue-eyed Supernatural guy Johanna seemed to trust.

"Don't mention it," I said awkwardly. I couldn't remember the last time someone had thanked me for destroying something, even if I'd had good intentions. It was nice, but I didn't know how to feel about it.

She tilted her head to the side a little, squinting her eyes before laughing. What was she looking at?

"Come on, Alec, let's get you to whoever this Love bloke is before you lose that bloody leg. A little help, Oli?" She tucked herself in on Alec's other side.

The blue-eyed Supernatural holding him let out a short laugh as they basically carried him out the door and toward the infirmary under Alec's directions.

I shook my head as I headed down to the bunker. *What an odd girl.*

Since Lily still occupied my sister's bed, I put Alexandra into mine and climbed in after her. No more than a few hours had passed from when I'd come out of limbo and walked into the simulator, but I was dead tired. I told myself I was only going to rest my eyes, but it didn't even take thirty seconds for dreamland to swallow me whole.

CHAPTER 27

This time, when I opened my eyes, it was neither limbo nor the living world that greeted me. Dreamland, as I now not-so-affectionately referred to it, had transported me back to my childhood bedroom—powder-purple walls and all.

"What are we doing here this time?" I groaned. I couldn't even see child-me, but the paisley black bedspread and training weapons on the wall didn't lie.

"You'll see," my other said quietly, looking out the window just as a scream erupted from the front yard.

A door slammed and footsteps rushed upstairs. I had a bad feeling as my bedroom door swung open, and my father ushered me in. Child-me was older still. My legs were longer than last time, my hair darker. Mother used to tell me I was born blond, like Lily, but that my hair had turned black within days. Maybe my soul had known even then just how dark I was to become.

"Analysa!" He yelled for my mother, and she was at the door before he even finished.

He rested child-me on the bed, and only then did I

notice the writhing. Black and purple encased me in a shield even he couldn't break, with all his might. If I'd ever questioned before whether my father loved me, I didn't now. His brown eyes were softer than I'd ever seen them when he turned to face my mother.

"What is it?" she asked softly, looking down at my crumpled form. Her white-blond hair billowed in the breeze that carried through my bedroom window. Whatever angelic glow I'd always associated with her faded when her eyes darkened to a charcoal black instead of their usual gray. There was nothing angelic about that.

"What did you do, Eric?" she demanded, striding forward. My sisters' heads peeked around the doorframe.

"Is she doing the weird shadow thing again?" Lily asked.

Alexandra bonked her on the head then grabbed her by the collar of her shirt to pull her away. She looked guilty, and I didn't question why. Dressed in her training leathers, Alexandra looked like some type of ancient child warrior. Child-me was dressed much the same, and I could only guess what the dreamland's version of my father had had them do. How far he'd gone before I'd snapped. She'd snapped. Child-me.

"They were training, Ana. I didn't realize until it was too late," he whispered.

Alexandra released Lily by the stairs, and my other sister wasted no time running. Not Alexandra, though. Her small brown eyes watered as she stared at the dreamland Selena on the bed. Her chin quivered, and fire sprang to life between her fingers—but she didn't seem to notice.

"You never do," my mother whispered, bringing my

attention back to my parents. She hummed a calming tune, in between scolding my father. "How many times have I told you not to push her? How many times do you need to beat her before you realize she's a child? She isn't a warrior, and if you don't stop, she'll never live to be one." My mother's words were harsh, with more grit than I remembered.

Before my parents could say more, Alexandra ignited— consumed by a guilt that wasn't hers to bear. Whatever my father had done to us in dreamland, it was his burden, and his alone. She was a child, and I was a child, and the world was cruel.

"Take care of Alex, if you can manage not to hurt her too," my mother snapped. I'd never heard her so angry or spiteful.

My father leaped to his feet, closing the door behind him on his way out. The last I saw of my little sister was her firedrop tears hitting the ground before she turned and ran. Was that fear in her eyes when she looked at our father? Or was it concern? I didn't care to know. This dream left a bad taste in my mouth.

"I don't understand why you brought me here," I said harshly to my other. She may have been a figment of my imagination, but she watched the scene before her with a bored interest that even I couldn't have feigned.

"I didn't bring you here. You did." She arched a perfectly shaped eyebrow, daring me to contradict her.

Bullshit was on my lips just as my dreamland mother started crooning to the body of a girl locked in her own mind.

Run, run, girl of fate.
Your dark mistress is here to stay.

Run, run, and I pray.
The madness won't take you away.

My mother was somewhere between singing and praying in her devotion to child-me. The energy was snaking back into my tiny body, but the trembling remained. And I remembered.

Run, run, child I made.
The darkness wants to come and play.
Run, run, don't delay.
She will take you far away.

I hadn't thought about the lullaby in years, or what it meant. She'd told me once that her mother had sung it for her, to guide her when the path became too dark. Now that I knew she was adopted, I wondered if it was all just a lie. The more she sang, though, the more uneasy I became.

Run, run, Mother of fate.
They are here, you cannot stay.
Run, run, don't delay.
They will burn you at the stake.

A shiver made its way down my spine. I'd never considered the words before, but instead wiped them from my memory. Was this a warning of what was to come? Or was her melancholy lullaby simply her own madness seeping through?

Run, run, daughter I made.
So you can come back one day.
Run, run, soul in pain,
So you can make them pay.
And pay.

The mists of swirling color had all but disappeared from child-Selena's body. The shaking had lessened to a slight tremor. My mother's soothing tone may have calmed the child, but did nothing for the daughter watching. I'd always known that the madness came from her, that something in her mind had slipped after we were born, but I'd never guessed how deep her darkness ran until she murmured the last line of the lullaby.

Run, run, they will say.

You will take revenge one day.

"What is this?" I snapped at my other. The memory was so detailed it looked completely real—from the way the hairs on my mother's head shone to the texture of the fibers of my bedroom carpet   but this couldn't be real. Could it?

"Maybe it is, maybe it isn't. You talk to the voices in your head, so who are you to say what's real and what's not. Eh?" my other said, her violet eyes glowing with mild amusement.

I glowered at her, but it wasn't worth debating when that would just prove her point. My mother's sobbing brought me back to the scene.

"I see you, Selena. I know the realm you walk in. It's time to come back though, baby girl. The darkness is gone." Her words calmed me, even though I wasn't the child she was talking to. Not anymore.

"It never leaves," the child and I said as one.

Returning from limbo was never physically difficult; it was making the choice to come back that was hard. I had the power, but I'd lacked the strength to abandon the safety of my mind even then. So many times—too many—my mother had had to pull me from the darkness because I couldn't do it myself.

"One day it will," my mother promised. She was a

damned liar, but I guess the apple never falls far from the tree.

"No. I don't think it will," the child said. She peered up through her rain-colored eyes at her mother, who was wasting away before her. I'd never realized it growing up, but looking back through the memories, she was thinner now than I'd ever seen her. Those cheekbones could've cut someone, and the collarbones sticking out beneath her crewneck sweater weren't any better.

"What do you mean, honey?" she said softly, running her thumb over my hand in gentle circles. She brushed my hair away from my face so softly that I couldn't recall ever being touched that way. Like I was fragile. No. Like I was precious.

"Violet is the darkness, Mama, and she's here to stay," the child said darkly, but it was my other I looked to.

She'd known this was coming. I could see it on her face as she gauged my reaction. Violet? There was no one I would've referred to as Violet other than her, with those glowing purple eyes.

"Who is Violet?" my mom asked, an edge in her voice. A tense note that hadn't been there before.

I glanced back at the mother and daughter pair, unsure how this was going to play out, but unable to write it off completely. Unable to say for certain that dreamland wasn't real. That it hadn't happened.

"She's the voice I hear in the darkness, when it hurts too much. She comes to me, in limbo. She speaks to me in my dreams. Don't be afraid, Mom. Violet's my friend," the child-me said, her bright eyes showing a hint of purple.

My mother gasped, grabbing my face roughly so she

could get a better look at my eyes. Her mouth went slack, but only for a moment, before she slapped me.

Crack.

What the hell? That was uncalled for on so many levels. My mother would never have treated me like that. I glared at the cowardly woman. Child-me turned away as fat tears slid down her cheeks.

"I'm sorry. Oh my god. Selena, I'm so sorry. I don't know what came over me," my not-mother gushed. She moved to hold the child, but the girl flinched, pulling away. Dreamland mother opened her mouth and closed it again three times before backing away from the bed.

"Violet isn't real, Selena. I'm sorry I hit you, but you must understand that. The darkness isn't real. It's all in your mind, and only you can defeat it." When she pulled back this time, it was like she'd made up her mind. Like she really wanted me to believe that there wasn't something in those eyes that scared her. That I really was chasing boogeymen.

"And if I don't want to?" child-me asked. I got the impression it wasn't just me speaking, as I now knew just how easily *Violet* could step in when she wanted to.

"Then you'll die like the rest of them, always chasing shadows," she whispered. Her back was to us, but the vein in her neck was bulging. Her hands trembled, but with fear or anger, I didn't know.

"Who?"

"You know who, Selena," she answered, making her way to the door. It grated on me that the second she knew I was fine she fled, like a damned rabbit in a wolf's den.

"The matter manipulators?" child-me asked, her voice

sharp with interest.

I'd always wanted to know more as a child, about why they were afraid of me, why I was supposed to be afraid of myself. It wasn't like I'd picked the darkness. It wasn't like I'd chosen to be strong. Or crazy. My dreamland mother reached for the knob, but the door wouldn't move. She sighed, and swung her gaze back to the person responsible.

"Open the door, Selena," she said, her voice more exacerbated than anything. I suppose that was better than fear...or pity.

"The matter manipulators died a millennium ago. How am I here? How is this possible?" Child-me was up now, out of bed with her arms thrown wide in a plea. My heart ached that it kept coming back to this: me asking for answers, and them only keeping secrets.

"Goodnight, Selena," she said, and that was that.

I turned to my other—Violet, as the child referred to her. Her long black hair was tied back in a wild braid, and her eyes held mine.

"If you didn't do this then why am I here?" I asked. Bluntness seemed to work best with her.

"Why did you go into limbo?" she asked, answering a question with a question.

I scowled, but tried another tactic. "I need space to figure stuff out."

She pulled a knife from the wall and picked at her fingernails with it, digging the crud out while she made me wait. "Has it not occurred to you that maybe you're still searching?" Another question, but at least this one was getting somewhere.

"Through some twisted version of my past? I fail to see

how that helps me," I said.

She smiled, just a little. Violet was going to make me work for whatever answers I got from her. "Sometimes you need to remember the past to see the future and live in the present. If one doesn't know who they are then what do they know?" Her psycho-mumbo-jumbo was getting on my last nerve, but I was never able to wake myself up, not in dreamland anyway. May as well go with it, for just a little longer.

"So you're saying I need to remember who I am?" I asked, raising an eyebrow at the absurdity of that statement.

"I don't know. Do you?" she shot back, a twinkle in her eye. She was enjoying this.

"I know who I am. What I don't know is who you are. You weren't around when I was this young. My mother didn't look like a damn wraith, and my father wasn't an abusive prick. I don't understand why I'm seeing any of this..." I gritted my teeth, waiting for a response, but she just gave me that pretty, awful smile.

Child-me was curled up in bed again, staring at a wall, probably talking to some godforsaken hallucination she thought was her friend. Not much had changed.

"Just because you don't remember doesn't mean it never happened, Selena. Even our own minds can lie, so who's to say what's real or fake? At the end of the day, we're all liars. I'm just along for the ride." She smirked.

Something about what she said grated at me, though— the idea that I didn't remember my own past. That my parents were actually these kinds of people, and I this kind of daughter.

"Let's say you're right. Why would I not remember this? Why would it be coming back now? Years after they died. Why?" I asked, running a damp palm over my eyes, pinching the bridge of my nose.

Breathe... In. Out.

"That, I think, is the best question you've asked in a very long time." Her eyes flicked to the child-me lying curled in my own solitude, no longer trusting the world to care. Something close to warmth crossed her gaze as Violet looked down at child-me. Almost as if she cared. But not quite.

I thought of the questions child-me had asked, and the one it always came back to. How was it possible for a telekinetic child to be born to into a non-telekinetic family? How did I even exist?

Something told me Violet knew, but I wasn't ready to know. There was work to be done, people to slay, Fortescue bitches to hunt. I needed time to think, time to contemplate what this all meant, and if it was real—but here was the crux: how do you tell real from hallucination when you can't even trust yourself?

They all looked the same to me.

"Time to wake up." Violet winked.

The dream faded, and I had no desire to linger. Dreamland could go back to whatever forgotten recesses of my mind it had inhabited before.

"This isn't over," I said, and her laugh echoed until the moment I opened my eyes.

Gold stared back.

"Your sister's awake. Thought you ought to know," Johanna said.

CHAPTER 28

HER HAIR WAS STILL BLACK AS NIGHT, BUT HER EYES WERE BROWN, so that was something. She moved almost hesitantly as she trailed her fingers along the cotton sheets of Alexandra's bed. She sat with her legs close together, quivering ever-so-slightly, and I didn't think she even realized I was awake.

"You're alive," she said, looking nowhere in particular, making me jump just a little.

Silently, I crept across the cement floors; Johanna trailed me quietly, more ghost than girl. Her head snapped up when I sat down directly across from her.

"Did you think otherwise?" I asked. The dark energy that coursed through her veins came to the surface, swirling across her skin like moving tattoos. I doubted she noticed.

"I heard them. The voices. The whispers that beg you to kill. I felt their darkness, and your pain... I saw your demons," she whispered, her voice more impassive than I would've expected given the horrors she'd endured.

"How are you feeling?" I asked slowly, scared that her eyes were seconds from turning purple and my other, Violet, was going to come out.

Her lips quirked up in a weary grin.

I loosed an unsteady breath, my chest relaxing a fraction as I waited for her to reply.

"Shouldn't I be asking you that? You did tell me not to do it." Her voice was still too unfeeling, but this wasn't Violet. Of that, I was sure.

"For good reason. You nearly killed yourself, girl," Johanna said.

Lily jumped a little, more skittish than normal, but that wasn't terribly strange given the ordeal she'd been through. She glanced sideways at the mysterious, golden-eyed sphinx, who'd settled quietly against the side of the bunk while we spoke. Even I had only noticed her out of the corner of my eye, and she never made a sound.

"Who are you?" Lily asked. Her tongue clicked, and she scrunched her nose. She didn't appreciate Johanna's input, but was trying to be polite.

"A friend," Johanna said, glancing between my sister and me.

Lily laughed, but it was hollow. "Selena doesn't have friends. Well...not outside her roommates and Lucas," she said with a snort.

I would've facepalmed right then, if I hadn't tensed up instead. I glanced across the aisle at Aaron, and waited for the outburst. He lounged against the concrete wall, his arms folded across his chest. Had he intentionally picked the spot next to the door for a reason, or like me, did being in this concrete prison make him edgy? His eyes were black again—I thought I saw a gleam of gold, but it was gone so fast I couldn't be sure—and he gave no indication that he cared. I didn't know how to feel about that, given that I still didn't even know what being my signasti meant. Maybe if I avoided it forever, I would never have to find out.

"She's friends with Blair," Johanna pointed out.

"Blair is blood. It's not the same," Lily mumbled.

"Johanna's a friend, Lily. Let's just leave it at that," I said as I turned back toward her.

"Where's everyone else?" Lily asked, more perceptive than I'd been.

I must've been so wholly focused on her that I hadn't noticed that the rest of my team wasn't here—apart from Johanna and Aaron.

"The others needed some fresh air, after everything that happened," Johanna said, mostly to me. It wasn't like Lily knew most of them—I barely did myself. After the war zone simulation, some things were going to be changing around here.

"Did something else happen?" Lily asked, her skin going ashen.

"Can we have the room for a little while?" I asked, glancing at Johanna and then Aaron so he knew the request extended to him too.

Her eyes glowed gold for a moment before she said, "We need to talk, but it can wait for now."

She took one last look at the two of us, before walking through the door Aaron was holding open. His eyes settled on me for a moment, all-consuming. I shook my head, turning away to clear my thoughts. The door clicked shut behind him, and with it, the ability to breathe easy returned.

"So you know?" she asked, wasting no time at all.

"What are you talking about?" I said, wanting to gauge how much *she knew* before I went there.

"That he's your signasti?"

What the hell?

"How do you know?" I snapped, mentally backtracking to the last time we'd spoken. It was before I went off in the simulator the first time, when I tried to kill him. Which meant there was only one person who could've told her.

"Blair came to me after your panic attack, and the fallout in the bathroom... I figured you had enough crap of your own going on that it was best just to give you space. Until Tori came and found me, and now...here we are," she said. Her eyes darted to the sides, like she was still seeing shadows. She rested a palm across her chest, taking deep, steady breaths. Her heart pattered in her chest, like a hummingbird in a cage of bone. She didn't need to know I could hear it, though; it was best to let her adjust as the swirls receded again.

"Blair told you? I thought it was Alexandra, given how much she blamed me," I said.

I wasn't as bitter about it as I had been, though, not after the war zone. For a girl who didn't know how to be anything but selfish, she'd sacrificed herself to the fire to save us. I was just glad I'd gotten to her in time.

"Who do you think trained with me every morning? Blair took over for you and kept me updated. Honestly, I think she just needed someone to talk to. She felt like she couldn't tell you, but it's not like she really has any other friends," Lily said. Her eyes were a clear, undiluted brown, not a hint of darkness in sight.

I clenched my fists in my lap, swallowing hard. Blair shouldn't have needed to take over for me. Lily shouldn't have been the only one she felt she could talk to. Here we were, though, because I kept shirking my responsibilities.

"Now's not the moment to feel guilty. Save it for your pillow at night," Violet whispered, and I rolled my eyes skyward.

"Heartless," I scoffed.

"They used to say the same about you."

I shook my head, clearing away her voice and the whispers so that it was just Lily and me.

"I've been a crap friend the past couple of weeks, and an even shittier sister," I said.

She smiled, almost amused but also a little sad. "Well, I can't imagine it was easy finding out you're soul bound to your sister's now ex-boyfriend," she said, reaching out across the narrow aisle between us to take my hand.

"I don't even know what it means, Lily." I sighed deeply, and moved beds to sit next to her.

Lily stilled, her hand fell away from her chest, and the shaking stopped entirely as she said, "You haven't talked to him?"

"No, there hasn't been time. And even if there had been, I doubt talking will make him go away," I grumbled. I stared at the empty room, silent apart from the sound of breathing.

Lily grabbed my face roughly and forced me to look at her. "You need to talk to him. If you don't even know what a signasti bond is, or what he's gone through, how can you dismiss it so easily?" she asked, her voice rising a little.

"Get off me—" I said, pushing her hands away, but she didn't yield. She wasn't weak, no matter how tired she looked.

"You need to talk to him. I did some reading, while you were *busy*—and I think this bond is part of why you're having issues controlling yourself. It's making the demons worse."

What? The bond was making—That prick. Why was she feeling sorry for his ass?

"How?" I asked, trying not to be too snippy with her just yet.

"If you'd talk to him, you would know," she snapped.

Okay...

"Seriously? If he's making it worse—"

"Don't try to manipulate me, Selena. It's hurting you, but by the same token, it could also help you," she said. Dropping her hands into her lap, she pushed back to lean against the wall.

"What if I don't want help?" I asked, being pedantic now because I was tired of being told what to do.

"Too bad. That ship sailed a while ago." She smirked, not even taking me seriously.

"I don't want his help. He can burn in hell."

She tensed, just a little. Oh crap...

"It doesn't help him that when you look at him you see a demon, quite literally. He's probably the only person who can help you, and he's also your biggest trigger," she said.

I stilled, because her observation went beyond what she

could read on my face. She was recalling what she'd seen in my memories.

"How are you really?" I asked.

She stretched her arms out, splaying her fingers before settling back again. Taking her sweet time deciding how to answer.

"I'll be okay," she said eventually.

I could live with that, but I didn't like it. Being okay eventually meant she wasn't okay right now.

"Do you want to talk about it?" I asked, not really sure how to proceed with this type of conversation.

She snorted again, glancing at me. "Do I want to talk about your nightmares? Hmm...let me think about it," she said. "Smartass." She laughed again, this time a deep throaty sound that reverberated off the ceiling of our empty cell. "They're not *my* fears, or my demons. While part of me feels like I should be asking you that, the rest of me knows it's not my place. I took a chance when I tried to shut you down, and your mind bit me in the ass for it," she said. "I'll live."

I could tell that part of this was an act, that she wanted to be more okay than she was. Maybe there was some truth in the saying *fake it till you make it*, though, so I let it slide.

"Well, what do you want to talk about?" I asked, trying to give her as much space as she needed to sort it out. She didn't look like she was falling apart, and like I had with Alexandra, I needed to trust that she would tell me if she ever hit that point.

"So, this is where you've been living?" she asked, taking in the more-than-humble abode that was the barracks.

"Yep, me and the fifteen other unlucky people who got dragged into this mess," I said.

The concrete walls didn't seem as foreboding as they had a few weeks ago, though, and the space wasn't quite so cold. On the surface, it was easy just to see the gray stone walls, and feel like you were in a prison. It was the little things, though, like our unmade beds, and the occasional trinket here and there that gave the smallest of glimpses into the minds of those who lived here.

"It's...cozy," she lied, cringing as the words fell short.

"Liar." We laughed for a moment, before she went quiet.

"Do you have a bathroom?" she asked, more hesitant again.

I was going to tell her we pissed in a pot, just to see the look on her face. She was fingering her now-black hair, though, so I was pretty sure this wasn't a normal bathroom break.

"Yeah. You want me to come with you?" I asked, though I wasn't really prepared if she had a breakdown or a panic attack.

"Please," she whispered. Her smile fell at the bathroom door. She was playing with her hands, rubbing them over her stomach and pants.

"Just remember: it's only hair. We can always dye it," I said solemnly.

She nodded, pushing the door open for herself and turning to face the mirror.

Her mouth plopped open as she ran her fingers through her dark waves. It didn't look like she was panicking, but I wasn't really sure what she was thinking either as she turned to see herself from every direction.

"I look like you," she gasped. A wide smile broke across her face, and I let go of the breath I hadn't realized I'd been holding.

"Is that a good thing?" I asked, even though I knew she thought so. Best to keep her excited. Happy.

"We actually look related now. Come see," she insisted as she dragged me in front of the mirror with her.

Two black-haired beauties stared back, one with eyes like chocolate, one with eyes like steel. Our faces had always been similar, but she was right—we looked even more alike now. Her skin had a light tan from her mornings training, making her eyes stand out. While she wasn't as muscled as I, she was definitely getting there.

"You don't look so bad," I said, grinning so she knew I was kidding.

"If you mean bad as in badass, why, yes, I do." Her reflection winked at me in the mirror, but my own smile didn't meet my eyes.

"Speaking of being badass...we need to talk about your training," I said.

She nodded, turning and sliding up onto the counter so that she was facing me. "I'm leaving with you guys when you go."

What?

That was not where I'd expected this conversation to go. I opened my mouth to object, but she held her hand up to explain first.

"Ever since we came back, no one will speak to me. I tried to go to the boxing gym, and even though the coach would've taken me, no one would fight me because they didn't know what you would do if I got hurt. Boys won't talk to me. Girls just whisper about me. Even Bella won't sit next to me in class anymore, because she's afraid of being associated with me. I'm completely and utterly alone here." She paused, swallowing hard before continuing. She didn't break, and she didn't cry—I had to give her that—but her eyes were as cold as the sterile bathroom walls.

"You and Alexandra are my only family, and you're leaving me to go fight in a war. I know you don't want me fighting—you've made that pretty clear—but you need to think about what I want. And understand that when I say I'm leaving, it isn't up for debate. This is me telling you I've made up my mind, and you can either help me or not."

We stared at each other, but I didn't know what to say. I'd told her I wanted her to get better, so that she could take care of herself when I couldn't. I'd told her she could choose her own happiness. Now she'd made her choice, and I couldn't just say no because I didn't like what she had chosen.

"The others aren't going to like this," I warned.

"I don't really care. I can hold my own, and I'll do what I can to contribute even if I'm not on the front lines. At the very least, it couldn't hurt to have a healer around," she pointed out.

I couldn't disagree there.

"You sure this is what you want? No doubts?" I asked, not believing what was coming out of my mouth. My book nerd, dorky sister...was dropping out.

"Things have changed, Selena. Everything has changed. We lost our parents, and so I clung to you and Alexandra.

Then we came here, and I clung to Bella and my other friends. Sooner or later, though, I've gotta stand on my own two feet. I have to move on." she said quietly, running a shaky hand through her hair. "It's not that I don't feel the sadness anymore, because I do. It's always there, making me feel too much and reducing me to this withering, worthless bundle of tears and snotty shirts. I hate her, this girl who can't control herself or the anxiety." She paused so long I didn't think she was going to continue, and I would've left it if she had.

I didn't know what to say to her, and every time I'd tried in the past, it just came out wrong.

"So, I evolved, and in finding a purpose I've made her go away—at least for now. I still feel the crippling sadness, but now I know it has an end. Nothing lasts forever. Mom used to tell us that, but my brain never seemed to grasp it. After six years, it's like waking up from a really long nightmare. I still feel it. I still see it. I know it's not real, though, and that's made all the difference." Her voice was like snow falling on a sunny day, soft and beautiful.

"We've both got our issues to work through. Maybe when all of this is over, we can settle down somewhere and try to have a life," I said.

The faraway look in her eyes cleared as a bittersweet smile made its way to her lips. "We already have lives. Sometimes, it's a matter of choosing to live, and that's why I'm coming with you."

The world was changing, and so were we. For better or for worse, it was time to start living.

"We'll continue your training like normal, and when

the time comes for us to leave, I'll make sure you're coming with. Be ready, but don't tell anyone yet," I said.

"You promise not to back out on me?" she asked.

"I promise."

She nodded once, holding up her pinky. I almost laughed at the idea of a pinky promise; we hadn't done that in so long. But if that was what made her believe me, a pinky promise it would be. I took her little finger in mine and hugged her tightly to my chest, hoping I hadn't just agreed to something I couldn't do.

CHAPTER 29

The next few hours passed way too fast. After sending Lily on her way, I lay in bed with a sleeping Alexandra, trying to figure out how to get my life in order. I'd been gone for five days. Suspended in limbo. I was back now, though, only to find that time was almost up. We had ten days left of training, and it felt like we'd only really started.

I still needed to talk with Johanna and the others to find out more about how they'd ended up here, and answer their questions. If they could stick with me in a war zone and sleep next to me at night, there wasn't much point in keeping some of the simpler things from them. And it would probably help if I took the time to learn their names.

Man, I'd been such a shit leader. A shit friend too. I couldn't recall the last time I'd talked to Blair, and after she was nearly blown up, she probably could've used some support. I needed to do better. If people were willing to throw their lives down to stand by me, I needed to be worthy of that kind of loyalty. I still saw this as a prison sentence, even if I would get a shot at revenge when this war ended, but the time for moping was over. Alexandra and Lily both needed their sister. My friends needed me to be there. My team needed me to get my head out of my ass and lead them. Lucas...well, he needed to get his own shit together. He was in no place to ask anything of me after getting in a slugging match in the middle of an elimination. It was a good thing Aaron had been there.

Aaron.

Did I really want to think about what he needed?

Lily had said he could be part of the reason I was getting worse, but I didn't have the first idea why. I didn't even know what a signasti bond was. I was reluctant to ask Aaron, because that seemed too real. Too concrete. I would've asked literally any of the others—Alexandra, Johanna, Blair, hell, even Lily—but they all were adamant that it came from him. If I wanted answers, I was going to have to get them on my own, because I sure as hell wasn't ready to go to my sister's ex-boyfriend.

A thought came to me, and I slipped my phone out of my pocket. Maybe the internet had some ideas. Just like this morning, though, the screen stayed black as the red battery icon flashed in the corner.

"Seriously," I grumbled, slipping it back in my pants.

I rolled again, blowing the hair out of my face as I stared up at the ceiling. I really didn't want to talk to him, especially when I knew nothing about what this stupid bond was. It gave him an advantage over me, and how did I know he wouldn't lie? He'd obviously been lying for quite a while about it, which didn't help my confidence in him.

But maybe...there might be a way to find out.

I shimmied down to the end of the bed and jumped off,

landing lightly on my feet. Alexandra didn't stir. I ran my hands through my hair, looping it around into a bun on top of my head. My mouth tasted foul, even though I'd eaten nothing in days. Come to think of it, all of me was gross. I grabbed my bag of toiletries and a fresh set of clothes, heading into the only working bathroom. I stripped quickly and sighed in almost-contentment when the cold water hit me. Wonderful, bringing an icy bliss like nothing else could. I hummed to myself while scrubbing my scalp clean with the citrusy shampoo Alexandra always got me, and five minutes later, I was already patting myself dry. I dressed quickly in jeans and a Daizlei t-shirt, after putting my hair back in a bun. I really needed to cut it, but as impractical as it was, I'd never sported short hair, and I didn't plan on starting now. I scribbled a quick note letting Alexandra know I would be back, and stuck it in her outstretched hand. Heading out the door, I felt lighter already, more centered and like myself.

The walk to the library was brisk, and I didn't see anyone I knew. I had no doubt my face would draw attention, but I hoped wearing a shirt without any visible weapons would calm some of the rumors that I'd skin anyone alive who talked to my sister. I only did that to those who meant harm.

The bell dinged when I walked in, and I found Professor Rivas, the librarian, sitting behind a broad oak counter. I breathed in deeply, inhaling the scent of old books, teenage hormones, and something like smoke. There wasn't a fire going, but there was the faintest scent of something wild that had passed through a while ago and was probably long gone. I shook my head clear, and walked up to the counter.

"Yes?" she asked, peering up from behind the rather large collection of encyclopedias she was organizing.

"Hi, Professor Rivas, how was your summer?" I asked, wanting to butter her up a little before getting to what I'd really come here for.

"Short, unfortunately. I was exploring a particularly fascinating Mayan temple when our Council sent out the distress alert, ordering us back. What can I get for you, Ms. Foster?" she said, straightforward as usual.

I liked that she didn't waste time, and wasn't the type to dally much. Like all underappreciated faculty, though, she wanted students to treat her with the dignity she deserved.

"I'm looking for a book," I said, pausing while I thought about how to phrase this.

"Well, you are in a library, dear. I would hope that's what you came for," she said, cracking the briefest of smiles before motioning for me to go on.

"Have you ever heard the words *signasti animam*?" I asked her, lowering my voice even though no one was paying us any mind.

She cocked her head for a moment, assessing me. "I have. Might I ask what you want to know?"

"I need to know everything," I said, backtracking a second later with, "For a school project."

"Right," she drawled, before coming around the counter to lead me into the heart of her books. We passed shelf after shelf, and the quiet whisper of students soon turned to true silence. The shelves back here had an inch of dust, and books with titles in languages I'd never seen before. In the very back corner on a smaller shelf were about half a dozen books with *signasti animam* and variations printed on the spine.

"This is it?" I asked. Surely a place this big with a budget like ours should have more than a few...but it would have to do.

"The bond is rare, and old. Most Supernaturals never find their signasti, and those who do don't usually recognize them. Other species have better luck, but in the last few centuries, it seems Nyx's turned away and taken the concept of predetermined mates with her. These are all we have on the subject," she said.

I took a step toward them, but something made me hesitant.

Once I knew, I could never unknow. Blair and Lily had excused Aaron because of this. Alexandra hated him for it. This bond had already made a mess of my life. Did I really want to know?

Professor Rivas turned to leave, pausing only for a moment to say, "I hope you find what you're looking for, Selena. Be careful."

I had a feeling that warning had nothing to do with the books. For a woman who spent her days in a library, she knew more than she let on. Wasting no more time, I took my tiny collection of answers and settled down against the far shelf. The first book was small, not much bigger than my hand, with faded gold lettering that read: *anima vinctum*.

Soul bonded.

That was a slightly nicer term than the one they'd told me, even though they clearly meant the same thing. I took a deep breath and opened the book.

The first few pages made no sense. It was just a bunch of drawings of men and women, some morphing, others splitting. Several depicted what looked like two people being cut open to search for their souls. The author noted their death, and lack of results.

Well yeah, idiot. You can't cut a soul out.

The journal was handwritten and badly faded. As the pages went on, it transitioned from drawings, to discussing the theoretical concept of a soul, to talking about something like divine intervention. The passages were barely legible, but I could pick out some terms the writer kept using. Anima Vinctum. Signasti Animam. The list went on, and some were more depressing than the one they'd given me. The books talked about forever, two souls always seeking each other out—which made it seem like they believed in reincarnation—but the books were old or fading. The English wasn't modern, and that made it difficult to decipher. Forever sounded pretty long, though… How the hell did you end up bonded anyway? I flipped through two more journals until the pages came up blank then turned to the next book.

The History of Us. Who named a book *The History of Us?* Sounded kind of pretentious, but I'd give it a try. This one had more of a textbook quality, with an actual table of contents, and right there at the very bottom was *signasti anima*, printed in small black letters.

"Close enough," I breathed, turning to page one hundred and sixty-seven.

Seriously? One lousy paragraph. Well, at least it confirmed what I'd already gathered—that this was some kind of archaic view of soul mates. Which, oddly enough, would explain the weirdness of the last year surrounding Aaron. If this was to be believed, it was because he'd known the moment he saw me. An otherworldly 'tether' had snapped into place, binding us forever. It seemed oddly convenient that Supernaturals hardly ever saw these bonds, and when they did, it was only after the 'claiming' had happened.

"What the fuck is a claiming?" I muttered, slamming the book shut and tossing it away. Tossing was an understatement, actually, as it flew ten feet and landed with a *thud* on top of a pair of dull black boots. Boots? What the—

"I was wondering how long it would take you to start looking," a deep, distinctly male voice said.

I glanced up into coal-black eyes as the smell of smoke and the wild enveloped me. I should've known he was here. I'd smelled his scent when we fought. He took slow steps toward me as I stood. His eyes heated, like a predator on the hunt.

Oh hell. Not happening. I flicked my wrist and put away the books. They made a *thack* sound as they hit the shelves a little harder than I'd intended.

"You have claws, but you're running like prey. Do I intimidate you that much? Does this?" his voice was a whisper in my ear.

I froze, my body instinctively tightening, as if it knew he was no good for me. Knew I would have no choice in how I reacted. I didn't want to turn around because he was there. Right there. How he'd moved from five feet away without a sound...

"Intimidate me? You're more likely to smother me with

that ego. My answer hasn't changed, Aaron," I said bitingly, hoping my venom would keep him off my tail.

"What do you want to know about the claiming?" he asked, moving to lean against the shelf. His eyes were a burning black, the gold already peeking through like embers dancing in the depths of the darkness. My throat went dry, but at least I didn't blush. I had a pretty damn good idea what claiming meant when the words 'mate' and 'forever' were involved—oh, and let's not forget bound.

"Fuck off, Aaron."

I turned to walk away, but didn't even make it half a step when he wrapped his hand around my wrist, giving it a small tug. Like a string wound too tightly, I snapped right back into him. His scent was as intoxicating as it was assaulting, and I was in big trouble—because I didn't pull away.

The inner heat that seemed to radiate from him hit me like a wall. My body went loose, as I let him wind his other arm around my waist. His hands were so *warm*, filling an ache in my bones I hadn't known was there. Unlike last time, when he'd given me ample warning, this time, he was going for the kill. This time, he didn't let me be dissuaded. And this time, when he brought his mouth down on mine, I liked it.

That was an understatement. It was the kiss that made people see stars, and think they could reach them. It was a wildfire raging through my body, needing an outlet, and he was ready to take it all. The restless beast inside me had been seeking something, and she'd finally found it.

I brought my hands up around his neck, curling my fingers into his hair. He groaned, pulling me closer, as he slid his hand away from my wrist and wrapped it around the side of my neck, using his thumb to guide my face higher. I stumbled in his arms, my legs weak, and then the damn doorway appeared in my mind. The heat. The fire. The beast inside me. It all came back to the door, and the way his lips set me aflame.

My emotions ran raw, and every nerve ending in my body came alive. When he let me slam him into the library shelf, we were wrenched apart for the briefest of moments, and his eyes glowed gold with an unnamable emotion. I reeled him back in, pulling his face to mine with all the strength my shaking arms could muster.

Something was building in me. Burning in me.

The door shook so violently that I wanted to reach forward and touch it. Caress it. Open it. Until it was all ripped away, and I found myself gasping for breath.

Aaron sidestepped me, untangling himself so fast that I fell forward, clutching two bookshelves for support and snapping one of them. I recovered my footing, pulling back to face him.

"I've waited a year to do that, and it was worth the wait." He winked, but underneath that cool exterior, there was something in him that burned at my touch. His breath was nearly as unsteady as mine, and his heartbeat drummed in my ears. He wasn't as together as he wanted me to believe.

"Why did you do that?" I snapped, my cheeks still flaming.

He was as cocky as the day I'd met him, sexy as sin, but it was the way he looked at me—like I was everything— that made me uneasy.

"Because now I know your soul recognizes me, and you won't be able to stay away anymore."

He turned away, leaving me open-mouthed, red-faced, and fuming, but I made no move to stop him.

Of all the arrogant things that bastard could—

"Oh, and Selena, darling?"

I looked up, into the dark eyes that saw past my cold exterior into the blazing fire of my heart. He might've seen me, but I wasn't his. "When you want real answers, you know where to find me."

And just like that, he was gone, and with him, any warmth.

"You're an idiot to ever turn that down," Violet said, ogling him from the back of my mind. She was a beast in her own right, and I shuddered to think what would happen if she came out when he and I were fighting. There was already enough...tension without throwing her into the mix.

"I don't want a relationship, least of all with him," I fired back, even though my body was telling me otherwise.

I'd just told Lucas there was nothing going on between Aaron and me, and even though I didn't want Lucas, that didn't mean I wanted Aaron—or his signasti bond.

"You know, for someone with so many issues, you judge an awful lot," she said.

"Put a sock in it," I hissed back.

Deep down, I knew she was right, but that was a secret better left buried in the graveyard where I kept my heart.

CHAPTER 30

"Mind if I sit here?" I asked.

The entire table went silent as Johanna glanced up at me, and motioned to the stool across from her. "By all means."

I'd come back so late last night that everyone was already asleep, and I'd left before anyone woke. They probably thought I'd ditched them all again. Quiet chatter broke out as I settled in, glancing up and down the table. I took care to avoid a certain male gaze, but noticed that too many people were missing. Alexandra was still in bed, but...

"Did Lucas come back?" I asked.

Wrong question, apparently, as the Graeme girl on my right ground her teeth.

"Vonlowsky had to have a talk with him. He's out blowing off some steam," Alec said vaguely.

Wait—Alec?

"How are you back already? I thought your leg—"

"Was nearly blown off?" he finished for me.

I nodded, taking in the dark circles under his eyes.

"It was in pretty bad shape, but Love managed to save the leg. That woman is a bloody miracle worker. She let me out this morning with a cast."

"Well, that's good." I'd been under her care for days after the warehouse. He was lucky.

"It is, and I have you to thank for it. Johanna told me you came into the simulator and said you weren't leaving until you'd found us. My mistress would've let us die. Thank you," he said solemnly.

Any ideas I'd had about him and Anastasia had gone out the window when I'd seen her lack of empathy for her servants, particularly when he'd been bleeding to death.

"No problem," I mumbled, picking through the fruit on my plate. People thanking me wasn't something I ever thought I'd get used to.

"I don't think you ever got a proper introduction to the rest of your team," Alec said, alleviating some of the awkwardness.

"Scarlett and Sebastian from House Graeme," he said pointing to the German twins on my right.

"As in one of the ruling families?" I asked.

The blonde on my right, Scarlett, gave a sly smile. "Yes, and I'm the heir," she said. It almost looked like the word *commoner* was on her lips, when Alec continued.

"Camilla Divin and Constantine Berg." Alec motioned to the two I already knew on my left. The small girl with cloudy eyes gave a wide smile. Her curly brown hair was pulled back into three bunches on top of her head, going straight down the middle.

"Berg, that's another family. You're a…" How could I say half-breed without actually saying it? They'd wanted to kill Lucas, and I wasn't trying to burn any bridges quite yet.

"Constantine is part-Witch, as is Camilla," Johanna said, noticing my effort and giving me the answer.

"I've just never read about ruling families that were—"

"History is written by the winners, Selena. There's much I doubt your school has told you about the Council," Johanna said quietly.

I nodded and kept my head down. There was a clear power struggle between the half-breeds and full-blooded Supernaturals...but it could wait.

"Liam." Alec went on to the boy with curly, red hair. He looked gangly, and hardly more than fifteen.

I offered him a small smile to ease the tension, but it may have looked more like a grimace. His gaze dropped to the table, focusing on the eggs in front of him.

"And Oliver," Johanna finished for him, rolling her eyes when Oliver gave a little bow. He was the one with blue eyes who'd helped take Alec to the infirmary yesterday.

"At your service," he flirted, throwing his arm around Johanna as if she were his little sister.

She just shooed him away, muttering about daft boys. I would hardly have called Oliver a boy; he was probably as old as Alec, who sat on the other side of her, laughing to himself.

"You knew each other before here?" I asked casually.

The playfulness in Oliver's eyes died.

"In passing," she said cryptically, leaving me to put the pieces together.

I piled fruit into the crepes. "Does it have anything to do with a prison break?"

Wrong.

Wrong.

Worst thing I could possibly have said.

The table went stone cold silent as they turned to me. Johanna was the only one who didn't look like she was about to murder me.

I sighed, setting my fork down.

Please don't make me fight my way out of this room.

"What do you know about that?" Johanna asked, and her eyes had gone completely yellow. Black slit irises were all that remained, making her look distinctly reptilian.

"Your mistress likes to talk," I said slowly.

"She's no mistress of mine, girl. Let's be clear that while you may not have been raised into this world, ignorance is not bliss."

"I'm not trying to be ignorant. I'm asking questions. If you won't answer them, you can't blame me for how I put snippets together. I'll tell you what I know, but I have questions of my own you still haven't answered," I said, hoping I hadn't just overstepped their gratitude. I wasn't going to be walked over, though, for a misinterpretation.

Johanna settled back, running her thumb over her bottom lip. "Fight me," she said. It wasn't a question.

"Umm...I'm not sure I understand," I said.

Oliver laughed, and he wasn't the only one. Most of their group was now either grinning or rolling in their laughter. "Oh, but you will, mate. You will," Oliver said, wiping his eyes.

Johanna didn't smile, as she stood and motioned for me to follow. "Shall we?"

What had I just gotten myself into?

"I really don't understand the relevance here," I said.

We'd decided to take this fight outside, since the simulator was still broken. We all jogged to the other side of campus where no one would hear us. I was never one to back down from a brawl, but this was lunacy. We had no weapons, but she exuded an easy confidence, almost a swagger, as she approached. The others stood off to the side, watching with arms crossed and sly smiles. Her nine thought she would win without question, and my friends never doubted me.

Guess we'll see who really belongs on top.

"Everything has a price. You want answers, and I want honesty. I've never known someone to lie to me during a duel. I will be able to tell if you try," she said.

She's lying... But her lips were turned up in an easy grin. Her eyes never left me as I approached, and that should've been my first indication that this fight was going to be different. That she wasn't kidding.

It should've occurred to me that I'd never seen her use her ability. A lot of things should've occurred to me before I'd agreed to this, but by the time she was swinging, it was too late.

I narrowly escaped her punch as I ducked to the side, and her knee came for me. Pain exploded across my abdomen, knocking me back a few feet.

What is she?

In the time it took my stomach to start healing, she was already on me again. I dove to the side.

"What do you know about the prison break?" she said, coming up fast while I was still down.

In the half second it took her to advance on me, I shot my foot straight for her face. Her eyes went wide an instant before my foot met her chin. There was a wicked snap as her head lurched back so hard she stumbled.

Whiplash is a bitch, isn't it?

I rocked forward to get back up, landing nimbly on my feet. Dirt danced in the wind, but with the sun on my face in the heat of a late August day, I felt peace.

"I told you that Anastasia ran her mouth yesterday before I went into the simulator. Something about how unimpressed she was with Vonlowsky's teaching, and that she was more amused by your prison break."

Johanna watched me as she stretched, cracking her neck all the way. The sound sent shivers up my spine, and not in a good way. She wasn't a hulk like Aaron or Lucas, nor was she incredibly fast like Amber. She couldn't teleport me like Tori, or use flame and ice like Alexandra and Blair. She was something entirely different, something I'd never encountered before. I just didn't know what.

"Truth. What's your question?" She grinned.

I smirked back, wiping my sweaty palms across my pants. My scars tingled as sweat rolled down my back, and the tiny white tank top I was wearing became see-through. Dirt was already smeared all over it and me, but Johanna didn't look any better.

"Who was the prisoner?" I asked, letting her advance on me.

She cut her hands through the air like knives, changing her fighting style completely. While I was used to dodging punches, this was different. With her fingers held together stiffly, she made jabs left and right. I moved to shield myself with minimal success. For every blow I blocked, one landed. At first, I didn't understand the madness behind her movements, or why it felt like her fingers were shattering bone. Even as quickly as my body healed, the pain didn't immediately recede. I moved to escape her hands, but she slipped through—striking a very small point just below my jaw.

"Me," she said just as pain blinded me.

"Ugh!" I cried out, stumbling forward. My legs weakened, and my knees cracked when they hit the floor, but the white in my vision was receding. I was coming to, and Johanna was ready for it.

Brown boots crossed my vision. She was going for a final blow to seal the win. A quiet trance took me as I let my eyes fall shut.

"Why did you want to know who it was?" she asked, but her voice was slow. Warped, even. Or maybe that was just me.

The way she moved was unnatural and eerily similar to someone else I knew. I felt the tautness of her arms through my power as she pulled back, preparing to land the blow.

You are the master puppeteer. You control everything! my subconscious screamed, snapping something in me, and somewhere deep down, I knew I couldn't let Johanna strike my head.

It was as if time itself slowed, and a wave of sudden clarity washed over me. I reached up and plucked her hand from the air then threw her to the ground with all my strength. Her body hit the dirt like a bug meeting a boot. I couldn't pull my gaze away from the impact as I stood. She stilled for a moment in the hole her landing had created, and that was that.

"Because I want to know what you did to land yourself here," I said, waiting for her to get back up. Seconds ticked by, and I started to feel a little uneasy with all the glares being thrown my way.

Really? She can try to take my head off, but I throw her in the dirt, and we have an issue? Assholes. At least they were loyal.

I took a timid step back in the direction of campus. Johanna wasn't moving, and thirteen pairs of eyes were glued on me. The tension settled in, and I was starting to regret agreeing to this.

"I was born." Johanna coughed.

I whipped my head back around, staring wide-eyed at the source of tension. "What?"

"Anastasia Fortescue killed my best friend, and the Council sentenced me to death for it." Wisps of brown hair had come loose from her braid and now fell strikingly around her tanned face. This story kept getting darker and darker at every turn.

"But your friends...their families are on the Council..." How she could bear to be near them if they'd endorsed this?

"The Council is divided, Selena, but every time a family stands up to the Fortescues, they find themselves wiped off the map. My friends risked their lives to break me out, and now we're paying the price for what I am."

"Because you're not pure-blooded," I whispered.

It finally made sense. Why I'd never heard of mixed Supernaturals before a few days ago. Johanna had a voice, and power of her own, but it wasn't a purely Supernatural one. And that made her a threat.

"I'm happy to see you're not quite as ignorant as I thought," Johanna said. Beneath her wild hair and impassive demeanor lay a person who was boiling with contempt—because of the hand she'd been dealt in this world. And I understood that.

"I'm here...because I didn't have a lot of choices," I blurted. Telling the truth, but still not breaking Anastasia's rule. We were all brought here as prisoners, and even though I couldn't say what Anastasia had blackmailed me with, I could say I wasn't willing. I didn't want this any more than they did, and her offer to get revenge suddenly didn't seem quite as appealing. There was a reason she'd put me here, with her other prisoners, and I wanted to know what it was.

Johanna paused, regarding me carefully. She looked at her friends, and then mine—who were not looking very pleased with me right now. Blair in particular looked like she wanted to take a swing at my head, and it didn't take a genius to know why.

"You told us she asked you, and you thought it was the right thing to do!" Blair said, striding forward.

I held up my hands and nodded slowly, swallowing hard. "Yes, it was the right thing to do given my options. I'm not *allowed* to say more than that," I said, trying to put as much emphasis on the word as possible.

I got that she was a bit pissed, but honestly, I hadn't known that this was a group of prisoners when Anastasia brought me on. I'd really thought we were just going to be a hit squad, and when the Vampire/Supernatural tensions died down, I'd go free with a shot at hunting whoever had sent the Vampires after me, and the demons before them. Johanna's story...changed things. I needed to give them something, because I wasn't going to be a pawn in whatever game Anastasia was playing. Not anymore.

"I can't say I'm terribly shocked. You're not exactly the type to fight for glory, or what's right," Johanna said. She laughed quietly to herself, and I wasn't sure what she found so funny. Maybe she was the one losing it.

"And you? Why are you here?" Johanna asked, turning to Blair.

My cousin looked at me, clenching her jaw like she wasn't going to answer at all. "Because she said she needed us," she said eventually.

"And the rest of you?" she asked, turning to those of my team who were here.

Aaron, my sister's ex and the man bound to me in ways I didn't yet understand. Tori and Amber, my roommates who'd become more, who'd become my friends. Blair, my cousin-turned-protégée, and closest friend. They'd stood by me through it all. I didn't deserve the loyalty, but somehow, they thought I'd earned it. And yet, they all gave Blair's answer. They were here because I'd said I needed them. I'd just never come clean about what I really meant— that I needed them to put me back together when the time came, and not just as punching bags or Vampire bait.

"I didn't know how to bear this sentence alone," I said —making every head turn toward me. I hated being this open. I hated the vulnerability. I hated the shields I couldn't seem to keep up, as every facet of my life came down.

But they deserved the truth. My team deserved my

thanks. Johanna deserved to know that she wasn't the only prisoner, and her friends needed to know that I didn't want to lead anyone to their death.

Johanna laid a hand on my shoulder, turning me to her. She was smiling despite what had brought us all together.

"You're not like the others raised in this world, but I don't think the one who raised you was any kinder. Guard your heart, and tread lightly. You never know what mask evil wears…but you, Selena, I trust you." She paused, glancing at something behind me. "Get through the next week, and then we'll talk."

The tension was thick, and I still didn't have all the answers, but some part of me knew that they truly meant me no harm. We all had our reasons for ending up here, some simpler than others, but at the end of the month, we were going off to fight—whether we liked it or not.

The only thing that was abundantly clear was that Anastasia was planning something. I hoped I'd get the chance to end her before whatever it was came to light— because knowing her, it would already be too late if it ever did.

CHAPTER 31

On the third day, the simulator still wasn't fixed.

I suspected Vonlowsky had finally opened his eyes and was trying to save us from Anastasia's games. If he was, though, it would only bite us in the ass when she came knocking.

Breakfast was drawing to a close, and my friends were preparing themselves for the worst. Alexandra had only woken up yesterday, and I'd filled in the gaps as much as I could within the concrete bunker. Johanna had said you never knew what mask the enemy wore, and I wasn't taking chances. After the fight, the day had gone by slowly, and the night had been restless for everyone. Blair had tossed and turned below me until early morning, when I made a split-second decision and woke her up to train. When I'd pulled my head out of my ass three days ago, I'd taken over Lily's training again, and though Blair and I had never spoken of it, I suspected the tossing and turning was about more than just the coming elimination. The time for war was drawing near, and everyone needed someone. Even Blair. Even me.

She said nothing as we dressed and headed out, training for the few short hours before dawn. We were back in the barracks before anyone woke. Well, before anyone got up. About half the room was breathing too unsteadily to still be asleep, but I paid them no mind. How they chose to prepare was up to them; my job was to keep my demons in check—even if one of them had taken it upon herself to make sure I didn't do anything stupid because of my 'sentimental heart.'

Violet was good at it, making little comments about my team throughout breakfast. Nothing much, but just enough to distract me, until Lucas entered. The veins in his neck stood out too much, as he looked at the only open seat, next to Aaron. Had the shadows under his eyes been so dark last time? Had he even slept in the last few days?

I didn't know.

We weren't friends anymore. Friends didn't hit friends, but I wasn't going to blame myself when he'd hit me first.

I didn't leave when he took the seat across from me, and I didn't balk at his presence, like most of my team. I simply ignored him, letting my shields of iron will and icy wrath keep any and everything from entering my mind.

I drained my cup of black coffee, savoring the bitter aftertaste that fueled my indifference. I'd once said that the only thing worse than hate was never caring at all, but at the time, I hadn't believed it. I hadn't believed I'd had it in me not to care what he chose to do, or what he was thinking. I didn't love him, not the way he wanted me to, and he loved me too much, in a way that had broken him. Broken us.

I shot a look at Aaron, silently asking if he could control himself, and Lucas gave me a pointed stare.

"I'm going upstairs to wait for Anastasia," I said. My footsteps were quieter than their breathing, and the door clicked shut behind me. I paused for a second, wondering if he'd speak when he thought I couldn't hear. No one said a word, though, and I continued up the stairs. With each step, my jeans slid more than I liked, and my black shirt was looser than it should've been.

"Damned limbo..." I muttered to myself.

It hadn't even felt like hours, but five days had passed in which I hadn't eaten a thing, and my body wasn't happy with me. I needed to eat more if I was going to keep up with Johanna. That girl was a beast, just waiting to be cut loose. I should've wondered what hid behind those somber eyes the moment I saw her.

"What do you mean the simulator is *not* ready?" Anastasia Fortescue's voice carried, not as a shout, but as a whisper of darkness.

I debated turning back, but when the stairwell door two floors below opened, I knew there was no avoiding this.

"The simulator is still down from the last elimination, Council Member. I have the technopaths working on it around the clock, but the structural damage needs to be repaired before they can work on the rest of it," Vonlowsky said. It wasn't quite the groveling he'd done before, and she saw it too.

"They haven't even started?" she seethed.

"Council Member Fortescue," I said briskly, interrupting her before she gutted him like a fish. "I'm glad you were able to make it," I lied, plastering a strained smile on my face. I prayed that saving his ass didn't get me thrown in prison or, worse, killed. After all, that was what I was here to avoid.

An aloof stare was the only acknowledgement she gave me, before she turned back to him. "When will it be ready?" she asked. Bluntly. Brutally.

"I was told another week. With the modifications you—"

"A week?" she repeated, her voice devoid of any emotion.

"Yes, Council Me—"

"Then I will be back in a week, with something special for the last elimination. Just to make up for lost time," she declared as the others walked in behind me.

I was overjoyed that we had another week, and no one had lost a limb this time, but I knew deep down that this was very, very bad.

"What does that mean?"

Oh shit. I'd said that.

Not good. The way she was looking at me was very not good.

"I own you. It means whatever I want it to." Her heels clicked against the smooth surface as she walked away, but fire raced through me with a heat that made me not care who she was—or if she would make me regret it.

"I work for you, but I'm not your slave. We made a deal, Anastasia, in case you forgot that little detail." The moment the words were out, all the fire in my veins turned to ash.

She looked back at me with death in her eyes. "Speak to me that way again, and your life is forfeit."

Anastasia waited a moment, ensuring she had the last word, before leaving. The door swished shut, closing me in. *Count to ten*, I told myself. Alec had warned me, in his own way, that she was a liar and would abuse our deal. I was an idiot for not recognizing that she and I were the same.

"Selena?" my sister said.

I didn't turn around, but my body shook with power, barely contained. "What?" I said softly. There was no point snapping. I knew what she was going to ask.

"What was the deal you made?"

I let myself cool for another ten seconds, let the ash settle in my bones. I didn't want to lie anymore, but the truth had consequences. So, I would settle for another truth.

"I made the best choice out of the options I was given. I'm sorry I can't tell you more."

"But—"

"When you stepped in front of the fire to save us, did I ask you why you did it?" I said, still staring at the door. I could feel every body in the room as easily as my own. Their energy writhed through my fingers like chords of powers just waiting to be played.

"No."

"Then trust me when I say that that's all you need to know. I have my reasons, just like you had yours." Calm claimed me as Violet settled over me like a blanket of shadows.

"Control. There is peace in control," Violet whispered.

She didn't ask me again, and I didn't bring it up.

THE NEXT TWO days passed in a blur, and then the invitations arrived.

"Why the bloody hell would she send us invitations to a ball, five days before we're leaving? Has she gone mad?" Scarlett asked, voicing the question for all of us.

"I don't think it's an invitation," Blair said quietly. She looked at me, as did the others, for some kind of reaction.

I took a tight breath, running a hand through my hair.

"I suppose there's no way to get out of this?" I asked, looking at Alec and the others who knew her.

"I'm afraid not. She would take it as an act of defiance," he said, stretching out on the bed with his damaged leg elevated. It may have been a blessing for him that the simulator wasn't fixed, but something told me these invitations were a bad omen.

"And what doesn't she consider an act of defiance?" Alexandra asked, rolling her eyes and sending her own invitation up in flames then blowing the scattered remains through the air like a lover's kiss.

"It's not so much what you do, as it is your frame of mind. Your actions don't matter, unless you truly want to serve her—and she knows that. So, she'll make her demands displeasing, just to see how far she can push before you snap," Alec said. There was a wicked sharpness to his voice, and I didn't want to consider how many times he must've *displeased* her for him to understand her motivations so thoroughly. Intimately.

"This is a power play as much as anything. She's holding it on the last day of the month. I think we should just go and get it over with. She's not going to pull anything in public," Oliver said, holding up his own invitation and tapping the perfect script stating the date and time.

Five days from now, right after the last elimination.

"Well, it can't be that bad if there's booze," I muttered, shutting out the other monsters that were having much darker thoughts.

"*Lush,*" Violet griped at me.

"*I haven't touched a drink in months. Hush you,*" I said back.

"And eye candy," Amber drawled, glancing at Constantine. He cringed slightly, and Johanna snorted. While Amber was a true man-eater, I suspected that half her brazen comments were just for kicks. It clearly made Constantine uncomfortable. Then again, her wolfish grin wasn't exactly encouraging.

"And who doesn't love an excuse to blow my mother's fortune," Blair said lazily. She eased back onto her bed, cellphone in hand. I wondered if she was looking at dresses already, or, realistically, weapons that could be hidden beneath them.

"Well, I guess it's settled then. We're going to a party."

CHAPTER 32

Each day that led up to our final elimination dragged a little more, and the feeling that something was coming for us, the all-consuming sense of doom that had never steered me wrong had me doubled over, gasping in the bathroom stall. Blair held my hair back, and I emptied my stomach for the umpteenth time in the past twelve hours. Morale was in the toilet, like the contents of last night's dinner.

But here we were, on the last day of the month, more united than when we'd started.

"You're in no condition to do this today, Selena," Blair said. She ran her chilly fingers over my forehead. I let out a small moan at the wonderful coolness that gave me the shortest of reprieves.

"It's not like I have a choice. I'll be fine. You should be worrying about you." I groaned, leaning back against her. Sweat beaded at my temple as my pulse hammered in my veins.

Something is coming.

Something worse than ever before.

But I couldn't tell her that.

"You're burning up," Blair said as she smoothed my hair back while I wiped the vomit from my mouth.

"Everything is hot to you," I grumbled, gripping the toilet seat as I pulled myself up. My body swayed, and Blair locked her arms around my waist in a frozen grip.

"Get-off-me!" I said, pulling away. The bathroom door banged open, and I knew who it was, *smelled* who it was, before he ripped the stall door off.

"Animal," I muttered.

"What's going on? You've been sick since dinner last night," Aaron asked.

I turned in Blair's grip, and had to reel myself in when his black eyes threatened to consume me.

He's not a demon. He's not a demon. He's not—

"She's fine. Just give her some breathing space," Alexandra said from just over his shoulder.

They both turned to look at my redheaded sister, leaning against the doorframe with arms crossed.

To me, she said, "It's the feeling again, isn't it?"

I nodded, breaking out of Blair's arms to empty my stomach again. So much for being strong. Rough hands scooped my hair away from my face, and I groaned into the smell of bleach and vomit.

"What feeling?" he asked. I could tell he was gritting his teeth, but I didn't know why he even bothered to care. Pompous idiot may've been bonded to me, but he was a fool if he thought this was going anywhere.

"Blair, get him out of here," I said, as I tried to right myself again. This time I had more success than the last, but that probably had something to do with his strong hands pulling me up with ease.

"What feeling?" he repeated.

"I said, get out!" I snapped, whirling on him. The monster in me eased an eye open, and smiled.

His eyes were entirely black, as if that shimmer of gold that seemed to come out around me was locked down tight.

His breath was fresh as cold water on a summer day, but the wildness in his scent drove me nuts. While Lucas reminded me of the forest, Aaron was wind and smoke.

"Excuse me," I snapped, shoving him aside.

Blair followed me out of the bathroom, past Alexandra. I didn't turn back when the door closed behind us, even though neither of them had walked out. Maybe they had unfinished business they needed to sort out, or maybe he'd gotten tired of waiting to get a piece of ass. I still remembered the way he'd talked about his ex a year ago, before he knew me or my face.

After wiping my palms on my black leather pants, I got to work gearing up. My black combat boots were wonderfully sturdy, and great for holding my thinner knives, while the curved blades meant for slower killing hung from my waist. My leather jacket had been destroyed in the last fire, so I went for a different look of badassery—a simple black tank top that let me sport my scars with pride. With power.

"You look good," Blair said quietly.

I nodded. "You too. No matter what happens today, I'm proud to be your teacher. But I'm even prouder to be your friend."

She smiled softly and nodded. "Me too."

We walked down to breakfast together, where we sat at

the end. The room felt as somber as my thoughts. When Alexandra and Aaron finally came down, we were most of the way through breakfast, and only two seats remained. Alexandra peeled off right away, and took the chair next to Lucas, leaving the one on my left for Aaron.

The seat creaked as he swiveled it toward the table, respectfully avoiding my gaze and trying to give me space. I rolled my eyes, but found my attention snagged by Lucas staring. And so I stared back for a moment. And then another.

"Do you have something to say?" I asked, breaking the silence.

Lucas's gaze turned cold instantly. Maybe I shouldn't have engaged him—he seemed to be having a hard enough time as it was—but I was tired of the way he looked at me when Aaron was around. I wasn't trash just because I hadn't picked him, and never mind that I hadn't picked Aaron either.

"You kind of did when you jumped him in the library," Violet muttered.

"He jumped me!" I fired back, and her cackle reverberated through my pounding heart.

"Why would I? Going to sic your dog on me?" He sneered, glancing at the male on my left.

Fire spread through my chest, but I willed ice into my veins. Blair reached under the table, putting a firm hand on my knee. It was a silent anchor that let me keep my control just long enough for her to reply instead.

"If you're here to pick a fight, get out. She doesn't need to put up with your bullshit any more than the rest of us do." The air turned icy as the frost of her breath carried across the table. A warning if I'd ever seen one.

"Oh, so she saves dear Alec, and suddenly all is forgiven?" he shot back at her.

Alec was half a table down, and had gone bone-white. "Leave us out of this, Lucas. You're being a prick."

That only seemed to rile him up more, though. "Is that the best you've got, brother?"

"You can't handle the best I have," Alec responded without skipping a beat.

I damn near spewed my coffee across the table.

"You're crippled, so let's see how that works for you in the elimination," Lucas said darkly.

I gaped for a moment, and the hand on my knee had turned cold, so I wasn't the only one appalled.

"Is that a threat?" Alec asked, taking a chunk out of his apple.

It bothered me more that he wasn't upset by this, that he almost expected it, and I didn't know what to think of that. Or what to think of him, this new, harder, crueler Lucas—a Lucas I'd never known.

But for once, I didn't have it in me to fight with him. Didn't have it in me to stop him from digging himself an even deeper hole. I didn't know how to help, so I didn't waste my time trying, or even look his way when I stormed from the table to the stairwell.

Something was eating at me, clawing at me, but instead of facing it, I ran. The panic wasn't subsiding, and by the time I reached the ground floor, my coffee was already on its way back up. I grasped the cold metal handle in my slick palm and pulled so hard the door groaned and the top hinge broke.

I'd taken two steps into the room when a pair of cold blue eyes in a too-familiar face looked my way. The source of my panic. The reason for the dread that filled my veins.

Anastasia.

And she'd brought friends.

"Council Member, I didn't expect to see you quite so soon." My voice was clear and unwavering as I worked to keep my breakfast down.

"Where is the rest of *my* team?" she asked, not even bothering to address me.

I pursed my lips slightly before putting a falsely subservient smile on my face. "They'll be here shortly."

Anastasia narrowed her eyes but said nothing.

I took the chance to observe the people she'd brought with her. Both the men and women were obviously Supernatural in skin and eye coloring. They stood tall, looking arrogant, and smiling coldly at what they perceived as weakness. Their whispered words were clipped, short and without emotion. I caught the glances of a few and the slight widening of their eyes when they flashed between the Head of Council and myself. Their clothes were fine, higher quality than I was used to wearing, and far more refined than the leather pants and tank top I wore now.

Another moment passed before the door two stories down opened. Anastasia gave me a cold, calculated smile as the first of the footsteps cleared the stairs. I didn't move an inch as the door flew open.

"What is the meaning of this?" Johanna said, striding

forward with mighty steps. She didn't quake under the cold stares of the people surrounding Anastasia.

"I would watch your tone, half-breed," a burly Supernatural man growled. He was taller than any other male in the room, save Aaron, who tried to step in front of me and was snarling quietly under his breath. I understood his aversion to the term half-breed, but I most certainly didn't need him trying to protect me.

"Likewise, Council Member Branislav," Oliver said, stepping up next to Johanna. She stilled them all with a death stare that said the words she couldn't—that one day she would murder them in their sleep.

"Silence," Anastasia barked, only settling herself when her orders were obeyed. She splayed then fisted her fingers, stretching as if she too could feel the veins of power that thrummed under this explosive tension. "The Council has come for a demonstration. A proof of power and worthiness, if you will," Anastasia purred.

Half my team tensed while the other half started walking to the simulator, already resigned to what a 'demonstration' likely entailed.

"Not so fast." She paused, and dread unfurled in my belly like a raven spreading its wings.

Goose bumps broke out across my flesh when the Head of Council looked right at me, a cruel smile on her lips. "We only require a final demonstration from the team leader, to ensure that we chose the most capable person for the job," she continued, a huntress who'd waited far too long to spring her trap.

"I was under the impression I'd already proven how capable I am, given what happened last time," I said softly.

A subtle reminder that I wasn't without claws. Memories of smoke and rubble came to mind.

"And I've decided to reconsider that decision. Now, a demonstration, *please*. We will not ask again," she said, not-so sweetly.

We. I liked how she used them as a weapon while never asking for an opinion other than her own.

Cold fingers wrapped around my left hand and burning ones around my right. I looked back and forth between my sister and cousin, at the raw emotion in Blair's eyes that she gave to no one, and the love in Alexandra's. I nodded once to each of them, letting only the smallest sliver of my gratitude show. Anastasia was playing a dangerous game, and I wasn't about to give her the only ammunition that could take me down.

My friends. My family. For them, I would shatter the very earth.

So, when I stepped inside the simulator, I didn't show any fear. I didn't turn back and let them see my apprehension.

No. I kept my eyes open and wits about me, until the ground moved, like a monster opening its jaws to swallow me whole.

CHAPTER 33

The simulator floor broke apart like the teeth of a kraken, shifting back toward the walls to reveal an antechamber of true terror below. A lake of dark water so deep I couldn't see its bottom. The drop itself was no more than the sixty feet I'd jumped off the ravine, but in this arena, the floor was moving.

Down below, stepping stones created a circle of sorts around the outer rim of the lake. Four massive poles rose out of the water, looking like power lines with an impressive trunk. Sheer terror seized me as the piece of the floor I was currently standing on slid rapidly away, leaving me in a world of water...and I didn't know how to swim.

My mother had been afraid of water, and it was the only fear she'd passed onto both me and my sisters. While I could do a shower, and even a bath, anything more than two feet was not happening.

I was going to drown.

Swallowing hard, I forced my legs to move, positioning myself just so. If I didn't do something now, I was going to fall off the edge too far away from the stepping-stones that were the only land. Violet rested a reassuring hand on me, a will of steel leaving her fearless despite the very real possibility of drowning if I planned this wrong.

"Aim for the stones. On three. Two. Jump!"

The jump down was daunting when I knew what was coming if I missed. The brutal impact on my legs ricocheted through my spine and rocked me so hard my teeth chattered, because I couldn't roll. I let the force tear through me, preferring it to the building panic that had my heart beating so fast it was hard to breathe. The lake was even more terrifying up close. A harsh wind whipped my braid back as I surveyed the waters that splashed over the stone's edge and onto my dark pants.

Black. They were truly black, and a shiver ran through me.

How had Anastasia known? Was it sheer luck that she'd pieced together the only physical obstacle that had a chance of ending me?

I doubted it, but down here, that doubt would serve no one. If I wanted to live, I needed to be clever and figure out exactly what I was fighting against. In the center of the lake, a ripple ran through the water, too swift to be a lazy current. I stood my ground, staring into the waters, when another, more defined shudder ran over the surface. Closer this time.

My breath hissed between my teeth as I inhaled sharply and sprang to the nearest stone. And then the next. I had cleared four stones in fifteen seconds when the air swished behind me. I looked back just as the water parted, spiraling down like a massive whirlpool. Water poured over the three-foot-wide stepping stone as a creature of nightmares leaped over the spot where I'd been standing not a minute before. Nine heads homed in on the empty rock, their serpentine eyes so predatory it made my blood run cold. Each head had a snake-like neck that eventually merged into one massive body, with short legs and webbed feet. I say short, but each of those legs was as tall as me. One of the heads swiveled around at my gawking, as if the creature realized why I'd been sent here—just as I did.

"You have one hour to kill the Hydra, or you become its dinner," Anastasia said over the intercom.

Her voice ignited my rage, and I abandoned all self-doubt, forcing the fears down. I strangled the panic, and I used it to fuel me. To jump.

The beast gave a mighty roar, but I didn't stop leapfrogging from one stone to the next. Hydra. *Hydra.* I'd heard that before. As I fled, I searched my brain for what I knew of this beast. When I'd gone on a learning spree last spring, I'd studied many creatures. The species that controlled this world, the Supernaturals, and the ones that, if given the chance to reproduce, would take it back. Like the Hydra.

Fucking huge? Check. Many heads? Check. Lizard body? Check. Acid spit?

Oh shit.

I glanced behind me in time to see it leap from the water again and emit a vat of acid, aimed right where I stood. It was clear—so clear against the ever-changing black scales of the Hydra that I almost missed it. The acrid smell hit me mid-jump, and I faltered on landing. My foot slipped off the stone disk, and a girl screamed as my body hit the water.

Cold. So cold.

And dark.

I reached out into the nothingness, grasping for something, anything, that could pull me out of here. I opened my mouth to scream, and icy water rushed in, filling my lungs until they burned. That thing was probably swimming around here somewhere, waiting to eat me, but I couldn't find it in me to move or lift my arms to attempt to claw to the surface. I couldn't swim, not that it mattered since I didn't know which way was up—or down.

The burning in my chest reached a climax then faded into a warm blanket as I floated in the icy depths of a lake that never ended.

"Is this what peace feels like?" I asked myself, but no one answered.

"Violet?" I asked again, unease flickering somewhere in the back of my waterlogged mind. Where had she gone? And why did this silence feel so *cold?*

Something reached into me and ripped my ease away, pulling on a thread in my chest.

Stop. I writhed, no longer wanting to feel anything at all.

"No."

My eyes snapped open, because I *knew* that voice. I knew who was tugging on that invisible line. I'd felt that warm touch against my skin only briefly, but I knew the smoldering it would bring out in me.

The burning was gone, and my eyes were open, but there was nothing I could do. I was going to die down here.

"You are not *going to die. Fight it."*

Some flicker of sense returned to me. Only an ember

of power, but an ember was all it took for the fire to spread. The world flashed in a kaleidoscope of colors as the invisible strings that controlled everything snapped into view.

"Violet?" My call was a whisper on the wind. I pushed further and faster into the recesses of my mind, but she was nowhere to be found. For the first time in my miserable life, I was free of the voices that plagued me.

But I wasn't free of all my monsters.

If Violet couldn't help me, there was another that could. A beast that lurked so deep underneath my skin that I didn't let others know it was there. I didn't let them see the savagery in my eyes. Or hear death's words on my lips, like a lover's kiss.

Aaron had awakened it, though, in his call to me.

This is it. Live or die, I said to myself.

"Get out of there, Selena. It's coming for you!" Aaron yelled down the bond.

I didn't give myself time to think. I knew what needed to be done. The beast knew it too, because the moment I opened the door, I was no longer the Selena the world knew.

I was no longer the prey.

I was the beast.

And I roared.

A new fire burned in me as power consumed my veins. Water rushed far and fast from me. Fleeing like it would for no other.

The hounds of darkness were chasing the tide, though, and even the water couldn't move fast enough as I forced it out. My feet hit the bottom of the lake as I parted it into two mighty walls. The Hydra was here, though, and it still thought it was hunting.

Little did it know the huntress had come.

Violet's presence came back to me when the water cleared—joining mine and the beast's, meeting as one, an unholy trinity. We didn't speak as I parted the walls further, forcing the water higher on both sides of the chamber. In the middle stood one of the lone poles—my fishing rod, for all intents and purposes. I didn't let myself think as I wielded my knives like picks, and climbed.

Water drenched my clothes, but I wouldn't falter. Exhaustion made my muscles burn, but I wouldn't fail.

Higher. Higher, I urged myself, until I sensed its eyes on me from where it was waiting me out, seeing what I would do. When the acid came for me, I was prepared. Swinging myself up by the hilt of the knife now firmly planted in the wooden base, I didn't have to wait long until the acid began eating through the pole. But the Hydra was hungry, and that made it impatient.

When the monster jumped from one wall of water for me, I was ready. The wooden pole cleaved in two, and the top half, the one I was riding down, was already falling. The central mouth opened wide as it dove for me.

I flashed it a wicked grin and took off running down the pole as the Hydra dove for its dinner—only to find a mouthful of wood too wide to break. It didn't know what to do when I mentally thrust the forty-foot-long pole straight through its body.

It may have survived having its heads cut off, but good luck surviving being impaled straight down the middle.

I flung myself around as I fell to the earth, flipping off

the serpent as I went. The monster was still falling, but it wasn't quite dead yet. When my feet touched the ground, I didn't look back.

Not when I exploded the pole inside its body with a thought.

Not when blood rained down on me.

Not when a chunk of bone the size of my arm almost slammed into me.

Not even when its heads dropped like flies, and those cold reptilian eyes stared at me, almost as if it were acknowledging me in death as the more cunning monster.

I smiled to myself as I gathered the water under me, using it to propel me upward, then ripped a hole in the wall with a spear of water.

Cold settled in my bones, more comfortable than any heat. More natural than the burning. I stepped onto flat land, and beheld the faces of the Council.

Disbelief. Awe. Fear. Greed. Jealousy. Hatred.

I didn't give them the satisfaction of groveling, and only graced Anastasia with the briefest of glances, the smallest of acknowledgements, as I said, "Don't ask for a demonstration if you're scared of what you'll find."

I looked past my friends, past my cousin, who was frozen to the spot, and my sister, whose mouth was grim. I looked east, to where the sun was still rising, and I thought of my father. I still wasn't sure if dreamland was real, but I thought of the man who'd forged the beast in me—out of my own blood, and tears, and broken bones—and I thanked him.

CHAPTER 34

THE COLD DIDN'T STAY AS THE HOURS PASSED, BUT THE MONSTER lurking within me did. Prowling. Hunting. We moved as one when I stepped under the shower, and my sister came in after me. Naked as the day we were born, she was babying me, but I didn't think it really had anything to do with me being injured. She was calming herself as she scrubbed my skin clean of the Hydra's blood then passed me off to Blair, who wrapped a plush bathrobe around my shoulders. Maybe they were both shaken. I couldn't imagine what I would've felt seeing either of them go under... I shivered, leaving the memory of the lake where it belonged—in the past.

They whispered about me when they thought I couldn't hear. Or maybe they knew I could and were just waiting for an ember of the fire I'd felt in the simulator to resurface. The others, the nine, were stuck somewhere between fascination and fear. All but one. It was the heir to House Graeme who dared to approach me as I sat stiffly on Blair's bed, while she worked a comb through my matted hair.

"Remind me not to piss you off, matter manipulator," Scarlett said. She met my gaze, and nodded.

It had been bound to happen sometime, but I was surprised it had taken them so long to realize who I was and what I could do. Everyone in this room was deadly in their own right, but I didn't believe for one second that any of them were as bloodthirsty as me. And I was glad.

I didn't say anything to her before she walked away, but gave her the briefest nod of acknowledgment. Blair and Alexandra were the only ones who talked to me after that as the day wore on. The nine stayed on their side, and my friends stayed away. Aaron hovered, out of sight from the moment I'd left the simulator, but though I couldn't see him, I felt him. I still didn't understand what had happened in the depths of those waters, but I wasn't sure I wanted to. Not yet. I would need to go to him eventually, to figure this out, but not yet. Not today.

Inside, I danced with the monster—trying to put it back in its cage. Violet watched me from a corner of my mind. She wouldn't get involved, though. This was a test of wills I had to face alone. We were no longer bound as three, but that didn't stop her from lurking—and now that we were out, I had questions, and as usual, she evaded giving me answers.

"You weren't ready. Still aren't, but you're getting there. You're growing," Violet whispered.

A caress for my ears alone. Well, mine, and possibly Aaron's, judging by the way he shifted uneasily when she spoke. Violet was quickly becoming more than just some demon that lurked in my dreams, and I think he sensed that. Either way, she wasn't going anywhere long-term, so I didn't think too much of it.

"Why did you leave me, when I was underwater?" I asked, recalling those moments of confusion, when I'd called and she hadn't come.

"Even I have my limits," she said.

I didn't know what that meant, but no answer came when I said as much. I groaned in exasperation, and Alexandra's head snapped up.

"What's wrong?" she asked, more jumpy than usual. Fiercer than ever. I waved her off, kicking my legs over the bed to pace. The monster was restless.

"I'm fine," I said. My voice was nearly devoid of emotion, but I tried to show her that ember of heat so that she could maybe fan the flames. I didn't know how to control the monster, though, and so I stayed silent when she announced it was time to get ready—and left her to it.

Alexandra dressing me wasn't as strange as one might think, since I let her dress me for our birthday every year. It wasn't hard to sit in the cold metal chair, still as stone, while she applied makeup to my face and Blair arranged my hair. It wasn't odd to feel like a mannequin in my own skin, while the girl underneath recouped.

I used to think I was a dead girl walking, but that wasn't entirely true anymore. Because I'd learned how to live. Learned that I *could* live. But I still didn't understand happiness. The closest I came was the contented numbness that Violet's presence pushed onto mine, helping me build weak barriers around the monster while we all regained our strength.

It wasn't as easy, though. While I'd kept the monster in

a cage before, it didn't want to be caged anymore. It shot fire through my veins, only to be turned to ash as Violet weighed in. It was an exhausting process, rebuilding the barriers while the monster lurked. They wouldn't be built in an hour, though, or even several hours. It had taken a lifetime to lock the creature in the dungeon and keep it there, and the monster was fighting tooth and nail to never return. I didn't move a muscle, though. I didn't flinch when it roared, or buckle when it stared me in the eye with more emotion than I was capable of feeling.

I sat straight as bone as my sister and cousin prepared me for the final test of my power and restraint. A ball with Anastasia Fortescue, where I assumed the Council would be watching our every move, no doubt seeing how tight a leash she had me on after my demonstration.

My hands curled into fists, the only sign of my internal struggle, as Alexandra finished painting my lips. She took two steps back, her own cherry red lips curving into a sly smile. She was as gorgeous as always, a living flame in a dress of dark red satin. She motioned for Blair to come around and have a look.

"She's...perfect," Blair said. Her eyes were frigid but glowed with pride and something else. Her gown was more ornate than Alexandra's, with a tight bodice of ice-colored lace that fell freely past her waist and all the way to her feet. A single split to mid-thigh revealed a pair of pristine white ankle-boots. An odd choice for this type of party, but if it came to a fight, she was prepared. I had no doubt she'd strapped weapons where no one would see them, as had Alexandra.

My own arms were bare, though, and my legs were

entirely visible through the chiffon fabric. No weapon's belt or straps adorned my body. I wasn't even wearing a bra.

"Are you ready?" Alexandra asked, reaching out for my hands, which never moved.

The monster quieted when I slammed down another brick in an attempt at forcing it into submission. The wall climbed higher and higher, still fragile while the mortar set, but there, nonetheless.

No part of me had been left unscathed. Even my fingernails now shone like amethyst gemstones, and I wasn't sure I was ready to see what the rest of me looked like. Alexandra gripped my hands, spreading a pleasant heat across my skin and countering the numbness that threatened to overcome me. Whatever shoes she'd put me in didn't suck as much as the usual strappy heels. I glanced down, past the see-through chiffon, at the sky-high black ankle-boots, more edgy than Blair's but just as functional. They were similar enough to my combat boots that my feet didn't complain much, despite the added height. Two fingers went under my chin, lifting my face to the mirror.

The chiffon was draped over both shoulders, covering my breasts, but not my chest, not my scars. It bunched at the waist—where the solid black slip underneath formed the tiniest of shorts—then flared out like billowing smoke when I moved. Every inch of my legs was visible, and my arms were the barest of all. My scars on display as tattoos against my ivory skin.

"No weapons?" I asked stiffly.

Blair flashed me a wicked grin as she motioned to my hair. Lo and behold, she'd braided it around my head in an elegant updo, with intricate dagger handles sticking out like the jewels in a crown. My eyes were almost fathomless, but also inexplicably violet. It wasn't the same as my other's, not quite that hue, but it was there, and it paired beautifully with the dark purple lipstick that sealed the package.

"I approve," I said, turning from the mirror. I was death incarnate, with a beauty so dark only the bravest of souls wouldn't quiver.

"That's all?" Blair scoffed.

Alexandra shrugged, turning to the counter and playing with something there. "Coming from her, that's high praise."

I wandered over, stopping when I saw what was in her hands. "A mask?" I asked, marveling at the red feathers of the phoenix.

"It is a masquerade," Alexandra replied, slipping her new identity on. It was striking with the dress, and took her from elegant beauty to an unforgiving bird of prey.

"What do you think?" Blair asked.

I glanced in the mirror at her porcelain white mask, with delicate little ears. Silver glittered around the edges where there would've been fur. The nose made it unmistakable. I grinned at the white wolf, because she couldn't have chosen better for herself.

"Fitting. Where's mine?" I asked, startled when they fastened a mask of raven feathers around my eyes. Simpler then either of theirs, but a statement nonetheless. An animal of death. A warning and a promise.

I smiled in the mirror, and a shadowed goddess smiled back.

CHAPTER 35

"You look like a queen," Alexandra said softly.

"Of death," Blair added, and my sister nodded in agreement. I didn't disagree.

"Where is everyone?" I asked. The leaky faucet was the only sound apart from us, and that unsettled me.

Today had been a big day, and that demonstration had had a lot riding on it. Now, hours later, I was feeling spent, and the party hadn't even started. Rebuilding the barriers that kept the monster locked up had exhausted more energy than I was used to, and after facing the Hydra...I needed food, and sleep, and to never see a Hydra again.

"They left a while ago. You were pretty out of it, though...so I'm not surprised you didn't notice," Alexandra said.

I nodded in silent understanding, letting her lead me away from the bathroom. Something ate at the back of my mind. Something I needed to remember. When Alexandra stored her phone inside a tiny black velvet clutch, it came to me.

"Has anyone heard from Lily today? We leave tomor-row, and I told her I would come find her," I said. My voice sounded as scratchy as my throat felt, despite my ability to heal from pretty much anything.

"I talked with her a few hours ago. She told me to tell you that she'll be in the library after the party," Blair said.

I nodded, but despite her assurances, I checked my phone for messages and found none. Loosing a nervous breath, I typed out a quick message and stashed my phone under my pillow.

"Okay. Let's go," I said, lifting my dress with half a thought while we ascended the stairs.

The top level was dark, and the hole from the simulator hadn't been fixed. I shivered at the sight and kept walking, wanting to forget all about the Hydra, and the boogeyman that lived in my mind.

My sister didn't need to show us the way—we all knew where the ballroom was—but she did anyway. I suspected she needed to feel in control, and know that I was safe. I would've, if the situation had been reversed. I shuddered to think what the Hydra would've done to her, because in a world made of water, even a phoenix couldn't fly.

The soft strum of a waltz lured me to the doors, but it was Blair's hand on my back that made me cross the threshold into devastating beauty.

The room was painted in red and gold light, as the socialites of the Supernatural society gathered on the eve of our departure. Couples twirled around us under the colored lights, and the smell of citrus and mint permeated the room. My skin flushed under the intense heat, and the air tasted like sweat and lies. So many people were here, far more than I'd expected.

It was the perfect place to be forgotten, just another mask in the crowd.

I left my sister mingling near the door and made my way to the bar. Blair trailed me, a huntress in her own right as she eyed our bartender.

"What will it be for you, ladies?" the young man asked. His eyes glowed gold, and this time I knew why.

"Bone dry martini," Blair purred.

I vaguely wondered where Alec was, but it was none of my business to bring him up here.

"Double gin and tonic," I ordered, leaning back against the counter while I waited for my drink.

"Make that two," another woman said.

I turned sharply to look at Johanna, and, man, she'd really outdone herself. Modest and classy, she wore a long-sleeved dress of pure gold, and a mask of a dragon.

"I didn't peg you as a gin and tonic kind of girl," I said softly.

She chuckled quietly as the bartender slid my drink across. I winked at him, and downed it in one shot.

"Or I you a girl who drinks to block out the voices," she murmured.

I shot her the finger as she sipped hers daintily.

"Sometimes, you have to become a monster to defeat one," I said.

Her eyes narrowed, piercing my nonchalance. She opened her mouth as if she had something to say, when someone coughed to announce their arrival. She gave me a sly smile then disappeared among the crowd faster than should've been possible.

"May I have this dance?" Aaron asked, his voice huskier than usual.

I glanced over at the male who'd planted himself between me and Blair. Little traitor was preoccupied with the bartender and didn't even notice.

"No," I said stiffly, eyeing his well-fitting tux and…raven mask. A small gasp escaped my lips. *Traitors indeed.*

"Are you sure?" he asked, his gaze traveling down before meeting mine.

He was burning up, I realized, though I didn't know how. Something inside him was on fire when he looked at me, and this wasn't the first time.

"Quite."

I walked away, but only made it three steps before my feet refused to move. Lucas and Anastasia were wrapped like lovers in the tango of their lives. Her dress was like midnight, and his mask was a snowy white owl. I didn't cringe when he held her tighter. I didn't wince when he swept her away. And when the song came to a close, I didn't look away when he saw me over her shoulder. Even under this light, I could read the sudden tension in his jaw.

I wasn't jealous that he was dancing with another woman. I was livid that he'd chosen *that* woman. The woman who'd thrown me in a cage with a nine-headed beast not even twelve hours ago. The woman who'd watched his brother's leg almost get blown off, and hadn't cared. The woman who held my leash, because he'd done a shoddy job of wiping his sister's memory, and I was the one who'd gone down for it—and for the stupidity of trusting him in the first place.

I think I might've taken a step toward them, but only one, before the next song began, and I found myself being swept away to the sound of "Masquerade."

"You can thank me later," Aaron whispered as he spun me around.

I glanced up into his deep-set eyes, so much closer when I wore heels. We were only inches apart now, and despite my earlier performance with the Hydra, he looked completely at ease being this close to me. Not afraid in the slightest.

"I can thank you never," I muttered. The insult died on my lips the moment he brought me closer. His body exuded warmth, a heat more familiar than my own sisters', even though I'd only felt it once.

"Now where's the fun in that, *little signasti*?" he said softly.

I laughed in his face. "I like heartbreaker better." I smirked. Heartbreaker was the name I'd earned boxing last year. Man, that seemed so long ago now.

The music grew louder as the servers chimed in with, "*Masquerade!*"

The chandelier shook, just a little.

"I don't plan on letting you break my heart," Aaron said sharply, glancing up to see what I was looking at.

We spun faster and faster, dancing the same way we fought—like two halves of the same whole. I never would've thought him a dancer, but then again, most said the same of me.

"I'd have to have your heart to break it, now wouldn't I?" I said slowly. The words were a dare, a whisper lost in the thundering room. Another gin and tonic was calling my name, but this dance had saved me from what Anastasia would see as humiliation and so I would stay—but only one dance.

"*Masquerade!*"

I could've sworn the ground shook a little, as Aaron gripped my hand tighter.

"I know what you're getting at. Lucas was a damn fool to go after you, though, when he knew what you meant to me," Aaron said.

My heart stopped.

Literally stopped in my chest.

"What?" I asked. Demanded.

Aaron blew out a breath, making the air taste like rain. It would've been dizzying if I hadn't been rattled by the one piece of information everyone had alluded to, but I'd somehow never seen.

"You didn't realize...did you?" he asked slowly, almost pained. Something dark crossed his features, too quickly for me to read.

"Didn't realize that he's known for a year? Or didn't realize he's *lied* to me for a year?" I paused, looking every which way for Lucas—so I could ask him myself, and then kill him when he told me the truth. "I assumed he'd found out when the rest of them did. In the bathroom. I never— Why did you never say anything? Why didn't he? I'm going to murder him. I swear to Nyx, to the gods, to whoever the fuck is up there that I will string him up and—" I was speaking low, but my voice was rising with every second until Aaron silenced me with a finger pressed against my lips.

"*Masquerade!*" was thundering, causing the doors to shake and the room shudder.

"I wanted to earn your affection, but you'd made your choice before I ever got the chance. Part of you recognized me when you opened up as the year went on—your soul did, anyway—but you thought it was him." He paused, and I thought back to the summer, to Lucas telling me that I was the one who'd let him in. I was the reason he could read my mind. I hadn't believed him, and now I knew I shouldn't have trusted him with anything.

"When the summer came...you agonized over him, over feelings you couldn't understand. Insatiable urges you thought were more. But you didn't realize until you came back that it was never him. And even then, you didn't see it. You're just so fucking stubborn—"

"Do you hear that?" I asked, interrupting him.

Aaron said nothing as we stopped in the middle of the dance floor. My feet were no longer willing to move, as I grappled with the truth of his words.

That lying sack of shit had known for the last year that I was bonded—as in *life bonded* to Aaron—and never said anything. He'd made me feel guilty for not telling him about my father, and the secrets I'd kept. I'd fucking lost my freedom because of him—and had still been willing to try to forgive him up until he'd slapped me. But this? This was how he'd repaid me?

By lying to me about something that had nothing to do with him and everything to do with me.

I was going to kill him.

The room rumbled, and at that moment I spotted Anastasia, entirely alone on the far side of the room. She was smiling, the most cunning and wicked of smiles.

"*Masquerade!*"

Lucas was nowhere to be found as the double doors burst open.

Eyes, red and black, surrounded us instantly—and then the first scream came.

The Vampires were here.

CHAPTER 36

Utter silence was followed by a bloodcurdling scream, as I pulled one of the daggers from my hair and went to track down the rest of my team.

"We need to get out of here!" Aaron yelled, his back to me, as one of the Made lunged for him. The red-eyed Vamp snarled, but Aaron wasn't deterred. I let them battle it out as I searched for Alexandra and Blair.

The column of fire that erupted toward the back of the room gave me a good idea where to start looking, and I took off in that direction. The red and gold lights suddenly seemed dizzying, even sickening, as my heart thudded in my chest.

Where is she? Where is she? Where is she?

By the time I saw Alexandra, she was already facing off, one against three, but holding her own as she lit each of them on fire from the inside. The smell of rotted, burning flesh was stomach churning, but I couldn't afford to get sick. I slashed each of their necks, spraying both Alexandra and me in blood, as heads rolled.

"I had it, you know?" She pursed her lips, not seeing the dark-eyed Vamp behind her who moved to snack on her neck and suddenly found himself thrown into a wall. Alexandra spun around as a dagger went zinging through the air and nailed him to the wall by his neck. Black blood dribbled down, and I wasted no time beheading another of the undead.

Throughout the room, fights were picking up, as members of the Council tried to defend themselves, sometimes killing other Supernaturals in the process. I didn't know where the hell Anastasia had gone, but she was behind this somehow. Some way.

Why would she want us to train for a war, only to leave us blind when the war came knocking? Something wasn't adding up here, but I could figure it out after I killed her, or got everyone and ran. Whichever came first.

"We need to find Blair and get out of here!" I yelled to Alexandra, who was already facing another Vamp. The smell of blood and death called to me like the sweetest of lullabies, and I closed my eyes.

I was one with the world.

One with the universe.

One with matter.

And I was going to gorge myself on the snapping of bones and the feel of blood between my fingers before the night was over. The killing gene flipped on, the world slowed down, and I went to work.

Tomorrow, I would remember the next few faces I killed, and the ones after that, but then I started to forget as the battle drum beat inside my chest, compelling me to march. To slaughter.

Using only the daggers in my hair and my ability, I alternated between dismembering and beheading, while Alexandra baked them to ash. We were fighting our way across the room, when a low cackle brought me to a grinding halt.

"Anastasia," I breathed.

She was watching me like a bug she was going to crush. The condescension and certainty were staggering, but I lunged nonetheless. She danced out of my way, but I brought my boot up in a roundhouse kick to the chest, sending her flying into the bar. Her back bent unnaturally as the stone top cracked in half. Plumes of dust and wood chips went everywhere, stinging my eyes as I stared her down. My muscles ached from my earlier fight with the Hydra, but now wasn't the time for weakness.

"You knew they were coming. You told me this was all to stop a war. Why bother if you planned on giving them our heads on a silver platter?" I spat, mentally reaching out and dragging her across the shattered glass and through pools of blood. She kneeled before me, blood leaking from her bottom lip, but whatever other wounds she'd sustained were already healed.

I reeled back to punch her, when she gave another gurgle of laughter and said, "I wouldn't do that if I were you."

She raised her hand and pointed a single finger at the stage, where spotlights snapped on, illuminating a terrifying sight. Lily. Bound and gagged like a piece of meat.

The person forcing her into submission?

Lucas.

Tick.

Tock.

Tick.

Tock.

Time flashed by, as I searched for an explanation, some reason for why he'd done this. But deep down, I wandered back over the past month, and, slowly, painfully, the pieces of the puzzle fell into place.

"Kneel if you want her to live," Anastasia said, but I didn't move an inch.

I didn't hit her again, though, as I stared up at Lily, who was half unconscious on the stage. Lucas grabbed her shoulder roughly and fisted his hand in her hair as he tilted her head to the side.

Someone had bitten her.

Not once in my seventeen years had I ever been so consumed by an emotion that I couldn't react. I was furious but I couldn't scream. I didn't know how to look away. All I knew was that the power was rising again, and this time, what I'd done to the Hydra would look tame. I was going to burn the world down, because a Vampire had defiled my sister in the most disgusting of ways.

Anastasia moved when I was frozen. A couple of Vampires jumped onto the stage and held Lily's arms, as if readying to bite. Or kill.

"Do. Not. Touch. Her. Unless you want to be wiped off the face of this planet like the dirt on my shoes." My voice was magnified by the loose grasp I had on my rage. Power crackled over my skin, making my hairs stand on end.

"You threaten me? The Head of the Supernatural Council? A Member of the Court?" she demanded, letting her own voice carry. The massacre was still going on, judging by the screams, but I didn't care who lived and who died in this fight, as long as I protected me and mine.

Instead of answering her with pretty words, I pulled the last dagger from my hair, freeing my braid, as I aimed for the spot between her eyes. So fast that even the Vampires who jumped forward to stop me couldn't protect her. But it seemed the Head of the Council could protect herself, and by the ease with which she caught the dagger, I was in some deep, deep shit.

"Why must you always be so predictable, Selena?" She gave an exasperated sigh, tossing the dagger in the air to catch it by its point. "First I send the demons for you, but you live and kill my darling Fernando. Then I send the Born after you, thinking you won't fight at the cost of your friend's life, since that's where it seemed to go wrong with the demons. And now?" She didn't smile or laugh as she twirled the dagger in her hands before throwing it straight between my eyes.

My powers were exhausted, from both the Hydra and the fight. My body too tired to try to catch it by the blade. The only option left was to move.

I flung myself to the side, spinning on my heel, but the dagger skimmed my ear and took a chunk of my braid instead. I didn't hear the weapon land, but the swish of my hair hitting the floor was enough to make me look down and see that most of the braid was gone.

"You're fast, girl, I'll give you that. But you're not the smartest." She went on, buying me time to find a way out of this, as her minions approached. Lucas was shifting back and forth uncomfortably, and while I wanted nothing more than to kill him with my bare hands, I didn't have the strength to take them all out. I didn't have the control not to obliterate Lily as well. Anastasia could thank the Hydra for that…but then again, maybe that was the whole point of my little demonstration. Not to kill me, but exhaust me.

"I've suspected you were behind the demons. What I couldn't figure out, though, was why. Why bother sending your pets after me in the first place if I'm so insignificant?" I asked, lying through my teeth, but deciding to kill two birds with one stone. If there was one thing I knew about Anastasia, it was that her pride was her downfall. She wanted to lord over me how much better she was, how much smarter, and I needed time to reach out to the others. To find a way to save my sister.

"Stay put. We're coming." The voice was distinctly feminine, and carried Johanna's essence. I didn't understand how, but frankly I didn't care, as long as Lily got out.

"You are insignificant, and I've made sure you stay that way," she purred, not quite buying into the lie as I'd hoped she would. I still couldn't piece together why she'd chosen to target me, or how I was a threat to her.

Unless, like most things in my life, it was my fault for simply existing.

"What about him? What's he got to do with all of this?" I asked, thrusting my chin at the dark-eyed stranger who held my sister hostage. I'd only just noticed that his eyes were black instead of green. At least they finally reflected his true nature.

"It's quite simple, really. You bought the story that he'd failed to do something he'd said he would, and I was punishing you for it. I was worried you wouldn't, that you would see what had really happened, that the Made had brought me your message. You bought his incompetence all too easily, though." She clicked her tongue, stepping into the spotlight, and dragging a long fingernail down my sister's cheek.

"I knew it would eat at you, that you'd gone down for what you viewed as his failure. You're predictable that way. You cut him out of your mind that very first night, and planted the seed that let me take him, like a crop ready for harvest. You fostered the jealousy and hatred all on your own, so when I came to claim his mind, there was nothing to stop me or protect him, from my gift—because you'd relinquished your control. His mind was ripe for the taking... I told him what I planned to do to you, and the poor boy had no chance, really." She switched to running her fingers through his hair, and Lucas didn't flinch.

"He was blind, because he loved you—and so he gave away his soul to save you. Little did he know that I couldn't kill you myself if I wanted to. But now that I have him...he'll destroy you for me." She started cackling wildly, uncontrollably.

When Anastasia raked her nail sharply across my sister's cheek and brought the blood to her lips, my gin and tonic fought to come back up. I had to say something. To get her attention back, to buy more time for the others.

"What are you talking about, you can't kill me yourself?" I yelled, and as I'd hoped, she paused and turned away from my sister.

"You think I'm daft enough to give away all my secrets to a pest I can't kill? No...You'll be gone long before you ever figure it out." She turned back to Lily and offered one of my sister's arms to the Vampires. They plunged their fangs into her, but Lily didn't cry out when their teeth pierced her skin. I couldn't stop trembling as I watched, unable to look away, too afraid of accidentally killing her to stop it.

Violet's presence was a numbness I couldn't afford as I rallied the power within me to try for one final shot. Aaron still wasn't here, and Johanna was nowhere to be found. With none of my team in sight, saving my sister and stopping Anastasia was on my shoulders. The pounding in my ears had reached its crescendo when Anastasia seemed to notice that something was amiss. That I wasn't bowing down without a fight.

"Selena!" a voice screamed. Alexandra's voice.

I turned—just a fraction—but it was a moment too long. Anastasia said, "Snap her neck."

"No!" I screamed, sending a wild shot at the stage. The power was unsteady, though. It didn't want to be contained. It wanted to break.

The power exploded against them, throwing Lucas and the others, but Lily... I missed, and Lily took the brunt of it. She hit the wall with a wicked crack, her neck hanging at an odd angle. It was only when the light left her eyes, and she collapsed entirely that I realized what I'd done.

Oh my god.

I couldn't breathe.

I couldn't see.

"*No!*" I screamed again, scrambling to get to her. To bring her back. To do anything.

She couldn't be dead. She just couldn't, because if she died...

Nothing was going to stop me from killing every living thing on the planet.

The ground rolled beneath my feet, but I didn't care. My knees hit the floor before I could even process what was happening, and I gave myself over to my demons. Fire ignited, pressing in on me like a mob after a murderer.

"Dormi, dea, propter manicaveris."

Sleep, little goddess, for you must rise with the dawn.

Those words wouldn't work this time, because madness had me. Grief claimed my every thought as I crawled on my hands and knees toward the stage—ripping concrete up by the chunk.

Oh my— I can't— I didn't mean—

I killed my sister.

The one I'd sworn to protect. To cherish. The one I'd held through every nightmare and panic attack. The one who was only just learning to live, and to save herself. She would never love again. Never laugh. Never cry.

"Lily!" I screamed, summoning an impenetrable dome of dark matter as I collapsed in on myself. Letting it disintegrate anything that dared attack me, and absorb their energy.

One moment, I was being swallowed up by the pain, and the next I'd been sucked away and was looking through different eyes. Clearer eyes.

Alexandra's face illuminated next to mine, like a warrior princess in battle. She grabbed me, this body, and brought my face to hers.

"You told me that you broke my heart for her. You told me that your entire existence depends on her. I can't save her and fight, okay? So I need you to come through on your promise that you'll get her out." Alexandra's eyes were glossy with unshed tears. Her voice cracked on a silent sob before she continued.

"You take her to the place I showed you, and if I don't return in twenty-four hours, you run. You run like hell, and you never look back. You hear me? You never let her look back."

Images flashed of her in the bathroom, worried that this party wasn't a coincidence. She showed him pictures of a house with a white picket fence and an alpine larch, and made him promise to take me away. Far away, if anything ever happened —as the only repayment for breaking her heart. He shuddered at the memories, and the lump in his throat at what he was about to do.

"She'll never forgive me," he said softly, but he'd do as she'd asked, and not because he'd promised, but because he thought it was the only way to keep me alive. It only took me a moment to realize whose body I was in, whose emotions I was feeling, and a moment more to understand that he loved her.

Aaron truly loved Alexandra. He loved her fire. He loved her will. He loved how she fought for me, but he wasn't in love with her. Not like she was with him, and they both knew that. They both knew that he cared for her like a sister, because his heart— no, his soul—belonged to another. It belonged to me.

"I don't care. As long as she lives, I don't care what you have to do to make it happen. You told me you're her signasti, right? That she's your one and only half?" Alexandra asked, not a shred of brown in her eyes as the fire burned.

He only nodded.

"Then you and you alone can heal her, and make her happy when I'm gone. That's all I ask. Make her happy," she whispered.

Aaron's throat caught when she hugged him tightly, briefly, and forgave him for dating her just to be closer to me. He turned toward the dark mass that was growing, eating everything that stood in its path as my body started to self-destruct.

Behind him, the fire grew as Alexandra faced off against my enemies, and trusted the man who'd broken her heart to save himself and the girl he was bound to. Letting her sacrifice it all in the process, just for one chance.

I tried to pull away, to go back to my mind as his emotions ran through me, one after another. So fierce and powerful, and yet I wouldn't let myself feel them. I couldn't stand the burn of them, and I screamed out to Violet.

Aaron broke through each layer of my shield, and when he looked at my face, the sight was one I never wanted to see again. I scrambled from his mind, wanting nothing more than to curl inside limbo and wither away. My consciousness left him, rushing back into my body the moment we touched.

He jolted for a second, as if he'd realized where I'd been, but didn't slow as he picked me up and ran—letting the world disintegrate behind him as my shield caved in and collapsed the ground.

I closed my eyes and surrendered to unending despair as I let the fire and brimstone swallow me whole.

CHAPTER 37

For the longest time, I'd obsessed about it, wishing I'd died instead of my parents, but I never truly understood the concept of ending. Never wrapped my mind around the very real truth of what it meant to be gone. Not until I heard the crack and saw the light fade from my sister's eyes.

For so long, I'd fought myself over what was right and wrong. I'd fought the killing gene, afraid of the monster I was becoming. I'd fought against Violet, because I didn't think she was real. I'd fought against the memories of my past until I could no longer deny what had happened. And still, I'd fought to hold on to the last shred of my sanity.

Lily was gone, though, like my parents, and she was never coming back.

It would've been so easy to give myself over to the light and fade away. They said that people couldn't die of grief or pain, but they also said that the matter manipulators were extinct, so what did they know? I could do it, and I was no longer scared, because the girl I'd been had died the moment Lily was taken from me.

I felt it the moment the killing gene broke free and the monsters overtook me. Trapped in my own internal hell, I stared them down with a promise in my eyes. A promise of what was to come. Of what I would become.

Lily had died, and I was never going to see her again. The absoluteness of that shook me to my very core, in a way my own near-death never had. It changed me, molded me, as I walked in limbo, watching my monsters fight each other for who would come out on top when I opened my eyes.

It had been four months since I'd nearly died and woke up no longer dormant. What would I be when I awoke this time?

That was the question I didn't know how to answer.

Not yet.

The pain that caged me was so resolute that I didn't know how to break out of it. I didn't know how to ease it, like I had as a child. That was wrong, though, because I'd never eased it, not really. Every time my father had pushed me too far, my mother had called me back from limbo. Who was going to do it this time, when no one knew how to reach me? No one saw my demons, or the inferno I'd let myself be trapped in.

No one, but one.

Violet.

She defied all reason, and even I didn't know how she was here, or what she was, but I knew what she could do. I knew she could end the pain and remake me into something more. Something stronger. Something so unbreakable that the heavens would shudder when I roared.

She could help me take my vengeance, when, alone, I couldn't.

"Is that what you want? More than anything?" she asked, eyeing me warily.

I was a withering ball of nerves and bones, but what I wanted more than anything was for the pain to end. For the suffering to end. For the grief to have an outlet, and for me to take revenge. That was all I wanted, and I told her as much.

She stared at me, with crystal-clear violet eyes. So bright, they looked like cut gems. I hoped they could cut. I burned to feel my enemies bleed.

"Then we will become one.

"We will become something new, something which has never been before.

"We will become death."

Her words echoed through me, speaking to the sorrow in my soul.

Death.

I liked the sound of that.

I would become the very thing that had taken every-thing from me. I would become *more.*

Violet reached out to me, tenderly, like she would've her own child. There was no warmth in her eyes when she took my hand, though, and I was grateful for that, because I never wanted to feel warmth again.

"Let's begin."

CHAPTER 38

When I opened my eyes, it wasn't a me, but a we. Pale purple bedroom walls were the first indication of where we'd gone, where Aaron had taken me, but I felt nothing.

Not a sliver of sadness. Not a shred of guilt. I felt absolutely nothing as I took in my childhood room for the first time in almost seven years. Outside, the wind howled, beckoning me on to begin my hunt. I had unfinished business, though, and a mild interest in what the voices downstairs were.

The bed creaked, ever so slightly, when I shifted to sitting, but made no noise when I stood. Footsteps echoed from downstairs, and the smell of lilacs and smoke drifted through my bedroom window. My mother had grown lilac bushes with Li—my sister. They had been gentle souls, but now they were gone, and I would hunt in their stead.

I walked around the room, examining the bits of paper where I'd scratched out my homework in Latin, and left every ounce of innocence behind when I stepped out of this house for the last time. I'd been in that very bed, with the black paisley bedspread, when the news came that my parents had died.

Somehow, I didn't believe that. I didn't believe a car crash was even a factor in their deaths, but that was just another secret I'd need to dig up when I'd killed each and every one who'd wronged me. Starting with the Council.

Wind chimes. Wind chimes pealed downstairs, and I knew then that this wasn't a dream. That while dreamland may have brought me here many times over the past month, I was here in the flesh this time. Hearing the wind chimes my father had created from the glass of the first window I'd shattered on command.

He'd been so proud of the little monster I was becoming.

What would he say if he could see me now?

I didn't care. Not anymore.

I didn't even need to flick my wrist to open the door silently, my mind loosening the hinges so they didn't squeak. The element of surprise was in my favor, and I needed to use it to greet my guests, before I decided how I would slit their throats. How *we* would slit their throats.

Violet and I were so tightly interconnected now that none of my demons could reach me. None of my emotions could overcome me. She'd once told me that there was peace in control, and for the first time in my entire life, I was at peace in my apathy.

Voices floated up the stairs, so mortal in their emotions. So breakable.

"It's only been twelve hours. No one's going to come looking here, not yet," Alexandra was insisting. There was a time when her voice would've made me weep for joy, but I wouldn't weep again. Never again. Not even when I'd built a throne out of my enemies' bones and slept soundly at night.

"We don't have time. Anastasia will recover, and what's left of the Council will side with her when she puts a bounty on our heads. If you want this place left in peace, we need to leave now," said another voice. A voice that wasn't entirely Supernatural, and tasted like the power of something that had left this earth long ago. I sniffed once, but only blood, dust, and smoke permeated the air.

"My sister is dead, and likely one of the Made by now. Selena is upstairs trapped in limbo, and I'm—"

Her voice broke off in a sob as she collapsed. From my place, four stairs from ground level, I could make out their reflections in the fireplace glass panels. My sister, an emotional heap on our dusty, old couch. Blair sat next to her, stroking her hair, her own eyes lost in something frigid and wrathful. I had no doubt that she would be useful in this quest for vengeance; I'd trained her that well.

Johanna paced, while Oliver sat on the floor nearby, watching her with guarded eyes. There were others of the nine here, though. I could smell them, even though they weren't in the living room. My breath hissed between my teeth when I spotted Aaron brooding in the corner. He was going to be difficult, stubborn.

He seemed to be the only one who heard my hiss, and his eyes flashed to meet mine in the glass. He strode forward just as I rounded the corner, still dressed as the queen of death, my newly shorn hair brushing my chin.

I couldn't imagine what they saw as they gaped at me now. Alexandra sat straight up, her mouth open in something almost like shock. But it was Aaron who got to me first—or at least tried to, only to be thrown back by an invisible shield that even he couldn't penetrate.

"What the—"

"Selena, are you—"

"How did you do it?" Alexandra asked. She was the quietest of them all, but somehow her voice was the only one that stood out.

I eyed her as I strode further into the room, relishing my remade body and mind. Savoring our strength.

"Walk out of limbo?" I asked, unsmiling but not quite bored. These people still had a purpose, even if they no longer meant the same things to me.

"Because your sister's not the only one with us," Johanna answered slowly. Her voice was hard, and unflinching.

I smiled lazily, showing my lovely, sharp teeth. "How perceptive. You smell of the ancients. From whom did you spawn?" I asked, in a way the old Selena might've considered brash. Then again, she'd died from that sentimental heart. I'd been remade from the ashes.

"The dragon. And you? Mother lost to time?" she asked, yielding to me, but not in complete submission. She would also be a problem, if I let it get out of hand.

"I am death, and I've come for the blood of those who've wronged me," I said, giving her credit for not shuddering underneath my otherworldly stare. I enjoyed the way it made the others flinch, as if something in them recognized that the girl they'd followed was no longer living.

A sharp knock rattled the front door of my parents' home.

Several jumped to get it, but I was at the door before anyone could take a single step. I sniffed again, parting my lips to taste the air, but it was ash in my mouth. I unlocked it, despite the protests, and opened it wide.

Leaning against the doorframe was none other than Elizabeth.

The cousin who'd once betrayed me.

"What's she doing here?" Blair snarled, and I suddenly found myself partially frozen as the doorway turned to ice.

A breath of fresh air wafted in with the autumn breeze as I took a very hard look at the girl who'd showed up on my doorstep. Elizabeth's hair was matted to her head, and she smelled of sweat, and dirt, and ash. Not an ounce of her was untouched by whatever had happened back at Daizlei.

"That is an excellent question. Why are you here in my doorway, uninvited? I'm certain I promised to kill you if you ever spoke to me again," I said.

Unlike Blair's, though, my voice contained no rage. Instead, I spoke with the softest menace and the promise of death. My energy reached out to caress her, and the mortal liar shuddered, pushing back against my power as she stepped away from the door.

"I've come to deliver a message to you," she said to me. Her voice shook like a leaf in the winter. She sweated like a sinner in hell.

"From who?" I asked, ripping my arm from the ice-covered doorway. I stepped out into the open air, tilting my head back to inhale the scent of life.

"From your mother."

My head snapped up, and I grabbed her by the throat. I took two steps in her direction, and she backed up, going right over the edge of our porch. Sweat dotted her temple in the few moments I held her there, just long enough to let her think I would kill her. Just long enough to make her honest.

"My mother is dead," I said flatly, not wasting my breath on the whys or hows.

"I—spe—speak—with the—" Her voice broke off.

"She can talk with the dead," Blair said from behind me, making no move to save the girl. Her loyalty to me was going to make this so much easier. Provided the others proved compliant.

"Is she reliable?" I asked.

"That's for you to decide," Blair said, not moving from her spot in the doorway as I threw the other girl down.

She choked on air, taking great, rasping breaths. Her heart beat in overdrive to make up for the lack of oxygen, and I gave her a minute before I spoke.

"I'm only going to ask once, and your answer decides whether you live or die. Understood?" I said, raising an eyebrow and daring that taut mouth to spit on me. The wind whipped around me, but I didn't shift an inch as she nodded.

Her eyes were burning, and I enjoyed watching the fire, because I would never again be burned.

"What's your message?"

She looked me up and down, as if weighing whether death was worth it just to spite me.

I smiled slowly, reassuring her that if she tried anything

funny I had no problem ending her here and now, on the porch of my dead parents' house.

"Find the Crone with the third eye."

I stared at her for a moment, debating the truth of her words. This girl was a coward, though, and had traded my life for hers. She wouldn't lie to me when the price was her life. I grabbed her arm and pushed her through the doorway past Blair, who stared at me in shock for what she saw as a betrayal. What she didn't realize, though, was that I had bigger plans than just surviving. No. I had plans to conquer. To kill.

The last words of my mother's song played for me, as eerie as when I'd first heard them all those years ago.

Run, run, soul in pain,

So you can make them pay.

And pay.

Run, run, they will say.

You will take revenge one day.

I wouldn't run anymore, because the time had come to make them pay. She'd known what would become of me, all those years ago.

But I'd had to die to see it.

And Li—my sister too.

I will avenge you, and when I'm done, there'll be no Council, no Anastasia, and most of all, no Lucas.

I will kill them all.

Acknowledgments

There are not enough words to express my gratitude to all you who have helped me get to this point. *Heir of Shadows* was just the beginning, and now that I am well on this journey, I realize it wouldn't be possible without a good many of the people on this list, and many more that I will never forget to thank should our paths cross again.

To my readers, thank you for making my dream come true. This book is literally my blood, sweat, and tears—risen from the ashes for your enjoyment—and I hope you love it as much as I do.

To my Academites, thank you for being amazing readers and helping promote my work. I want give a special shoutout to Kelly Donovan-Roberts, Allison Nicole Lucas, and Jessica Crosby for helping catch those last typo's before publication.

To Matt, you have been there for every long and sometimes terrible day. You make me dinner, take me out to go on walks with dogo, honestly some days I wonder if I would have survived school and two jobs if not for you taking care of me. I love you, thank you.

To Courtney, you're my best friend—the one who keeps me sane. You listen to my ramblings late at night and put up with me demanding your opinion on blurbs and covers at far too early in the morning. You have been one of the greatest friends that I will probably ever have, and I have never been prouder to have a Hufflepuff by my side.

www.ingramcontent.com/pod-product-compliance
Lightning Source LLC
Chambersburg PA
CBHW032210180726
48284CB00001B/275